DOCTOR WHO

HEART OF TARDIS
DAVE STONE

BBC

Published by BBC Worldwide Ltd,
Woodlands, 80 Wood Lane
London W12 0TT

First published 2000
Copyright © Dave Stone 2000
The moral right of the author has been asserted

Original series broadcast on the BBC
Format © BBC 1963
Doctor Who and TARDIS are trademarks of the BBC

ISBN 0 563 55596 3
Imaging by Black Sheep, copyright © BBC 2000

Printed and bound in Great Britain by Mackays of Chatham
Cover printed by Belmont Press Ltd, Northampton

Acknowledgements

I'd like to thank all the people who offered advice and examples for dealing with the Second Doctor as played by Patrick Troughton, what he might say and how he might be reasonably expected to act in any given circumstances. All of that advice was good, and the fact that I've *still* managed to get things completely and utterly wrong is a reflection on my own stupidity rather than on that of anyone else.

A number of the ideas in this book have been developed from a story I wrote for *Perfect Timing II*, a charitable publication which can be obtained in return for a fixed donation to the Foundation for the Study of Infant Death (FSID), of which one Colin Baker is chairman. Personally, I'd get it like a shot if I were you – if only for all the incredibly good professional and/or Who-related writers and artists who are in it and aren't me. Details can be obtained from 'Perfect Timing', 70 Eltham Drive, Aspley, Nottingham NG8 6BQ, United Kingdom, or, for the Net-connected, http://sauna.net/perfecttiming/ – all profits go to the FSID, so if writing via Snail Mail, don't forget the international reply coupon or SAE.

Preamble

Until comparatively recently, in novelistic fiction, it was a common practice to convey a particular kind of narrative break by way of three little asterisks, like this:

* * *

The form originated as a method of censorship, self or otherwise, in more circumlocutionary times. The darkly smouldering hero, for example, would be reaching for the winsome heroine, ripping off such bodices as appropriately needed to be ripped, bearing her towards the nearest available flat surface and…

* * *

…we were suddenly catching up with them next morning, over kedgeree and a plate of kidneys and with no sign of the previous unpleasantness save for the resulting happy languor.

With the post-Victorian increase of permissible frankness, however, the primary function of the form atrophied and it took on secondary, intentionally structural connotations. Instead of simply meaning *later that day* – for which, after all, you just have to say 'later that day' – it came to mean a distinct kind of break, a switch between two basic and entirely distinct states, a plunge, in narrative terms, over the lip of what topologists call a catastrophe curve.

A fracture in place and time.

* * *

I mention all this simply because the form, of late, seems to have been devalued to the point where it merely crops up when a section break happens to fall at the end of a page, or as a facile typographic trick to set off every single section no matter what the context of transition – and which, coincidentally, helps bump up the page count like nobody's business.

Those are tricks I'm not going to play. So when you come across those three little asterisks in the following, be aware that they actually *mean* something.

DS, London, 1999/2000

How they strut and stammer, stagger and reel to and fro like madmen… A man once drunk with wine or strong drink rather resembleth a brute than a Christian man. For do not his eyes begin to stare and to be red, fiery and bleared, blubbering forth seas of tears? Doth he not foam and froth at the mouth like a boar? Doth not his tongue falter and stammer in his mouth? Doth not his head seem heavy as a millstone, he not being able to bear it up? Are not his wits and spirits, as it were, drowned? Is not his understanding altogether decayed? Do not his hands, and all his body vibrate, quiver and shake, as it were with a quotidian fever?

Besides these, it casteth him into a dropsy or pleurisy, nothing so soon; it enfeebleth the sinews, it weakeneth the natural strength, it corrupteth the blood, it dissolveth the whole man at length, and finally maketh him forgetful of himself altogether, so that what he doth being drunk, he remembereth not being sober. The Drunkard, in his drunkenness, killeth his friend, revileth his lover, discloseth secrets, and regardeth no man.

Philip Stubbs, *The Anatomie of Abuses*

A York man told Howden magistrates yesterday he felt 'violent' after seeing the James Bond film *Thunderball*. He pleaded guilty to stealing binder twine, assaulting a policeman, destroying a pigeon cote and damaging a police raincoat.

1960s news story, *Yorkshire Evening Press*

Gentlemen, of course I'm joking, and I know that I am not doing it very successfully, but you know you mustn't take everything I say as a joke. I may be joking through clenched teeth.

Fyodor Dostoevsky, *Notes from the Underground*

Prologue
The preliminary agronomy of cyclones

Lieutenant Joel Haasterman wrapped his windcheater tight around him in an unconscious attempt to protect himself from the sodden air – it wasn't the cold so much as the miserable dankness of the place that got to him. When Haasterman had first heard the term 'peasouper' he had never anticipated how literally and liquidly correct it was: he felt like he was stepping into an almost solid mass of filthy airborne sludge. It was a conscious effort even to breathe.

In the middle distance off to one side, the winter night sky flared, the source of light lost in the haze of smog. There was the multiple *crack* of cluster-bomb detonation. Instinctively, Haasterman made to duck, then caught himself and grimaced ruefully. With the memories of the Blitz so fresh, you'd think the Brits would have had quite enough of all things explosive, far less would congregate on parkland or unsafe bomb sites to let a bunch more off.

The thought of it gave him a kind of queasy pang of unease that was hard to define, and it was a moment before he pinned it down. It was simply that fireworks in the early winter rather than in the height of summer felt *wrong*. It was just another of those things that the USAAC overseas-operational familiarisation movies, supposed to introduce you to British folk and their quaint and eccentric ways, had never touched upon. It was another little basic wrongness that made arriving in a country that supposedly shared a common language and culture more like finding yourself in one of those parallel worlds they liked to talk of in *Astonishing Stories of Unmitigated Science*.

A grubby lee-tide wash of hat-and-overcoat-bundled humanity streamed past him, seemingly intent on picking him up and dragging him back down into Tottenham Court Road station in its wake.

Despite petrol rationing, the traffic here on Oxford Street was heavy, crawling at a snail's pace between cordoned-off and half-completed repair work to the road that barely allowed vehicles to travel in single file: squat black cabs and the occasional private car clotted bumper to bumper, their argon headlamps glowing balefully; the chugging, lumbering behemoth of a London bus.

An hour from now these streets would be almost empty save for the locals, the inhabitants of Fitzrovia to the north, and the denizens of Soho to the south. They would be heading for the watering-holes that skulked secretively in the side streets, their lights displayed with an air of furtive tentativeness even though it was two years since the blackout laws had reason to be in effect. Haasterman could have waited, could for that matter have avoided the fetid horrors of the London Underground in the first place and come by staff car when the streets were clear, but he had an appointment to keep. An appointment for which the place and time was set and non-negotiable.

For the moment, though, there seemed to be no easy way to even cross the street. In the end, Haasterman shouldered his way through the crowd and wrenched open the door of an idling and fareless taxi cab, crawled across the back seat and, oblivious to the indignant cry of the driver, stepped out the other side, slither-crunched his way to the pavement over a small pile of builders' sand beside an exposed pipe and bore left into Tottenham Court Road. It was only when he was walking up it that he chanced across another exit from the underground, and realised he could have saved himself the bother.

The warren of smaller streets running off the main thoroughfare were ill-lit. Haasterman became lost for a while and was after all late for his appointment with the Beast.

The saloon bar of the Fitzroy Tavern confirmed almost every American prejudice about a London pub: the battered hardwood counter top, the gleaming beer engines, old regulars' tankards hanging over the bar and, indeed, little caricatures of past regulars on the walls, drawn and framed and hung with varying degrees of care and accomplishment.

The Tavern seemed to be the haunt of the upper-middle classes rather than the lower, and had a hint of Bohemia about it. Pipes and cigars and trilby hats were in evidence, as opposed to abstinence and bowlers or roll-up cigarettes and flat caps. The pub was relatively crowded and rather boisterous – but there seemed to be an edge of desperation to the air of heartiness and hail-fellow-well-met, in the same way that the hand pumps showed distinct signs of worn disrepair and, Haasterman noticed, the complicated myriad of exotic bottles behind the bar had gathered a substantial layer of dust.

The only drink that seemed to be readily purchasable was beer. Of a certain and distinctly British kind. Haasterman accepted a pint pot of the warm and darkish, cloudy liquid from a barman obviously aspiring to the bit part of the Bluff Mine Host in a Noel Coward propaganda movie. At least a third of the drink was scum-like froth, but he had no idea if that was right or not and decided not to call attention to himself by complaining. He had probably been short-changed into the bargain.

Haasterman sipped at the foul stuff, the froth sliming itself unpleasantly around his mouth and cheeks, and wandered through the throng and the insinuating smoke, looking for the man he had come here to meet.

His instructions had been explicit and precise, he thought

dispiritedly, with no provision either way, and the man in question was probably long gone.

From outside there was another small explosion from a nearby bomb-site firework party. Haasterman felt secretly and vaguely pleased when he didn't react to it in any way at all.

'A not entirely uninteresting phenomenon,' said a voice beside him. 'The way that the postures and rituals remain while the old names are forgotten and changed.'

Haasterman turned to a man sitting alone at a table, puffing insouciantly on a pipe that gave off a sickly smell quite other than tobacco. A small cut-crystal glass was at his elbow, filled with a deep red tincture that looked too syrupy to be wine.

The man was elderly, bearded and gaunt, a shadow of the shaven-headed and plump figure Haasterman had first seen in the photographs in his preliminary briefing file, who had reminded him of a less avuncular Alfred Hitchcock. The white hair now sprouting on either side of the otherwise bald head was dishevelled, the disarray of one too old to bother, as was his tweed suit which had obviously been tailored years before for his former, more substantial frame. The eyes, however, were still the same and instantly recognisable. They...

The eyes burned with – not so much a sense of vitality as with a white-hot force of will. A sense of self so powerful as to keep the body alive, if not well, and keep it moving through the world in the face of any number of failures of the flesh.

'The Yuletide festivals of coming months are actually a time of hope and promise,' the man said inconsequentially, as though he were merely passing the time of day. 'A sacrifice to welcome back and nourish the reborn sun. *Now*, in November, is the time when we make noise and fires in a desperate attempt to drive off the wolves that are eating it – and burn our offerings in the vain hope that the wolves will treat us less harshly when the sun is at last eaten up. This is the year's true festival of terror, the true and ancient meaning of All Hallows

Eve – which in your country, I understand, is celebrated by sending children out to eat apples spiked with razor blades.' He chuckled dryly. 'Guy Fawkes and his fiendish plot have merely given us the opportunity to once again conduct the age-old rituals in the proper manner.'

Haasterman looked down at the old man. 'You're not serious.'

The other shrugged. 'Sounds plausible enough – and when you know as much about the Hermetic Arts as I do, you'll know that plausibility is almost everything. Sit, Lieutenant, sit. I'd all but given up hope on you.'

Surprisingly, given the relatively crowded state of the saloon, an empty chair was positioned invitingly across from the old man. A small part of Haasterman's mind wondered why it hadn't been taken – had some influence prevented another drinker from appropriating it, or was this merely an example of the well-known English reserve that made the moving of an item from its assigned place unthinkable?

He sat, and glanced behind himself a little nervously. Sitting with his back to a room made him slightly uneasy, even though he knew he was probably the only person in the room who was carrying a firearm.

'It's a bit of a public place to meet up, don't you think?' he said. 'I understand that you're a famous man.' 'Notorious' had been the word used in the briefing, but Haasterman wanted to start things on a friendly note. While the section had no intention of obtaining this man at all costs, a distinct interest had been expressed if the practicalities of the matter were possible. It would be a mistake to louse things up prematurely.

'The joy of coming to London,' the man said, 'is the anonymity it affords. It's easy to become lost in the faceless crowd.' He gestured sardonically to take in the saloon bar. 'And strangely enough, my *notoriety* is more of a problem in your own country than my own. I gather I'm a positive *cult* over there, amongst those who have read so little as to lack even the most basic understanding of my works and precepts extant.'

He took a measured sip of fluid from his glass with the regretful control of one who, in happier days, would have been happy to swallow the lot in one gulp.

'This establishment is perfectly suitable for our needs,' he said. 'At the turn of the century it was the haunt of genius, of writers and artists. Now it's the haunt of second-raters, backstreet journalists and latchkey so-called novelists too wrapped up in their own minuscule world to even notice, much less care about, anything not of their paltry and attenuated clique. I shudder to think of the state to which the Fitzroy Tavern might be reduced in another fifty years. Radiophonic actors and pulp-periodical writers, I have no doubt…

'Besides,' the man continued, 'for several years now, I've had a homunculus filling in for me in Hastings, taking care of my public appearance while I continued my true studies. Just a little something I knocked up from fungus and a word of power. In any event, of course, it'll have to die soon. I have plans for a funeral service well in hand as we speak. In Brighton, I think. It should be something of an interesting spectacle, given the rather overly strict bylaws in effect for public conduct…'

Haasterman attempted to bring the old man's ramblings back towards the matter in hand. 'And your reasons for requesting, uh, *repatriation* are…?'

The man snorted. 'Look around you, Lieutenant. Austerity has turned this country into a bleak and commonplace purgatory. Such a psychic environment is utterly inimical to my evocation – and damned little fun on the personal level, I might add, to boot.' He sighed. 'One had such hopes for Britain under National Socialist rule – did you ever meet the Mitford sisters? No, I suppose not. You people never quite understood how deeply spiritual Nazi ideology was, and still is in certain quarters – utter nonsense in the specifics, naturally, but the iron gullibility of the *Wehrmacht* would have given me all the power and, ah, material resources I should ever need.'

Haasterman found that he was growing angry despite himself, more at the old man's completely unapologetic demeanour than at what he was unapologetic about. 'You're talking about collaboration? Working for those bastards?'

'Oh grow up, Lieutenant, do. How many missile scientists have you spirited away by now? You're surely not going to tell me that your own hands are clean? Yours personally, the army and air force command that you claim to represent and the, ah, S*ection* superiors who are in actual fact your masters? We all of us make the best use of such opportunities as the world presents.'

The mention of the Section took Haasterman by surprise. His activities in Britain took place under more ordinarily covert operational guises, with no mention of the Section even by word of mouth. His surprise showed on his face; the other noticed it.

'Oh, you'd be surprised at some of the things I know,' the man said casually. 'I have a little man whose business it is to tell me these things – and I do, in a quite literal sense, mean a *little man*. That's one of the problems, in fact. If the war taught us anything it was that the sloppy, piecemeal way of doing things just won't hold water any longer. We have to think in larger terms these days, and for that I need the resources of patronage. And I happen to know that your Section operates under that precise same remit.'

He grinned suddenly – it was as if the corners of his mouth had been tugged up on threads and then instantly released. 'Of course, another reason for my haste is that England is becoming a little too "hot" for me, as I believe you'd term it. Rudolf Hess is in Spandau now, and it's only a matter of time before he lets slip about the *real* cargo of that plane, those years ago, the mystery machine-codes that not even the Enigma-crackers of Station X could begin to crack.'

The man sighed, a little regretfully. 'And additionally, certain of my, ah, *predilections*, shall we say, are now exciting more notice than is seemly – I'd have introduced the world *entire* to the joys of Thanatos and Tantra, of Daphnis and Thelema, if it hadn't been for those damnable youngsters... The forces of local authority, quite frankly, are on the scent and closing in as we speak. I have little time left if I am to take the appropriate measures.'

Little time left full stop, thought Haasterman, given your age and obvious infirmity. A year or so at the most, I'd guess. So what does the Section ultimately have to lose? 'OK,' he said out loud. 'OK. Let's say we can, uh, *disappear* you. What do we get in return?'

'Why, you get *me*,' the other said, simply. He opened the thick tweed of his coat a little and Haasterman finally saw what lay within. What on first sight seemed to be a crystal chalice, a pulsing and ablative light glowing from within. 'And you get this.'

Chapter One

The Creature from Existing Stock Footage (and the Unfortunate Consequences of Paratemporal Bravura)

In her antigravity Throne Dome of purest lapis lazuli and onyx, the High Queen of the Snail Women puffed out her tempestuously heaving chest under the voluminous and scintillatingly glittery samite of her shift, and waved her slightly dubious-looking ceremonial pigsticking spear.

'We have no need of your hu-*manly ways, Colonel!' she cried imperiously. 'Thousands upon thousands of your puny Earth centuries ago, we gave our men a special soup of rennet, lichen and* koogie-boola *beetles to sap their virile manly pride, and threw them into fetid and unending penal servitude!'*

The High Queen gestured languidly towards several of the lightly oiled and spiky-collar'd serving boys, who were crowding to observe the scene and twittering excitedly amongst themselves. One of them waved furiously at the camera until one of the others dug him viciously with an elbow.

'Jeepers, Captain!' the runty adolescent with the outsized tinfoil spacesuit and the unfortunately protruding ears exclaimed to Colonel Crator in a tense, hoarse whisper. 'A planet full of... a planet full of fairies with the women in control! What in the wide, wide wastes of Proxima XIV are we going to do?!'

'Hold hard, Scooter.'

Captain Crator scratched his blue-black chin with the back of a butch and blocky hand. 'No mere if fetching and extremely pulchritudinous female will ever get the better of a highly trained squad of EarthForce Combat Rocket Science Space-Marines! Have no fear of that, boys, for I have a plan...'

'Your so-called "plan" will avail you not!' cried the High Queen. 'Guards!'

The Queen of the Snail Women snapped her fingers and a rounded dozen top-heavy girls in patent leather and heels tottered forward, tentatively prodding the marines with their spears, looking for all the wide, wide wastes of Proxima XIV as if they didn't know quite what to do with them.

'Take them away!' commanded the Queen of the Snail Women. 'Throw them into the Pit of Utter and Excruciating Torture...'

'Take your hands off me right this minute, Norman,' said Myra Monroe. She said it lightly and with irony, but there was no mistaking that she meant it. Myra had distinct ideas about what she would allow when fooling around, and had no problem being friendly but entirely firm about it. A hand under the angora sweater was perfectly acceptable; a hand under the bra was not.

Norman Manley allowed the offending organ to make a tactical withdrawal and sat back on the Plymouth's seat, his other arm resting companionably about Myra's shoulders. On the Lychburg Drive-o-Rama screen, Captain Crator of the EarthForce Combat Rocket Science Space-Marines was being monochromatically shackled to a steel rack suspended from a winch, by a pair of domino-masked women in plastic bikinis.

Companionable, yeah, Norman thought. That was the word, he supposed. It was weird, when you came to think about it.

It was like the way that Myra didn't really *explain* much, in the way that girls in the movies explained everything that was happening, everything they were thinking – but you somehow got exactly what she meant without having to think about it. He was turned on by her like you wouldn't believe, it went without saying, and she had to knock him back on a constant if – he hoped – a slowly relaxing basis, but he'd found himself slightly unprepared for the real-life complexities of something so simple as being turned on, when it happened with some real other person, in real life.

Like any other male from the year dot, he liked to shoot the bull with the other guys at the Lychburg Food and Drug soda counter about his conquests amongst the female population of Lychburg High, but in fact Myra was Norman's first real girlfriend. In the two weeks since he had first asked her out, standing there outside her Home Ec. class, cold-sweat stammering all the while and wishing that the ground would open under him for the endless instant before she said yes, he had found himself completely unprepared for the easiness of manner they were establishing, the sense of mutual, friendly regard. It was something that the movies had never really touched upon, for all their flash and fireworks, and Norman Manley was coming to the vague realisation that the movies – any movie he had ever actually seen, in any case – hardly *ever* really touched upon things that were real and important, the things that really mattered way down deep. He didn't quite know what he should be thinking about that.

Myra arched her back to stretch it a little, then laid her head on Norman's shoulder and looked up at him. 'Do you know what I want? Do you know what I *really* want?'

'What do you want?' said Norman.

'I want a chocolate malt,' said Myra. 'A double chocolate malt with extra chocolate. And I want a corn dog, too.'

* **

For a moment, Victoria allowed herself a moment's pleasure in the impossibly smooth feel of the Chinese lacquer of the pen, the solid weight of it in her hand, the expertly crafted gold of the chasing and how it caught and held the light. In general form, the pen reminded her of the one that had resided on an especially constructed brass and ivory stand fixed to her father's study desk, costing an entire nineteen guineas and which – as a child – she'd been forbidden to approach by so much as three feet on pain of out-of-hand infanticide.

This pen, in some subtle and indefinable sense, made even the memory of the other pale; one could imagine it costing in the region of a hundred pounds, even a thousand, if such a thing were possible… as though it had in some way been formed from the transmutated material of some unearthed burial treasure of Sumatra. As an object, in and of itself, it seemed to carry some archetypical and priceless quality that might approach the classically tutor-taught ideals of Plato.

Some while ago, though, when she had asked for something with which to write, the Doctor had simply and absent-mindedly pulled this same pen from a pocket and tossed it to her without a thought, or, indeed, a second glance.

Now, Victoria turned her attention from the item in her hand and returned it to the Journal spread before her, in which she was recording certain events appendant to her latest adventures, attempting to put herself in the correct frame of mind to set them down, in some relatively clarified form, before she crawled beneath the counterpane and slept.

Mindful that (should she eventually return to her proper place and time) the contents of this Journal might have her dispatched to the confines of some conveniently out-of-the-way sanatorium without delay, she had inceptionally attempted to form them as a variety of fantastical Romance in the manner of Mr Verne, but had been defeated by the fact that the events detailed had been too true – too *real* in their particulars – to appear as some innocently convincing fabrication. Instead, she now settled for verisimilitude, distilled through certain minor fictions and evasions:

'... *and with the Baleful Influence of the Orb remov'd,*' she wrote, '*it seemed as though the foul Glamour that had turned the ordinarily virtuous and kindly People under it to purest Evil likewise dissipated. I am compelled to admit, it was something of an experience to see these poor Souls awaken to their true selves and propensities, and it gave me some small, salutary pleasure to participate in their resulting Celebrations. The people of Ma –*'

Here, Victoria thought for a moment, then continued:

'*The people of Madagascar, I feel, are decent Souls at heart, though frightfully Warlike in the way that they express themselves, if not in actual Fact. This is, says the Doctor, an integral part of their Culture, and as such he fears as to the consequences when the Missionaries of Civilisation encounter them, and mistake the Warlike pronouncements of their Tribal Elders for the literal Truth...*

'*But this, says the Doctor, is a matter for Another Day. As for ourselves, we at last repaired to the vehicular contrivance that had brought us here in the first place, the experimental dirigible that continually seemed to be blown off course...*'

The floor under her lurched.

For an instant, with a superstitious pang of fear, Victoria imagined that the TARDIS had in some strange manner been aware of her calling it a mere *dirigible*, had taken umbrage and was warning her that it would soon exact its Horrible Revenge. Then the room around her shook again – not with an air of imminent disaster, but with a feeling similar to that you might encounter in a hansom cab when the horse is startled, and uncertain as to which direction the jarvey wants it to go.

Victoria sighed. Obviously, the Doctor was tinkering with the inner workings of the TARDIS again – something he seemed to do with a remarkable if, in her opinion, rather inept regularity. Having only a passing acquaintance – as the Doctor himself would be the first to admit – with the technicalities of the processes by which the Scientists of his people had built the conveyance in the first place, the man seemed insistent upon divining them himself by a process of trial and error... an occupation which had thus far, uniformly and without exception, simply had the effect of turning things from bad to worse.

Sleep now did not seem to be an option. Discarding her William Morris bathing robe, Victoria opened her closet and selected a brightly coloured costume of some smooth, synthetic material. Donning it, she noted that the hemline was of such a cut as to leave her legs bare to the knees and recalled with a smile how, upon first encountering people from another time, she had been shocked and mortified to see how women had displayed so much as their *ankles*. At some point, she reflected, she would have conquered the effects of her upbringing to assay the wearing of an actual pair of trousers.

The TARDIS lurched again. Victoria glanced at herself in the mirror and decided that she might for this once forgo the application of cosmetic compounds in favour of seeing just what, precisely, the Doctor thought he was about.

* * *

The lovely young Proximan guard was all of a fluster, obviously having never before been exposed to the virile manliness of a so-called puny Earthling.

'Tell me,' she said, 'what is this thing that you Earth men call "kissing"?'

'Allow me to demonstrate, my dear,' said Professor Saunders, twirling his moustache and stepping forward to take her hand. 'When the time is slightly more propitious...'

There was a thump. The girl's eyes rolled up in her head and she swooned somewhat ungracefully out of shot, as though already in the process of working out how she was going to break her fall.

'Well done, Scooter,' Professor Saunders remarked, as that same youth appeared, hefting a component of Proximan religious sculpture that for some reason appeared remarkably similar to a baseball bat.

'Now we must find the good Captain – I fear that we have little time to lose!'

Captain Crator, meanwhile, his sinews cording like tensile steel, fought against the rather more intractable steel of the rack. 'You'll never get away with this!' he snarled through clenched teeth.

'Oh, but we will,' said the High Queen, from her levitating raffia and tourmaline viewing pagoda. 'The denizen of this Pit is a Ruul from the fetid swamps of Xanjax, the most abhorrent and bestial creature in all of Proxima XIV, trapped by our skilful hunter maidens and kept in a state of perpetual starvation – purely to deal with such irritants as you...'

A strangely archaic portcullis set in the side of the Pit rumbled upwards... and something came out of the gate. It had the body of a large and slightly moth-eaten gorilla suit and the head of a deep-sea diver's helmet, from which protruded a multiplicity of antennae and eyes on stalks. As it lumbered forward, its monstrous arms flailing randomly and the zipper up its back clearly visible, Captain Crator began to struggle all the more...

Norman headed back from the concession stand clutching his cargo of rustling foodstuff-packaging and paper cups, picking his way through the darkly, obviously occupied automobiles by the light from the screen.

Off to one side he saw a collection of motorbikes. Leather-jacketed riders were lounging next to them and passing around a flask of liquor while their girls, in identical pink blouses, held some private and animated conversation of their own. The East Side Serpentines: well-known juvenile delinquents and the bane of Police Chief Tilson's life. They didn't seem out for trouble, but Norman decided to avoid them anyway. He turned back the way he had come – and for an instant stared directly at the movie screen that had, the last time he looked at it, been showing *Attack of the Space Women from Proxima Fourteen*.

The screen was a shimmering blaze of colour. Complex, organic-looking shapes replicated themselves and expanded, their ragged edges becoming distinct as other shapes similarly replicated and expanded in a recurring and seemingly infinite succession. The effect was like some tangible force of suction, physically sucking at his eyes and pulling his body forward along with them. Norman moved towards the shifting light, unaware in any physical sense of the steps his feet were taking. It was as if he were in some way drifting…

Abruptly, the screen stuttered and blanked, to be replaced by the slightly overexposed slate-greys and whites of *Space Women*. It was as if the screen itself had suddenly realised that Norman was looking and had hastily covered up at a rate of twenty-four frames per second. Crator, the Professor, Scooter, a number of Proximan guards and, for some reason, the high queen herself in her distinctly down-to-Earth-looking underwear, were running through a tunnel as plaster flagstones showered around them. Rebounded off them, in several cases.

Norman stumbled, sticking out a hand to crush a package of Fritos against the wing of a pristine Mercury.

'Hey, watch the *car*, man!' The occupant was a BMOC from the Roaches, the Lychburg High football team. Norman knew his name as Joey Maven, and knew that Joey Maven wouldn't have recognised *him* from a dead dog. Maven was here with one or another of the cheerleaders, whose name Norman didn't know what with them being kinda interchangeable, and who looked at him with a kind of speculative spite as though considering whether to sic her boyfriend on him or not.

'Sorry...' Norman mumbled, noting that he was automatically ducking down his head and hunching his shoulders, just like the pack animals they were learning about in Mr Hecht's biology class. He slunk back towards his Plymouth and Myra – feeling kind of sick inside, as if his stomach were trying to tie itself in knots. The vision he had seen on the movie screen was lost in a complex, messy, animal mix of fright, embarrassment and subconsciously buried, completely unacknowledged white-hot rage.

* * *

The console room, Victoria had always privately thought, was in some sense inviolate. No matter what the past upheaval, no matter what the damage one might have seen when one was last in it, stepping into it *again* was to be presented with its perfect interplay of flat, white, pristine planes constructed from some substance reminiscent of ivory, extruded from some manufactory of the Alien and the Future. So much so, that even when she came into it from the minor lived-in disarray of her own neat and tidy apartment-chambers, the contrast between the two was a not unpleasant, but active, shock. The room was a place that contrived almost by its very basic nature, it seemed, to be impervious to disorder.

Now the scene was different. Cover plates on the surrounding walls and the console had been removed, great tangles of vulcanised black rubber tubing snaking from the one to the other. Galvanistic discharges stuttered and flared within the innards of the console itself, affording brief illuminations of workings Victoria could not even begin to describe, never having known the words. In her time with the Doctor, she had come to recognise the electrics, electronics and even cybernetics of times more advanced than her own, but the workings of the TARDIS did not seem remotely similar to these, even in kind. While not organic, the forms she could chiefly make out seemed to give the impression, in some sense that she could not quite define, of being *alive*.

The central column of the console (the time rotor, Victoria gathered, from some previous and off-hand Doctorial explanation) juddered and lurched through its usually smooth and graceful cycle, flashing with a fitful light that seemed to be forever on the point of catching into constancy, but never quite able to manage it. On the flickering zoetropic screens ranged about the room, Victoria saw the now-familiar chaos of the Vortex, that pulsing swirl of energies and masses that formed the very unformed magma of Creation – but it was jerking strangely, as though her point of view were constantly shifting and transposing.

Jamie was standing by the wall beside the outer doors – and Victoria's attention latched on to him gratefully. There was something about his solid, kilted, reassuring form that helped to counter the confusion of the surroundings. Of course, this might have been purely because he was tucking gloomily into a plate of cheese sandwiches – and it is slightly harder than otherwise to feel fear in a situation in which someone is comfortable enough to eat a cheese sandwich.

Jamie returned her unspoken, raised-eyebrow query with a shrug. 'Don't ask me,' he said. 'He's off again.'

The Doctor's head rose, grinning and unkempt, from behind the console. The grin made Victoria's heart sink. An otherworldly genius the Doctor might be, but it was the genius and otherworldliness, on occasion, of an idiot savant or a child. A fumbling, if fundamentally good-intentioned intelligence, with no real conception of the consequences of its actions. Victoria could quite imagine – should the circumstances ever arise – the Doctor going up to the Lord God Almighty and pulling on His beard, just to see whether or not it came off.

'I think I have it,' the little man proclaimed triumphantly. 'I think I do. At last, I really think I do.'

'Oh yes?' Victoria regarded him levelly. 'And what, precisely, do you really think you have?'

The Doctor rolled down his sleeves and plucked his coat from where it hung on a nearby hat stand that Victoria had failed to notice before, her mind being occupied with other things. He shrugged himself into the coat and became, for some short while, diverted into fussing over the slight fray on its cuffs – then, with a start, seemed to remember where he was and turned with a flick of his pudding-bowl-cut hair to regard Victoria again. Not for the first time, she found herself wondering just how much the mischievous little twinkle in his eyes was innate, and how much was consciously contrived for show.

'As I might have told you,' the Doctor said, 'at some point or other, I came to acquire the TARDIS under rather unfortunate circumstances. What with one thing and another, to avoid beating unnecessarily around the bush and, indeed, to cut a long story short, I ended up having to appropriate it by unconventional means...'

'Stole it, you mean,' said Jamie around the last half of his sandwich. 'You mean you stole it.'

'Yes, yes,' said the Doctor with a little moue of pique, 'if you really want to put things in the worst possible light. In any case, my, ah, people have certain procedures in place for when such a thing should happen. If a TARDIS is, as you say, Jamie, *stolen*, then self-proliferating, command-level polyviral autmemes are activated on an accretional and exponential time-delay basis, which...'

The Doctor looked around at the blank looks he was

receiving from both Jamie and Victoria.

'It's like chaining a penny farthing to a lamppost,' he said, 'or hobbling a horse. The difference being that my people are a bit more advanced and do things a bit more subtly. Instead of rendering the TARDIS immobile, they simply made it almost impossible for any thief to take it where he wants it to go. Set the controls for the late Byzantine era on Earth and you'll up in the Cool Cheese Millennium on Jupiter; head for the year 3000 and you end up last Thursday afternoon... *that's* why, I think, the old girl has become so intransigent as of late. It's not a question of me *not* knowing the first thing about piloting her at all.'

Now the Doctor gestured grandly, taking in the entire mass of tangled rubber tubing that adorned the room. 'I have now managed to bypass those processes; work around them with a number of quite brilliantly unorthodox and ingenious connections, even if I say so myself. Of course, that means the loss of a certain number of fail-safes, but with a complete regaining of control that's neither here nor there...'

'Fail-safes?' said Victoria uneasily. 'What exactly do you mean by fail-safes?'

'Oh, you know the sort of thing.' The Doctor waved an airy hand. 'Protocols that prevent us from materialising around some solid object, or in the heart of a sun, or in some universe other than our own. Not to worry though...' He rubbed his hands together in a brisk and workmanlike fashion. 'Such things are unimportant if one knows precisely where or when one is going. Allow me to demonstrate.'

And with that, before either Jamie or Victoria could even so much as draw breath to protest, he reached for the console and pulled a lever.

* * *

'Now I *think*,' said the Doctor, a number of hectic seconds later, 'I know what it was I did wrong...'

Chapter Two
A Meander Through the Relics

Species and their cultures evolve – but then, so does everything else. In biological terms, all *evolution* means is that a child looks different from its parents. Or applicable progenitory organisms. In general terms, evolution means that everything changes over time, even if only to collapse under entropy, to have bits drop off until it dies. The important factor in the process is that of *selection*. A change in basic nature happens over such immense periods, involves such extraordinary circumstances to bring it about, that in the terms of a generally humanoid life span any changes exist purely on the level of minor variations on a theme.

'Is here we come to big-nasty war on monkey-hominid planet called Dirt,' said the attendant, trundling through the chamber on the organically force-evolved rollers it used instead of legs. A complex limb sprouted from its grey, obloidular body and fashioned its appendages complexly so that they formed the outline of what could have been a graphically-designed arrow, pointing at one of the massive display cases to its left.

'Is phase one of big hitting everybody people with stuff type-thing that last almost all of monkey-hominidly local century, what is number of fingers aboriginal monkey-hominids have times number of toes, what come to eighty-eight proper years.'

The display case was crammed with artefacts, some of them genuine, some alien attempts at reproduction. They had been arranged in an illustrative tableau – again, by alien hands, with alien sensibilities.

'Is you see Tommies and the Fritzes all sitting in trenches,' the attendant continued informatively, 'with the clangy pinball machines and mustard gas masks, what are made from finest yummy yellow mustard and is made into nasty horrible devil faces, and is blowing poison gas to protect them from their enemy, the boorish Hun, what is riding towards them on big spiky-armoured pecky-battle Ístereich! Is above them flying bloody Red Baron in evil dirigible sausage-ship, and is very big impressive dogfight – with real pretend-move living dogs grown from Collection protoplasmic gene-banks all same!'

Romana looked up at the terrified and yapping chihuahuas as they struggled in the straps securing them to the conveyances that hung on wires inside the case. 'That strikes me as being unnecessarily cruel,' she said. 'And not entirely accurate in the historical sense.' She turned to her companion. 'Is it? Even remotely like it was, I mean. You're the one with the first-hand experience in these matters.'

'Well, these things get lost and found and misinterpreted over the millennia,' said the Doctor, smiling up at the scene. He seemed to be enjoying himself. 'You have to give them full marks for effort, if nothing else.'

'Even so...' Romana said dubiously. 'You'd think they'd notice little things like the fact of it being physically impossible for something like that to *fly*. What are the things the dogs are strapped into actually supposed to be?'

'I think,' said the Doctor, 'they're the Collectors' idea of Sopwith Camels. It's quite a feat of bioengineering, I suppose, that they managed to get the cockpits and flight controls between the humps.'

The attendant, meanwhile, had led his motley collection of sightseeing alien charges to another case. The Doctor and Romana hurried to catch up.

'Is here phase two of Big Dirt War. In happy Englandish springtime scene we see Good King Hitler on the beach and is playing with his ball, tossing it to Mother Brown and old Uncle Joe and rumpy-jiggy girlfriend Nancy Mitford. But is soon to come big and horrible tragedy! Is evil Eisenstein here on beach, too, with atomic Nazi doodlebugs! Is see how they burrow through the sand making big swirly marks (is from which they get their name) and is heading for Good King Hitler to crawl up bipedal-hominid leg and blow brains out of head! Soon whole planet Dirt is plunged into big hitting people with stuff-type thing again, and evil Eisenstein goes hoppedy-skip back to submersible nuclear battleship, what is called *Bismarck*...'

The race of creatures that had eventually become known as the Collectors had once been rather better known as a hideous galactic scourge. While they hadn't turned suns into supernovae, obliterated entire worlds with planet-crackers or killed populations on the level of genocide, as opposed to decimation, they had proved unstoppable in their own particular way. Their invention of the hyperwobble-drive and their use of psychonomic shielding on their swarms of ships meant that, while any planetary defence system might see them coming, the incalculably erratic progress of the ships themselves would prove too much for organic and artificial minds alike. Said planetary defences would suffer the large-scale equivalent of a nervous breakdown, allowing the planet to be completely overrun.

The only known defence from the creatures who would become known as the Collectors was, quite simply, to get the hell out of the way. Even the Daleks themselves had once, on hearing rumours of a band of Collectors in the vicinity, gone through extremely tortuous subterfuges to mask their entire home planet, pretend that it had been destroyed, and only bring it out from cover when the creatures who would become known as the Collectors had gone.

The creatures who would become known as the Collectors were not evil as such, but they were rabidly acquisitive. They had an insatiable desire for *things*, which they plundered from the planets that they overran, with absolutely no eye or other applicable optical receptor for the items' proper context or worth. The distinctions between precious gems or copralithic lumps of compacted silt, or finely crafted burial masks, or dead animals, or paving slabs, or slaves, or mangles, or jelly moulds...

All the values that other sentient beings placed upon the objects around them escaped the creatures who would become known as the Collectors completely. They were simply *things* and the creatures who would become known as the Collectors wanted them. And they acquired them in such numbers that mere words like *millions* and *billions* lose their very meaning.

Over their millennia of plunder, however, the creatures who would become known as the Collectors changed. One cannot come into contact with thousands upon thousands of other cultures – even via a process of violent mass theft – without certain attributes impacting and rubbing off.

Over thousands of years, the drive for pure acquisition waned; comparisons and contrasts formed despite themselves. The nature of the creatures who would be known as the Collectors evolved, by increments, until at a certain point they found themselves in a position similar to a gang of pirates looking at their booty, running their eyes over the haul of gold and jewels and suchlike treasures and wondering: *what the hell are we going to do with it all now?*

The upshot was, some tens of thousands of years beyond what in human terms would be called the twentieth century, if you wanted to find something your best bet was to go and look around the Big Huge and Educational Collection of Old Galactic Stuff.

The TARDIS had materialised in the hall of Big Pretend-Move Animals But Don't 'Cos They're Dead And Have Sand Stuck Up Them. The Doctor and Romana had wandered through the tangled taxidermic bestiary, past hairy mammoth-voles and hipogiraffes and behemoths and bandersnatches, until they had come to one of the transport tubes that wound and proliferated through the entire Big Huge and Educational Collection. The Collection was sorted and arranged by the kind of minds that would have been hard-pressed even to comprehend such a human term as 'random'. One could travel through it for weeks, for years – for centuries – and never find the same place twice, let alone what one might be trying to locate.

Fortunately, the Doctor had remembered to take along a reasonably sophisticated tracking device, its cannibalised twenty-second century bubble-circuitry packed inside the case of a hollowed out Pifco transistor radio. He and Romana had shot through the tubes on blasts of slightly noxious compressed air, occasionally shouting simple directions like 'Up!', 'Right!' and 'Down again!' until with some degree of overshooting and backtracking they had reached the near vicinity of their final goal.

Now, as they tagged along behind the sightseers being led through the hall of What Human-Type Monkey Hominids Got Up To On Planet Dirt, the tracking device began to bleep to the tune of 'Happy Birthday to You' via a cheap little sound-circuit that had been recycled from a musical greetings card.

'I think we've found him,' said the Doctor with delight. It was probably the first and only time in the history of the universe that anyone had been delighted by the sound of a musical greetings card.

'... is while Johnny Welfare plays folk rock on a stolen guitar,' the alien attendant was saying, 'his girlfriend is getting high on boogie tea and has fixed herself a California sandwich...'

'Do you think so?' Romana peered into the display case, which was showing a tableau from what had apparently been the Summer of Great Big Rumpy-Pumpy Love. 'I can't see him.'

'You're looking in the wrong direction,' said the Doctor. 'By the lava lamp and under the *I'm Backing Britain* poster. They've covered him with a throw-rug and sat a gonk on top of him, but I'd recognise him anywhere.'

Romana looked closer and, indeed, saw the familiar shape under the horrid orange and purple covering. 'Do you think he's intact, after all these centuries? Do you think we can get him to work?'

'I'm sure of it,' said the Doctor cheerfully, rubbing his hands together at the prospect of some serious tinkering. 'If the worst comes to the worst, we can simply extrapolate such memory algorithms as remain and transplant them into a new chassis. I'd been meaning to upgrade the little fellow for a while now, anyway.'

'Hmph.' Romana rapped the display case thoughtfully. She had been expecting glass, but the sound told her it had been fabricated from some extruded form of monatomic carbon and was diamond-hard. 'Any thoughts on the matter of how we're going to get him out?'

'I have formulated,' said the Doctor, his eyes sidling from the display case to the attendant and its charges as they moved on to another scene, 'a marvellously subtle and complex plan of action as we speak.'

Chapter Three

The Return of the Final Revenge of the Creature Part Two

The spaceship powered through the inky depths of outer space in a surprisingly stylish manner that was in fact a direct lift from an episode of Buck Rogers and the Mole Men *starring Buster Crabbe.*

In the control cabin, entered by way of a basic soundtrack-popping splice, Professor Saunders pulled a lever to activate a rather diminutive Van de Graaff generator, the immediate function of which was was not readily apparent.

'The Proximan Death Barrier was destroyed with the explosion of the planet,' he said, in his suave received-pronunciational tones, idly fending off the advances of a smitten pair of female guards, who were trying to stroke his brow.

'We'll have no problem getting back to Earth. Indeed, with the modifications I've made to our atomic space-jets, I believe we can make it in half the time.'

'Imagine that!' exclaimed Scooter, from where he was being partially smothered by the six-foot tall and strapping Commandant, who had previously presided over the horrors of the Slave Podiums. 'A trip of thousands and thousands of miles in a single week! You're a genius, Prof.'

'Yes,' said the Professor. 'I rather have to admit that I am. Just a little to the left, if you'd be so kind, my dear.'

Captain Crator looked up from where he was studying something that flashed its lights and went ping. 'I suppose I'd better check on our royal guest.'

The High Queen had, in some unexplained manner, been able to lay her hands on a fetching new samite gown, and a variety of soft furnishings which were variously hung and strewn around the formerly bare and spartan steel-plate-and-rivet-walled cabin. She now reclined upon a rather markedly luxurious couch, toying with the slightly insubstantial-looking chains that secured her to the wall.

'Ah, me,' she said despondently, looking up at Captain Crator as he came into the cabin. 'I see now how my intolerance and dictatorial ways have led my planet to its doom.'

Crator's face shifted expressions furiously as it attempted to convey how he was deciding to conceal the fact that it had been Professor Saunders, sitting on a lever, who had inadvertently set the Proximan bomb-rockets to explode in their own silos. He sat down himself down on the couch and took her hand. 'You'll have to stand trial on Earth for your crimes,' he said, with a lunatic disregard for any kind of comparative legality whatsoever, 'but, with the loss of your planet, I think they'll decide that you've suffered enough.' He became expansive, and not a little gesticulatory. 'A new life on Earth awaits you, High Queen – and one to put even the glittery minarets and weevil-swamps of Proxima XIV to shame!'

'One can but hope,' said the Queen, coolly, 'but you could tell that she was warming to the dashing Captain even as she spoke. 'The good Professor Saunders has been advising me as to how I might fit in there better.' She smiled at him through lowered eyelids. 'So tell me, Captain Crator, what is this thing you Earth men call "an expeditious bit of the how's-your-father"?'

The road back into Lychburg wound through a series of wooded hills, branching several times, and in the night it was easy to get lost. Norman swore under his breath and glanced between the two unmarked roads available at the junction. If other traffic had been around, he could have just gone with the general flow, but due to some freak of timing there was no other vehicle in sight. Norman was sufficiently adolescent to place a premium on looking cool in front of his girl – or at least, not looking the precise opposite – and to wander aimlessly through the back roads for an hour would look, he thought, uncool in the extreme.

'I think we should go left,' Myra said. It wasn't so much what she said as the way she said it, but he felt an almost physical paroxysm of relief. It was as if she had read his mind, and seen his secret dread of girl-contempt, and had made damn sure that what she said contained not a single trace of it. Mr Hecht had talked in his class about teenage hormones, Norman recalled, how they made you sorta crazy and confused, how they made you blow the tiniest of things out of all proportion – but knowing that it happened and *why* it happened were not much help when it was you who were going through it.

'Yeah, OK,' Norman said. 'We'll go left.'

The road led upwards, but in the dark the twists and turns contrived to mask how steep the incline in fact was – until they came to a bluff beyond which were sprawled the Lychburg city lights. You could make out the neon signs of Main Street, the lit-up clock face of City Hall which had stopped several years ago when it had been damaged by a lightning strike. You could see right across the city, even to the darkness of the hills and the tiny lights of the Drive-o-Rama beyond...

The towering embarrassment of adolescence hit Norman again as he realised he had parked in one of Lychburg's seriously notorious make-out spots without really meaning to. He started to apologise, but Myra was resting herself warm and casual against him.

'It's beautiful, isn't it?' she said in a voice that told Norman she had known precisely where the left turn she'd suggested led. 'I love it up here. I always love it when I come up here. What do you think? When you look at the City. What do you feel?'

'Well, yeah, uh…' Norman tried to sort out the feelings the question prompted. There was something vaguely disquieting about the way that Myra had said City, as though the word were capitalised, as though this was in some sense the only name Lychburg could ever have or need. 'Yeah, well, it's *home*, isn't it? It's our home town. It's where we grew up. Everything we know. It's just that sometimes…'

'Yes?' said Myra. Her voice was completely neutral: a simple prompt that triggered no fight-or-flight animal danger signals whatsoever.

'It's just that sometimes it seems so small,' said Norman. 'It's like we live our little lives here, go to school and go to work and to the movies, and none of it really *means* anything. I mean, there's a big wide world out there and…'

'There is no other World,' said Myra, voice still perfectly neutral. No human content to it at all. 'There is no World but the City.'

'What are you talking about? Just down the road from the drive-in there's…'

Norman's voice trailed off as his thoughts slipped over the edge of some mental cliff. A chaos of partially formed images struck him – images of a road similar to those which ran from Lychburg to the drive-in, only somehow wider and with any number of roads running in parallel, all of them packed with pod-like cars; images of places that were *like* the town of Lychburg but entirely different in some way that he could not pin down; images of *huge* and unimaginably complicated places with strange buildings and people who looked and moved in different…

Norman had been conscious of the outside, larger world in the same way he was conscious of having a right hand. It was something that you simply did not actively think about. The thought just never occurred. Now that it had, he realised, it was like falling into some mental void. There were places outside, and those places had names – but now that he tried to think of them, now that he tried to imagine some world other than, and outside from, the Lychburg city limits, he could not think of a single one.

Not one.

From down below, at the bottom of the bluff, he heard a sharply detonative sound like a rifle shot or a thunderclap close up – as though the air itself had split apart as something burst through it. There was the sound of some strange mechanism whirring to a stop.

'Your thought processes have become erratic,' Myra said in flat, inhuman tones, in the way that some science guy might discuss a bug under a glass slide. 'Complexity of the host-sensorium is resurfacing. Starting to remember. The signifiers of the World are collapsing, deconstructing under an atypical and excessive sense of psychic introspection. Clearly, it has been infected by the forces of Discontinuity.'

For the first time since they had parked here on the cliff-edge, Norman looked at her – turned to really look at her. Physically she seemed unchanged, but there was a hideous sense of *wrongness* about her, the positioning of her limbs, the muscles that moved them, set in postures that had no humanity about them; relaxed or tensed in manners that no human being could ever achieve.

Her eyes were clear and steady and direct, with nothing, absolutely nothing, living inside them.

'The Continuity must be protected,' she said, and with an entirely relaxed and casual manner reached up her hand to plunge its splayed-open fingers deep into Norman Manley's eyes.

* * *

Victoria would never have a complete memory of the events between the Doctor pulling the lever and her resurfacing into painful consciousness on the TARDIS floor. Such mental pictures and sensations that remained were fragmented and disjointed: megrimous and synesthesic fugue-amalgams that, even in retrospect, could not be forced into comprehensive sense. Images of ragged, faceless men with stunted parasites inside them marching in single file over some precipice to fall in impossible and somehow *multiple* directions under a gravity that no human had ever experienced. A flash of some fabricated, animated monstrosity, lashed together from paint-flaking driftwood and oiled rope. Pale-faced, god-like beings that pawed at her with long, segmented, wormlike fingers and plunged those same digits into the matter of her head. The wrenching, churning sensation of being, in some manner unrelated to the purely physical, turned inside out...

She hauled herself into what was more or less a sitting position with a groan. Her body felt bruised all over and her head was one enormous ache. She looked about: if the console room of the TARDIS had been in a state of disarray before, now it was in a state of complete disaster. Small fires spluttered behind the open cover plates and the air smelt faintly of ozone – the chemical compound rather than the smell of decomposing seaweed that people travel to seaside resorts to take for their health.

Jamie was off to one side, caught up in a clump of snapped-off vulcanised tubing, still insensible but beginning to stir. Of the Doctor there was no immediate sign.

'Doctor?' Victoria called weakly. 'Are you there? Where are you?'

'I'm over here,' came a voice from, as she had already assumed would be the case, behind the central console. 'I'm quite all right – although I seem to have become entangled with the hat stand.'

Victoria climbed, wincing, to her feet and walked around the console. The situation was, indeed, as the Doctor had described. The little man lay on his front with the stand on top of him, its length contriving to run at some slight crosswise angle beneath his clothing so that the top end protruded from his collar and the bottom from the right cuff of his checked trousers.

'If you could give me a bit of help,' he said, 'I'd be very grateful.'

'If you think for one minute I'm going to take off your trousers,' said Victoria, 'then you're sorely mistaken.'

'The thought, my dear girl,' said the Doctor, 'never crossed my mind. I do have some sense of propriety.' He lifted his right foot so that the protruding base of the hat stand bobbed up and down. 'I think the bottom, if you'll pardon the expression, screws right off.'

Victoria unscrewed the base and pulled the remainder of the stand through the top of his clothing. 'How did something like that happen in the first place?' she asked.

The Doctor stood up and dusted himself off – it seemed strange that he was constantly doing this, performing little fastidious gestures upon a general form that carried a vague but innate, and seemingly immutable, sense of shabbiness about it. It was as if, in some strange manner, he fully expected himself to be of some different form and was constantly surprised that he was not.

'I think we have been subject to some severe gravmetic forces,' he said. 'Forces that operate upon completely different principles from the galvanistic and magnetic with which those of your place and time would be familiar.' He frowned. 'It's a blessing that those forces seem to have spared us from more direct physical harm.'

Across the console room, Jamie chose this moment to regain consciousness, disentangling himself from the tubes and muttering some fearful Celtish oath. Victoria thought to herself that it was probably a blessing she couldn't understand it.

'What happened?' he asked the world in general, when the lapse into deplorable and untranslatable profanity subsided. 'And where are we?'

'Good questions,' said the Doctor. 'Astute and to the point, and I just wish I knew the answers to them.' His glance took in both of his young friends and became slightly apologetic, a little shamefaced. 'I was intending to take us to a place I know like the back of my hand...' (Here the Doctor happened to actually glance at the back of his gesticulating hand, frowned momentarily, shrugged and then continued.) 'London towards the latter end of the twentieth century, where I have a number of friends and, indeed, in some sense, family. The intention was to set a benchmark, to see if my modifications to the TARDIS had been successful...'

'So how successful were they?' said Jamie, sourly, rubbing at the side of his head on which a nasty bruise was already flowering.

The Doctor looked down at the dials and counters of the console and sighed. 'Not very. The instruments have been completely disrupted. There's no real way to tell precisely when or where we are.'

Victoria walked over to one of the viewing screens, which appeared to be showing nothing but a sizzling mass of monochromatic snow. She depressed the little switching mechanism set into its side and was rewarded by a flicker and then more though presumably different snow. She tried again. More snow.

'So the long and the short of it is,' she said, 'that we could be absolutely anywhere. So what are we supposed to do now?'

'Well, a great man of my acquaintance,' said the Doctor, 'once said that in moments of confusion the best thing to do is go for a walk and see what happens. Something almost always does.'

With that, he set his shoulders and strolled briskly to the doors that led to the outside. Victoria was of a sudden struck by a horrible recollection – a remembrance of what the Doctor had so recently said about how, with the fail-safes of the TARDIS disabled, it was quite possible for it to materialise in any place from the heart of a sun, to the etheric vacuum of outer space, to (and this was the personal dread that she immediately flashed upon) the crushing depths of the ocean bed. She opened her mouth to remind the Doctor of these salient possibilities, but it was already too late – he was industriously cranking the handle that manually opened the doors and they, in turn, were inexorably swinging back.

For some small while the Doctor, Jamie and Victoria gazed upon the scene revealed beyond.

'Well,' said the Doctor at length. 'I'm not quite sure what I was expecting, but I certainly hadn't expected *this*…'

Chapter Four
Developments of an Egregious Nature

The precise location of the barracks must, at this time, remain classified, save that they afforded easy access to the centre of London and the City. They tended towards, and achieved, an almost perfect anonymity. To the casual observer they were completely unremarkable: a set of lovingly maintained, post-war, prefabricated huts behind a fence and gate, and a parade ground that appeared to have been given over to the parking of a basic and generic collection of military vehicles, Land Rovers and transport trucks, rather than parades. Such personnel as might be seen appeared sporadically and unarmed, obviously about some specific errand as opposed to being any part of massed ranks. The pubs and residents of the surrounding area might notice a distinct lack of off-duty troops making use of their facilities, but this was, quite frankly, given the general nature of off-duty squaddies, more a matter of relief than of comment.

Of course, if these particular troops *had* been on the streets in force there would, as like as not, have been no local residents left alive to comment, and the pubs would have been blown up by creatures to whom a pie and a pint was the last thing on their minds, assuming they could metabolise them in the first place.

Katharine Delbane checked in at the gatehouse and strolled towards one of the huts, with a confidence that was less the result of knowing that she belonged here than of faith in the credentials she had presented, several weeks ago, when she had first arrived. The documentation had stated, with great sincerity, that she was a first lieutenant in the Women's Royal

Army Corps, with special expertise in the fields of computer science and tactical logistics, on secondment to the United Nations Intelligence Taskforce (British Arm) in an auxiliary capacity and with an honorary bump in rank to that of captain.

In fact – much in the same way that the lovingly preserved exterior of the barracks themselves hid what lay within – she was nothing of the kind.

Sergeant Benton was already in the tactical analysis room when Delbane entered, inexpertly tapping away on a brand-new Apple Macintosh, one of the several that UNIT had acquired by way of the sort of unconventional diverting of funds that Delbane was in fact, investigating. Benton was one of those NCOs who seem to have been built rather than born, fully formed to fill his rank – you couldn't imagine him as a private, and you couldn't imagine him as an officer.

For all this, he seemed remarkably casual in his manner – friendly rather than otherwise, and not exactly offensive, but with a complete disregard for the protocols and conduct common in the regular army when dealing with superiors. Indeed, his first words upon meeting Delbane for the first time several weeks before had been a cheery 'So you're the girl who knows how to work these bloody things, are you? Pains in the bloody arse they are, I can tell you. Want a cup of tea before we get cracking?'

In the weeks since she had come here, Delbane had noticed that the UNIT troops seemed to operate in a kind of family atmosphere, as opposed to a more traditional and hierarchical military discipline. Since she wanted to fit in as well as she could, the last thing she could do was haul people like Benton up for insubordination, but it preyed on her mind and never failed to put her in a bad mood. In and of herself, without really thinking about it, Delbane was the sort of person who believes that underlings are there to do as they are told and speak only when spoken to, if they really have to speak at all.

A bluff and distinguished-looking man of around fifty, in civilian Harris tweed plus fours and matching cap, was also in the room. Delbane had not met him before. He was leaning over Benton's shoulder, watching the computer screen with the frowning concentration of one who was even less of an expert than Benton.

'... so the incursions are remaining constant?' he was saying.

'Not constant,' Benton said. 'It's the rate of their proliferation that's constant, in line with their accelerating birth rate. And they breed like rats. Those damn Si –'

Both Benton and the visitor realised that Delbane was standing behind them.

'Those damn *Sicilians*,' Benton continued hurriedly. 'Bringing arms in with their, uh, Mafia contacts here in the Italian community and supplying them to...' He trailed off as inspiration seemed to fail him.

'That's the question, isn't it?' said the older man, barely fumbling the catch. 'I wouldn't be surprised if they're ultimately headed across the Irish Sea – though which side might end up with 'em I dread to think. Bad show, either way. And I'll remind you, Benton,' he continued, rather more sternly, 'national slurs about birth rates and so forth might have been... *allowed* in the bad old days of Empire, but they were loathsome and abhorrent even then. They certainly have no place under any command of mine. Do you understand me, Sergeant?'

'I'm sorry, sir.' Benton looked suitably chastened, as if he really thought Delbane was stupid enough to be buying their pitiful attempt at a smoke screen for one second. 'I spoke without thinking. I was out of order.'

This was merely the latest such automatic-seeming reversal Delbane had encountered. She would walk into the canteen to find the animated conversation of the private soldiers faltering into uneasy silence while they wracked their collective brains to come up with any subject other than the one they'd all been talking about. Divisional briefings by the divisional commander, Colonel Critchton, seemed to be a marvel of implication and double-meaning for which she could not quite find the key. Even the fact that the warrant officer, Smythe, had found lodgings for her in one of the better local hotels, rather than in the decidedly spartan and communal dormitory huts, seemed to be part of a concerted effort to keep her off-site as much as possible rather than the result of any consideration for her comfort.

It wasn't that she herself was actively under suspicion, Delbane judged; it was merely the blanket distrust of any outsider felt by people who had something to hide. And she was going to find out what they were hiding.

Benton now climbed to his feet and turned to Delbane with a slightly incongruous sense of formality. 'Have you met, uh, Captain Delbane, sir? She's on attachment.'

'I don't believe I have.' The other man likewise turned, and regarded her with the innate courtesy of an English gentleman of the old school. 'Lethbridge-Stewart.'

Brigadier Lethbridge-Stewart, Delbane thought. Commander-in-Chief of the European arm of UNIT and with a contingently effective rank – should certain and specific states of emergency be declared – surpassing even that of field marshal. Even in the regular army, and its rather more irregular divisions, the Brigadier was the stuff of legend. She tried not to seem overly impressed.

'Delbane's working on the deployment of resources,' said Benton. 'You know how it is at the moment. We have so many, uh, unconventional areas we can draw upon that they can get lost. Some poor sod at the blunt end doesn't call them up because it never even occurs to him that they might exist...'

The Brigadier nodded seriously. 'That business out in Haiti last year. I'd have killed for the proper kind of fetishes and a genuine obiman if I'd known how to get hold of one.'

Delbane decided to check a decent dictionary the first chance she could, just so she could be sure that she'd really heard what she thought she had. It seemed that certain frankly unbelievable elements of her preliminary briefing by the concern for whom she truly worked might be true.

'I should have a working database in the next few days,' she said out loud.

'Good, good,' the Brigadier said. 'I had thought to get in a few days golfing before I went back to Geneva...' He glanced down somewhat regretfully at his Harris tweed golfing outfit '... but circumstances seem to have conspired to keep me here for a while.' Another meaningful glance towards Benton. 'Contact Yates and have him put a tracking squad on those, ah, Sicilians.' He turned back to Delbane. 'Keep up the good work, Delbane. I look forward to seeing your results.'

His scarf flapping behind him, the object of his search still wrapped in its ghastly crochet throw-rug covering and cradled in his arms, the Doctor pelted back through the hall of Big Pretend-Move Animals But Don't 'Cos They're Dead And Have Sand Stuck Up Them.

From all around, from varying degrees of distance, came the cacophony of thousands upon thousands of bells, whistles, buzzers, hooters, sirens and other suchlike mechanisms that had been connected to the Collectors' equivalent of a security system. Behind, and slowly gaining, came a pack of Collectors shouting things like: 'Stop! Stop! Is horrible thief taking our valuable and lovely stuff!'

The Collectors were metamorphic by physical nature, their soft and gel-like flesh able to twist into myriad forms by way of a complicatedly interlinked skeletal structure and a large biological array of potential organs and appendages which could be force-grown in real time. At the moment they were collectively trying for something terrifying and ferocious – but it would only be a matter of time before they hit upon the idea of redesigning themselves for speed...

'Complex subtlety?' Romana snapped as she pelted along beside the Doctor, her skirts streaming behind her less dramatically, if rather more attractively, than the Doctor's scarf flapped behind him. She was coming to the conclusion, though, that crushed velvet and molecularly bonded gold-leaf trimming had been a bit of a mistake. She had also decided to regenerate herself a smaller, slightly more compact body the first chance she got, as soon as she could find a suitably elegant template. 'I'd hardly call that subtle.'

'I used the sonic screwdriver,' said the Doctor indignantly. 'Remarkably advanced Gallifreyan technology, the sonic screwdriver.'

'Yes,' fumed Romana. 'And you used that remarkably advanced Gallifreyan technology to smash a big hole, grab the thing and then run like Skaro.'

She decided that she sounded a little out of breath, so cut in her respiratory bypass system. 'And quite why you decided to come *here* to look in the first place,' she continued, her voice now completely cold and calm as she ran, 'I simply can't imagine and you never did tell...'

They had reached the TARDIS. Romana opened it with her own key and ran inside without breaking stride. The Doctor followed and she slammed the doors behind him in the enraged and monstrous face-equivalents of the Collectors.

'It was the easiest place to get to,' the Doctor said, skidding to a halt, 'all things considered.' Now that the immediate danger of being torn limb from limb was over he seemed completely and utterly relaxed, without a care in the world. 'It was one of the places and times where I knew for a fact the chap would be, with little danger of impacting on the timeline when I retrieved him. Imagine the effect if I'd whisked him away from that happy young man's birthday party in twentieth-century Manchester…'

'Yes, but you've really got to stop forgetting about him and leaving him somewhere,' said Romana, 'and then turning the known universe upside down looking for him again. He must be the oldest single lump of coherent matter *in* it by now.'

'Well, he was built to last, after all.' The Doctor set his burden down on the console room floor and unwrapped its garish mantle. 'Let's have a look at you, K-9.' He swung up an access cover in the side of the mobile cyberdynic unit and poked around the dormant innards with a not particularly gentle finger. 'The key systems seem to be salvageable, and the personality backups seem to be intact. A couple of new power cells, a bit of work with the quantum spanner and a buckyball-suspension-fluid change and he'll be good as new. You mark my words.'

Romana had been idly watching one of the glassblowers' bulls-eye mouldings which the Doctor affected on the white walls of the console room, and which had obligingly dilated to show the scene outside. The Collectors, having exhausted the cutting and sawing options of their various appendages on the TARDIS hull, were wheeling in a massive Chelonian matter-disrupter.

'I think it might be an idea if we left that for later,' she said.

'Quite possibly,' said the Doctor, looking over her shoulder. 'They might do themselves some serious damage if they try to fire it in an enclosed space. So let's not give them the opportunity.' He turned to the console and coaxed it into life. 'Where do you feel like? Paris in the spring? I've always loved Paris in the spring.'

The time rotor flared, and Romana felt the comforting sensations of translation into the Vortex, the place where some small, deep part of the time aristocracy consciousness truly lived – and then she felt a *lurch* inside, the spraining in her soul that told her time, as such, was out of joint. It was a feeling – if it could be called such – that was becoming distressingly, and not a little depressingly familiar.

'Oh no,' she heard the Doctor say, as an anaesthetic numbness infused and shut down her fourteenth and twenty-seventh senses. 'Not *again*…'

Chapter Five
In the Nation of the Solid State

As the jeep jolted down the worn-out farm track, Colonel Haasterman could feel every minor increment of the damage it was doing to his 64-year-old spine. The land for miles around seemed barren and disused, not so much from soil-banking but rather as a direct result of Reaganomics in the abstract: wheat fields reverting into dustbowl country, the life and fertility sucked from them as though by some tangible and baleful supernatural force.

'Supernatural,' Haasterman muttered to himself. 'Yeah, right.'

'Sir?' said the driver, a corporal in the State National Guard, a detachment of which had been called out to the Table City airbase to serve in an auxiliary capacity should the need arise.

'Nothing, corporal,' Haasterman told him. 'Nothing important to you. Keep your mind on the road.'

The jeep crawled on under a flat grey sky that seemed bigger than all outdoors. Eventually they came to a rusting chain-link fence. With a start of something like fright, Haasterman saw the bodies of small animals strewn along the wire. Had the overt effects of the flare radiated this far? Then he relaxed as his mind worked it out: the fence had been electrified again after long years of disuse, and the local animal population had long since forgotten it was potentially lethal.

Like the Golgotha Project itself, Haasterman thought, if it came to that. You build a catastrophe machine, and when you realise what you've done you try to shut it down. And then you bury it, and try to forget about it, jettisoning any number of lives and careers in the process – it was no coincidence that Haasterman himself had been sidelined into Project Blue Book and the mills of disinformation; a glass ceiling that had left him at the level where, in dealing with the overt Military hierarchies, he was pushing it to claim the authority even of 'Colonel'...

You bury the engines of destruction, and seed the ground with salt, and they lie dormant. Then they power themselves up again and *flare*.

A pair of armed guards were waiting in an insulated picket gate where the road bisected the fence. Over their fatigues they wore airsealed polyethylene coveralls with integral life-support packs. Duct-taped to the coveralls, seemingly at random, were totems of an antique-looking and strangely eclectic nature: head-shop hippie peace symbols, reproduction SS-issue swastikas, a pentagram, a Star of David, fetish-feathers and mojo bags, dog-eared minor arcana tarot cards and pristine, mylar-bag-wrapped major league baseball cards... the cumulative effect was of men built up from clotted-together scraps and junk.

Haasterman showed his ID to one of the ragged guardsmen who was eyeing him uneasily. 'The site is hot?'

The trooper shrugged.

'Not so bad, this far out. You wouldn't want to pitch a tent for long, is all.'

He hung himself off the side of the jeep and they rode with him, past the big Sikorsky Sea King choppers that had brought in the crash team and to the modular command centre that the team had set up.

Both helicopters and portacabins were daubed with sigils in liquid chalk, blood and other less palatable substances. Freshly slaughtered chicken giblets and dog entrails hung festively from the Sikorsky rotor blades. The canine offal, at least, had been rehydrated from its standard-issue code red vacuum packs, but all the same, Haasterman tried not to think of the scene if they had to evacuate and fire the choppers up quickly.

The trooper dropped down from the jeep, snapped off a casual salute and hurried to open the door to one of the cabins.

Haasterman turned to the National Guard driver, who was staring around with blank-faced horror. 'Get a grip on yourself, soldier, and come with me.' He hustled the guardsman into the cabin, then pulled a card bearing a minor Sign of Power and briefly showed it to him. 'Sleep. Forget.'

It wasn't what you might call *real* Magick, Haasterman reflected – but then, in the end, hardly anything that was called Magick really was. In the same way that certain patterns of conflicting data can crash a computer, there were certain images, certain shapes in the world, that shut down the higher functions of the brain. The guardsman slumped bonelessly. Haasterman put the card away again, being careful to keep his eyes averted. 'Keep him out of the way and look after him,' he said to the trooper who had escorted them inside.

The cabin was a cramped pandemonium of activity as totem-suited technicians worked their haphazardly bolted-together equipment. One wall was completely taken up by the big mainframe in its gimballed shock absorbers, its tape spools blitting and jerking. Its slaved terminals ranged from green-glowing, ultra-modern viewing screens with integral keyboards, to chattering print-out units adapted from electrified typewriters.

Dr Sohn was flicking through a sheaf of print-outs on a clipboard, circling various elements heavily with a scowl and a purple plastic Flair. She turned her scowl on Haasterman. 'How long until support arrives?' Haasterman was the vanguard of the heavy-duty mechanisms that would be arriving to supplant the crash team. 'And how much of it?'

'One Hercules, four ARVs,' said Haasterman, shortly, and regretted it. He had met Dr Sohn twice before, under distinctly different operational conditions, and had not found any way of getting along with her under either. It wasn't a question of anger or dislike, he told himself; it was just that he couldn't help *noticing*.

Technically, in Section terms, he had the seniority and rank on Sohn, but Haasterman was entirely aware that *she* was on the fast track upwards via several separate affirmative action routes – whereas *he* was just this embittered old has-been with the wrecked dregs of a career, who was only ever called back in because, when the heads finally started to roll, they needed an expendable head on the sacrificial block. And given the basic nature of the Section these days, *sacrificial* was almost entirely apposite.

Sohn gave a little sniff, and started tapping at her teeth with the barrel end of her Flair in a way that Haasterman found incredibly irritating. 'I just hope that's going to be enough.'

'It's all we've got.' Haasterman snorted with a kind of generalised contempt for the entire world. 'On this kind of notice. If it isn't, then the Powers that be have only themselves to blame for going along with Reagan and sinking everything into Christian Fundamentalism and Star Wars.'

Sohn shrugged unconcernedly. 'The symbols are where you find them, and the symbols change. That was the way to go. Besides...' She became pointed. 'Our resources would have been perfectly adequate if you hadn't *made* this mess in the first place. It's your mess, *Colonel*. You made it. All those years ago.' She gestured to a row of hanging totem suits. 'Let's go see what you have to clean up.'

* * *

'Well, I expected electrified ramps and death-ray installations at the very least,' said the Doctor, in slightly disappointed tones. He stuffed his hands in his pockets and looked around with a manner reminiscent of a schoolboy who had been refused some rightfully-deserved treat. Then he brightened again and rubbed his hands. 'I do fear, though, that this peaceful scene shall soon be rent by the horrific roars of who knows what hideous Evil...'

'What, really?' said Jamie.

The Doctor's face fell again. 'Not really, Jamie, no.'

They were in a sparsely wooded area, off to one side of a sharply inclined cliff face. To the other, the land ran down into a river-basin valley in which could be seen the lights of a town. To Jamie and Victoria, those lights seemed unnaturally regular, even over and above the fact that a town or a city could not by its very nature be called natural. In their travels with the Doctor, they had both long since become used to the strange brightness and constancy of electrical lighting, but *these* lights were laid out in a vast and utterly regular and mechanical grid. It would have taken gangs of labourers centuries to build up such an expanse.

'Now, yon place there doesn't look to be the work of any hand of man...' Jamie said dubiously.

The Doctor sucked his lower lip consideringly. 'I don't think so, Jamie. Unless I'm very much mistaken, that looks to me like a smallish twentieth-century American town. Relatively small, I should say, and quite possibly a city. The colonials tended to give things *big* names, I seem to remember...'

'So this was not built by some fearful and incursive alien force, then,' said Victoria, with a not entirely insignificant sense of relief.

'Not at all.' The Doctor considered a little further. 'Not in that sense, anyway. I have to admit, I've never really seemed to get *on* with America, really, what with one thing and another...'

Quite what that one thing was, was never fully elucidated. The other thing, too, remained similarly opaque, for at that moment there came the wrenching, tearing sound of metal sliding on rock. There was a burst of flame above them, and something hurtled down the cliff face. Both Jamie and Victoria instinctively made to dive desperately out of its way, then realised that this burning object was plummeting off to one side. For his part, the Doctor merely watched it with concern.

The burning object hit the ground with a second and rather more impressive explosion. It was a variety of automobile, and must once have had a squat but almost archetypical sense of *bigness* about it. Now it was a crushed and twisted wreck from which strangely liquid-looking and globular flames and greasy smoke poured.

Jamie turned to the Doctor, failed to see him and only then realised that the little man was running at full pelt for the wreckage. 'Stay here,' he told Victoria, who was staring at this sudden destruction in shock, and set off after him. The heat from the flames beat Jamie back before he caught up with the Doctor, but he was able to see the ragged and skeletal remains of a man, flame pluming from the empty eye sockets in his skull.

'Come along, Jamie,' said the Doctor, laying a sympathetic hand on his shoulder, though whether it was sympathy for the burning man or Jamie, Jamie couldn't tell. 'There's nothing we can do for the poor chap, now.'

'Doctor!'

The cry came from Victoria, who had seen something lying in the scrub land over to one side and had gone over to investigate.

'It's a young, ah, lady,' she called. 'I think she's alive.'

The young lady lay sprawled and unconscious in a patch of sage brush, in a scorched skirt and cardigan of some fine and hazy bright pink substance that Victoria for one thought a trifle immodest – if not in the actual cut then in the clingy tightness of it. Her face was painted in a way that had the words 'a certain sort' forming in Victoria's mind – but then she saw the bruised complexion under the cosmetic tinctures and instantly quashed such obdurate thoughts. The young lady was clearly hurt.

'She must have been thrown clear,' the Doctor said, arriving beside Victoria with a slightly winded Jamie in tow. He regarded the unconscious girl with a kind of sympathetic but critical detachment. 'I don't see any signs of severe injury. I think it might be safe to move her – but the sooner she has proper medical attention, I think, the better. Jamie – gently, now – if you could assist her, we'll see what we can do.'

Jamie gathered up the girl in his arms, and he and Victoria set off after the Doctor as he headed rapidly for the TARDIS.

'I have to admit, I'm not as well versed in the *medical* sciences as I once was...' The Doctor fumbled through his pockets for the TARDIS key. 'I'm sure I've got some books on medicine somewhere, though, and there are of course a number of interesting and quite advanced devices I've picked up here and there on my... Oh, hello, Jamie, Victoria. What are you, ah... oh.'

There had been no sense of transition. The Doctor had opened the TARDIS doorway, stepped into the darkness behind it and had instantly stepped out again. Now he turned and tried it again – and once again stepped straight out.

'Oh dear,' he said, not exactly worried, but in a tone that had uneasiness as a distinct possibility in its near future. 'Oh dear. That can't be right, can it?'

In their totem suits Haasterman and Sohn prowled the concrete blockhouses that had once housed the Golgotha Project and had been subsequently – and extremely hurriedly – converted into a skeleton-staffed observation and early warning station. In addition to the portable life-support and radio systems in their suits, there were snag-free graphite-coated air lines and cables for communications and power. These linked them umbilically to the crash team's encampment over two miles away, via heavy-duty booster pumps, transformers and land lines established outside the installation itself by advance-party support technicians. This was purely belt-and-braces procedure, but it put Haasterman in mind of Theseus and the Minotaur – had him wondering as to what, precisely, might still be living in the installation maze.

As it turned out, nothing was. Definitively so. The skeleton staff seemed to be making a profound effort to live up to their name, but the dry and effectively sterile air had mummified them to a certain extent. Intestinal tracts had bloated, eyes had fallen in and tissues had desiccated, but they had not as yet started to rot.

'Looks like the wave front killed them instantly,' Haasterman said, inclining his suit-bulked body from the hips so that his faceplate and the camera bolted to his helmet could take in the view of a body slumped over a desk. The residue of the coffee it had spilt by tipping over a cup fanned out irregularly across a collection of report sheets. 'Dropped them in their tracks. Is there anything we can learn from the bodies?'

'I doubt it, very much,' said Sohn. 'The fact of temporal-fracturing means that by our very nature we are living in the universe the fracture creates. Any number of things could be different and we simply wouldn't notice.' She paused, looking at another body that had collapsed while apparently on the way to the women's rest room off to one side of the main control chamber. It was impossible to guess what Sohn was thinking, through the layers of her suit. 'Then again we might get something,' she said at last. 'From the hair and fingernails, from the post-mortem anabolism. They died in a state of quantum flux, broadly speaking, before their physical processes could adapt. We might be able to gather some data as to the basic nature of the transitions.'

'Conclusive?' Haasterman asked.

'Inferential,' said Sohn, 'at best.'

Haasterman nodded, equally opaquely, to the world outside his helmet. 'So let's see if we can gather something direct.'

The installation generators were EMP-blown and the on-site power was out. The basic nature of the Golgotha Project meant that this did not affect the processes of Containment, but it did mean that the servomechanisms that controlled the blast shutters over the lead crystal observation windows were inoperative. Haasterman pulled a bitless electric drill from the tool kit on his belt, plugged it into his suit's outlet and applied it to the socket bearing of the manual override.

The shutters opened up with a groan, like the slats of a massive armour-plated Venetian blind. Beyond them, Haasterman and Sohn caught their first sight of the crater, the five-mile half-globe scooped out of the bedrock with such clean precision that its inside shone like a mirror. On a clear day, from the installation, it would have been possible to see clear across to its burnished other side. At least it would have been, had it not been for the shifting glow of the thing that hung in its centre.

Haasterman had been in the process of bringing up the optical enhancement systems of his suit, designed to translate subatomic phenomena into models that the eye could see. Now he stopped.

'Oh dear God,' he said. 'You can *see* it. You can see it with the naked eye.'

'This is not good,' said Dr Sohn, her voice very carefully neutral in the manner of one who does not trust the quality it might have if it were otherwise. 'Not good at all. I hope you have contingency plans, Colonel, because I somehow think that a Hercules and three tanker trucks are *not* going to be enough.'

Chapter Six
Meanwhile Back At...

Outside the UNIT barracks a big, articulated tanker truck rumbled its ponderous way along a street which had been widened some years before to accommodate military transports – and had, incidentally, cost the Ministry of Defence a community centre and a water flume for the local swimming baths to squeak planning permission past the Greater London Council. After several years of Tory government the community centre was long shut down and the swimming baths were bone dry and squatted by an anarchist performance-art collective.

The tanker truck was misfiring, roadworn and plastered with Long Vehicle and Hazchem signs, but the one thing it didn't look was suspiciously sleek, black and menacing. It churned to a gear-stripping halt and the driver, a perfectly nondescript little man in unkempt greasy overalls, swung himself down from the cab and wandered over to the guardhouse clutching a clipboard and an impressive sheaf of dockets.

It is a sad fact that, due to the influence of a certain kind of Hollywood movie, any patently innocent vehicle or man approaching a secure location is quite obviously up to no good. The patently innocent driver will bumble around asking for directions, mutter something about the regular driver being off sick, opine that there must have been some mix-up with the paperwork and then pull out a gun and shoot the guards before they can move to check up on it.

This being reality, or some reasonable approximation thereof, the nondescript little man simply pulled out his gun and shot the guardsmen without preamble.

Crash-hatches in the side of the tanker truck racked themselves down, and a collection of what, on first sight, appeared to be men in full combat body armour swarmed through the barracks gate.

* * *

Romana peered through the dilated viewing port with a kind of disdainful unease – the sort of emotions she might feel when looking at some pathetic human attempt to build a crude atomic bomb: the feeling that she was looking at something ludicrously inept and simple-minded on any number of levels, but with an awareness that *one* of those levels would be able to obliterate anyone in the vicinity if it went off. Beyond the viewing port, the complex polyfractal swirls of the Vortex had been replaced by a static crystalline structure that had never moved, would never change, for the simple reason that there was no accessible dimension for it to move or change within.

In a certain sense, the very world around us is linked with the consciousness of its observer – with what that observer, on the quantum level, is physically capable of conceiving. The world outside the viewing port had been conceived by someone who had never heard of fractionated dimensions and was fundamentally incapable of conceiving of an integer greater than three.

The Doctor was worriedly pecking at a set of buttons on the console. A readout illuminated itself briefly and then faded with a discouraging little gravmetronic *blurp*.

'The TARDIS exists in her own temporal bubble,' he said, 'so we can move around inside her. Outside, we're trapped. Trapped like a –'

'Braxellian fly in *oogli*-tree amber,' said Romana. 'I gathered.'

'I was going to say like a toad in a treehouse,' said the Doctor, in a slightly hurt tone of voice. 'Or do I mean in a hole? Ah well...' he shrugged. 'Doesn't matter. The fact remains that we're completely and utterly stuck. Again.'

Romana looked out again at the fixed and motionless metastructure of the world, at the half-resolved images fixed within, caught between one living breath and heartbeat and the next. 'You know I wouldn't mind,' she said, 'if it didn't happen every other day of the week. It's not as if they haven't already given us enough to worry about with the Key to Time. How long do you think they'll leave us here?'

'Oh, I don't know,' said the Doctor. 'They're getting a bit better about it lately, I think. Could just be a couple of hours.' He pulled something from a pocket and waggled it meaningfully. 'Quick game of cards while we wait?'

Romana considered. The Doctor tended to play with an ancient deck of tarot cards blessed by several magi who had been adept in the physical manipulations of reality that human beings knew in a corrupt form as Magic. In locations like the TARDIS, where the fundamental nature of reality was different from what it was commonly held to be, this could lead to unexpected and sometimes quite remarkably unfortunate results. Even a game of Happy Families could end in tragedy, depending upon which particular family it invoked.

'Better not,' she said.

'Suit yourself.' The Doctor pocketed the deck. 'I just thought it might help to pass the –'

'Time has no meaning, here, Doctor,' said a scratchy and slightly cracked-sounding voice, as though the speaker's vocal cords were desiccated from years, and possibly centuries, of disuse. 'Space itself has no meaning, here, in any proper meaning of the term, for you have been taken…' The voice paused dramatically. '… Out of Time!'

'Well, yes, fine,' said the Doctor a little irritably, uncharacteristically, as the ordinarily broad and cheerful patience of his current incarnation began to wear a little thin. 'We've already worked that out. Through constant practice, I might add. Why have you done it this time?'

A vaguely humanoid shape was forming by the console, or rather partially inside it due to a small miscalculation of positioning. An insubstantial, hologrammatic figure in flowing, metallic-grey robes. It resolved itself into a bald and elderly man, with deep wrinkles around his mouth and a jutting, beak-like nose. The tiny, almost imperceptible signs that distinguish a particular type of face from any other allowed the Doctor and Romana to recognise this man as Gallifreyan and a high-caste Time Lord, nearing the end of his second or possibly third regeneration.

'The very fabric of space/time is in danger!' the Time Lord pronounced, still in his dry and scratchy voice. 'The universe itself is on the very brink of being catastrophically torn apart!'

'Once again,' said the Doctor, 'this is hardly a surprise. That's the only reason you people in the High Council ever seem to want to talk to us these days, and I really wish a subjective fortnight would go by when you don't.' He scowled bad-temperedly. 'What have you gone and done to the basic underlying fabric of space/time now?'

* * *

The black-clad, combat-armoured figures swarmed through the UNIT barracks, shooting everyone and anyone they could find. They hammered open every door they came to, using a compression-wrench that pulled the locks from the frames on those that were locked, checking that the rooms behind them were clear while more of their fellows advanced, spreading through the barracks in an unstoppable leapfrogging tide. The UNIT troops themselves were able to offer little or no resistance, not through any lack of skill or training, but from the sheer reaction-time factors of responding to such a swift, decisive and wholly unexpected incursion.

An advance party hammered open the tactical operations computer room. There was no one there, no sound or motion save for a chattering golfball-printout from a terminal slaved to the UNIT mainframe, which occupied several chambers underground and was actually less powerful than the newly acquired Apples.

Katharine Delbane was in a completely different wing of the barracks. One of the great joys of knowing something about the new developments in computer technology is that those who don't tend to completely overestimate the time a task will take – if things go well and the damn things don't crash three times out of five. Delbane had completed the transfer of files into the database a week before, learning quite a lot from them in the process as she became familiar with the resources at the UNIT organisation's command. Names on the active and inactive lists, names and contact procedures for suppliers of items ranging from industrial lasers to live marmosets, archaeological tools to rocketry components, Watusi tribal masks to dedicated time on US college-campus particle accelerators...

None of it, however, was any direct use – the nature of logistics being that they detail the possible courses of an action without describing that action's ultimate purpose. It was all very well to know that UNIT had access to, and the use of, any number of people and things, but that didn't help with discovering what they were being used, precisely, for.

Delbane remembered her briefing before coming here. She could hardly do otherwise; it was etched on to her mind like her childhood name and address – rather more so, in fact. In her work for the department she'd adopted a number of new names and addresses.

The department (or more properly, Divisional Department of Special Tactical Operations, open brackets, Provisional, close brackets, with Regard to Insurgent and Subversive Activity – commonly and more colloquially known as 'the Provisionals') was ostensibly an arm of Special Branch with direct funding from the Treasury. Its duties, though, were slightly more abstruse and indefinable than that. The Provisional Department reported directly to the Prime Minister, was in a sense her personal hand in any number of covertly operational areas. A department operative might find him- or herself infiltrating an NUM ballot-meeting for surveillance purposes, taking a job as a teacher to blow the whistle on some headmaster's Marxist leanings or being positioned on the bridge of a Royal Navy battleship, purely so that he or she could fire off a round of shells at some boat travelling in a completely innocent direction and then go, 'Whoops.' The department existed, quite simply, for the application of a precise force of influence to counter the forces of subversion, as and when it might be needed.

Although the head of the department, Crowley, had daily contact with the Prime Minister, the briefing had been Delbane's first meeting with her face to face, in her private dressing chambers in the House of Commons. The experience had been more intense than somewhat, to say the least. The Prime Minister had looked down at her over her nose, with the kind of flat contempt that certain senior army officers had reserved for her as a chit of a girl getting above her station.

Delbane had seen all the obvious images in the media, and heard the jokes by 'alternative' comedians about how the PM was the only real man in the Cabinet, but in this first direct contact she realised that this wasn't precisely true. The Prime Minister contained within herself a bludgeoning and utter force of will that is often only achieved by men. Looking into those cold, hard, slightly deranged eyes Delbane had understood that she was there, so far as the Prime Minister was concerned, to perform a function, a function that did not require sympathy even on the level of patronisation, and that outside the limits of that function the Prime Minister could not care one iota if she, Katharine Delbane, lived or died.

'You have experience as a military officer?' the PM had said, shortly.

'Well, yes, I...' Delbane began, meaning to say how she had tried to follow in the footsteps of her father, how she had enlisted and trained and then realised that the only opportunities of promotion for a woman were in the precise areas for which she had no aptitude whatsoever. She had wanted to explain how an instinct for computer programming had put her on the fast track to being a jumped-up typing-pool secretary instead of resulting in her programming the weapons of the future, but the Prime Minister had abruptly cut her short:

'Then I suppose you'll have to do. I'd rather have a man, quite frankly. Men know how to follow orders, take command when they have to and do what has to be done, without all that confused emotion that women tend to exhibit. But we need an army officer with training in this "new technology"...' You could hear the distasteful quotation marks with which she wrapped the words, as though the only proper avenue for the scientific mind involved the chemical manipulation of a new flavour of ice cream, '... and you're the only one available who fits the bill.'

Delbane found she was reminding herself that this forthrightness of opinion was precisely why she herself had voted for the Prime Minister in the first place. If you can't take it when it's directed at *you*, she told herself sternly, then you're indulging in hypocrisy of the worst kind.

The Prime Minister had gone on to explain the basics of the situation. The United Nations Intelligence Taskforce, so far as its British arm was concerned, was a disruptive internationalist holdover from the bad old days of Labour governments and the soft Conservatism of Heath. Its abstruse means of funding gave it a degree of autonomy from governmental control and even market forces (a term which the Prime Minister pronounced in the same tones that an apostate might mouth one of the names of God), and this was quite unconscionable. It had used its entirely unearned status, time and time again, to block and countermand the processes of the nation's central government – its most recent and blatant act being to requisition fully a third of the gold reserves from the Bank of England without explanation. The failure to replace those reserves had led more or less directly to the chaos that ensued after a catastrophic stock-market crash, the true magnitude of which had necessarily been hushed up. Indeed, it had only been Scottish oil revenues, and the funds received from the US in return for allowing the establishment of several bases on this sceptred isle (the Prime Minister had actually used the words 'sceptred isle') that had allowed the government to stay in power by knocking half a penny off the basic rate of income tax.

This state of affairs could not be allowed to continue. Simply by existing, any organised body in the world had secrets that could be used to hang it out to dry, and Delbane's job as a DISTO(P)IA agent would be to root out UNIT's secrets.

Thus far, however, Delbane had met with little luck. There was some big secret here, she was sure of it, but it had the general flavour of the punch line to a joke – blindingly obvious if you guess what's coming, but totally unknown if you don't. All allusions to it had been carefully, if sometimes hastily, deflected, like Benton's recent mention of 'Sicilians.'

Even looking for something as basic as misappropriation of funds had been a dead end. The paymaster's files showed a number of entries for special duties compensation and for deaths in the line of duty, but there was no mention of what those duties were or what the deaths were from. The only real anomalies Delbane had found were references to a certain Dr John Smith, a so-called 'scientific adviser' with a hideously erratic and exorbitant rate of pay and a file attachment to the effect that he had been 'deactivated'.

The lead was so thin as to be laughable but Delbane was nothing if not thorough, which was why she was currently in the workroom once used by Dr Smith. They were in disarray, as though their occupant had merely stepped out for a second and might return at any moment, but covered with a film of dust – the gritty and particulate dust of London grime rather than the shed skin cells that would suggest visits by other human beings since Dr Smith had gone. Delbane was reminded of the untouched, shrine-like way in which some of the people in Belfast (her first and only real direct experience with such things) kept the rooms of loved ones who had been roughly deleted from their lives.

With the uneasy sense of defiling such a shrine, Delbane wandered between benches crammed with complicatedly breadboarded electronics that her trained eye saw could never work and strange arrays of twisted glass tubing that reminded her of every mad scientist's laboratory in old movies and could probably fractionate a reasonable moonshine. Even stranger devices appeared to be nothing more than the sculpture installations of a deranged artist, cobbled together from any number of mismatched materials, the intended function of which – if there had ever been one – she could not even begin to imagine.

Here and there were scribbled notes, written on an eclectic collection of yellowing chit forms, torn newspaper squares and bus tickets in anything from fountain-pen ink to crayon and what appeared to be nail varnish – this last, over an old and cheesy newsprint portrait of a smiling, hourglass-figured Diana Dors, used for a set of perfectly calligraphed ideograms that she recognised as Japanese.

Standing out from the clutter, in the sense that it did the precise reverse, was a gap where a large document cabinet or the like had been removed from its place against a wall. There was something odd about this, and it took Delbane a second before she realised why: the cabinet had been removed in some manner that had left absolutely nothing else disturbed.

Something caught her eye on the floor where the putative cabinet had been and she picked it up. It was a garish comic book from the 1960s, creased and flattened, that had obviously been dropped then mashed down by the weight of the cabinet and subsequently forgotten about. Without much interest, Delbane flipped through pages of International Retrieval, Joey Mindswap, Goron killer robot-units surfacing from the Thames and exploded diagrams of second-stage Saturn probes. There was one particularly opaque strip that had something to do with an ineptly delineated farmer in an incongruous porkpie hat and gabardine macintosh running away from walking scarecrows that were turning into irascible-looking old men in flowing robes.

The comic had obviously been dropped by some semi-literate public works contractor or private soldier years before. All the same she put it in the zip-locked PVC folder she carried, along with her collection of Smith's notes.

The doors of the hut that contained the workroom were of heavy steel plate, and looked as though they could withstand the force of a small nuclear blast – if not the hordes of ragged and bloodthirsty mutants that would subsequently appear, if you could believe in garish comic books. The doors had no locks and the hasps that might have accommodated padlocks had been painted open with layers of thick and liquid-looking military green paint.

Delbane pushed the doors shut behind her with a clank and headed along the gravel pathway towards her proper place of duty. Her route took her around the back of the kitchens so it was a small while before she reached one of the more well-travelled areas. When she did she realised that something was wrong.

Soldiers' bodies lay here and there, dragged and dumped in an effort to conceal them not from those within the barracks but from any casual observer outside them. They lay against walls and by doors and against the ductwork that protruded from the huts looking like a collection of rag dolls scattered in a tantrum by a child who'd received yet another rag doll for Christmas. Delbane stopped dead, her startled eyes darting from one body to another.

There was a blur of motion from behind her, from the direction of the big Calor Gas canisters outside the kitchens, and something hit her hard, to bear her down into the gravel.

Chapter Seven
Strangers in Purgatory

Victoria sat on a fallen tree trunk by the side of the road and rubbed her ankle, wishing that the footwear she had chosen in the TARDIS had been more suited to healthy outdoor pursuits. Fetching though her calf-length patent leather boots were, the spiky heels had sunk deep into the woodland earth and now, on the tarmacadam of the road, had allowed no greater pace than a tottering walk until one of the heels broke off. The new leather had cut into her and she had turned her ankle to, as it were, boot. All things considered, she considered herself fortunate not to have broken it.

'Come along, Victoria,' the Doctor called from further up the road. All but lost in the dark, he and Jamie were dragging the unconscious girl on a makeshift tree-branch trellis. Or rather, Jamie was dragging her, the Doctor having directed the original fashioning of the trellis by way of much helpful advice, before declaring that all that brain work had quite tired him out. He was subsequently flitting around and about to pick and sniff indiscriminately at various items of roadside vegetation, in the manner of one prancing happily about in a meadow on a summer's eve. Possibly, he was putting on this performance in an attempt to keep their spirits up. If so, thought Victoria glumly, it was meeting with a noticeable lack of success.

After finding it impossible to enter the TARDIS through the front doors, the Doctor had tried several alternative routes, involving first one of the back panels, then what he referred to as the occasional cat flap and, finally, clambering on to the roof and attempting to prise open its central beacon. Each of these had met with the same degree of fruition as his current attempts to lighten their spirits. At length he had admitted that they were, in all probability, stuck here for what he termed the duration – whatever the duration might happen to be. The first priority was still, the Doctor had continued, to find medical assistance for this young lady here, and with the TARDIS inaccessible that meant taking her into town – trading off the advisability of moving her against that of leaving her, and any of them, alone in the comparative wilds. Who knew who, or what, might come along.

It had taken them an hour or more so far to spot a road and then to travel it. The lights from the city ahead were just enough to see by, but Victoria's journeys in the TARDIS, to worlds and lands with rather more advanced methods of transport than her own, had spoilt her. What she wouldn't give, now, for a hypergravity belt, or a jet-skimmer, or an atomic-powered ornithopter. She would settle, she admitted to herself ruefully, for a pony-drawn omnibus.

Victoria sighed, broke off her remaining heel, pulled her boots on again and flatfootedly hurried to catch up with her companions.

'You're just in time,' the Doctor said happily, when she did. 'I think I hear a vehicle of some sort coming.'

Victoria couldn't hear anything at this point, but this did not surprise her. She knew that the little man possessed senses of a remarkable acuity. All the same, hope did not precisely spring in her breast. Thus far they had encountered a grand tally of two automobiles. One, a big, growling, smoking article with blazing headlamps and fins on its tail that gave the impression it was about to take flight – or at the very least *swim* at the first opportunity – had slowed down as it approached Victoria, but speeded up again as it got close enough for the pale man within it to see that she was not alone. Victoria tried to think as charitably of this as she could

– that the poor man had simply found his nerve insufficient to cope with what was obviously a rather problematical state of affairs – but she was finding this a bit of a push. The second occurrence had been, if anything, even less ambiguous: a large, blocky vehicle like a motorised cart with, in a trailer, a collection of rough-looking young men who had thrown beer-smelling tin cans at them and then roared off, laughing mockingly, to a drunken cavalcade of rifle shots aimed, one could but hope, into the air.

'Don't worry,' the Doctor said cheerfully, entirely aware, it seemed, of her misgivings. 'It's only a matter of time. People are only too happy to help those in distress, most of them anyway, if you only give them the chance.'

'Can't come soon enough for me,' said Jamie, who had taken advantage of this pause to set down the trellis and the girl, and was rubbing at his shoulders. 'I think my arms are coming loose.'

The lights of an automobile came into view from around a curve in the road. In addition to the ferociously dazzling electrical headlamps that Victoria was coming to realise were quite common in this place and time, she saw an arrangement of flashing blue and red lights arranged across the roof of what she thought of as the vehicle's steering cab.

'What did I tell you?' the Doctor said, triumphantly, waving frantically at the approaching car. 'Unless I'm very much mistaken, that vehicle belongs to the local forces of law and order. Our troubles are over.'

It was not exactly common for a chief of police to be awake and out of bed (or at least, awake and out of the certain kind of establishment to which senior officials the whole world over tend to gravitate) at 2.15 in the morning. Police Chief Clancy Tilson, on the other hand, was an uncommon police chief.

His dedication to the law was unwavering and had never been corrupted – not because of a refusal to take advantage of the more *interesting* opportunities his position afforded, but because they had simply never occurred to him.

Legend had it amongst Lychburg's proponents of organised crime (Big Vinnie's Bar and Deli – accident insurance, boogie pharmaceuticals and introductions to accommodating young ladies a speciality) that he had once and in all innocence given a sizeable wad of greenbacks back to Big Vinnie's cousin, Diminutive Norris, thinking he had dropped it by mistake. And, tellingly, he had completely failed to notice the rather boisterous and illegal poker game going on in the next room.

While his basically somnolent nature would ordinarily have him tucked up in bed with a malted milky drink by the early evening, his willingness to be called out at all hours to deal personally with any tricky situation or case was just one of the qualities that had the good people of Lychburg voting him back into office for twenty years in the face of all comers. The question of whether any of these tricky situations or cases were actually *solved* was neither here nor there.

'As I said before,' the unkempt, battered little man across the table from him in the interview room in the South Street Precinct House said, 'myself, my niece and her young friend were on a camping holiday, rambling through the mighty and majestic redwoods and pines of your splendid country and so forth, when we happened on a car accident. The young man – I assume it was a young man – who was in the car was clearly beyond help, so we were simply trying to get the young lady… how is she, by the way?'

Tilson turned to Sergeant Smee, who stood by the door. 'What about the girl?'

The sergeant shrugged. 'Mercy Hill, I think. That was where the paramedics came from. I'll have it checked.'

'I'd be very grateful,' said the little man.

There was something a little wrong about that, Tilson thought. It was as if the little man just naturally assumed that Smee was going to check up on the girl for *him*, as a special favour, rather than merely following the orders of his chief.

'So anyway,' the little man continued, 'two of your officers happened to come along. and so I naturally flagged them down. Mr Wijikwaski and Mr Garcia, I think their names were, from what I saw of those little name tags they had. I said, "Could you be of some assistance, officers?" and either Officer Garcia or Officer Wijikwaski – I forget which – said…'

The little man scratched the head under his Three Stooges cut for a moment as though trying to recall.

'Ah, yes. "Down on your face, dirtbag. Don't move. Don't even breathe. I can make a hole you can *see* through." Yes, I think that was it…

'So, while myself and my young companions were lying on our faces, not moving and trying our very hardest not to breathe, Officer Garcia or Officer Wijikwaski, one or the other, made the comment that we didn't come from around these parts. I mentioned that, to cut a long story short, we were visitors from the British Isles and he muttered something or other about Benedict Arnold and they arrested us on the spot. I'm afraid I had to prevail upon them rather hard to call an ambulance for the injured young lady before they dragged us here.' The little man sniffed. 'My friends are still in your holding cells, hopefully making lots of new friends. It seems a bit of a harsh reward for trying to help a victim of a road accident.'

Put like that, it was difficult to deny what he said. A patrol car had been dispatched to Coogan's Bluff and confirmed that there was indeed the still-smouldering wreckage of a car there, registered to a Norman E. Manley and containing, so dental records would probably confirm, the body of that same Norman E. Manley. In that respect, the stranger's story checked out… but there were other suspicious elements.

Chief Tilson opened the manila folder before him and extracted a number of items.

'You were brought here and we took mugshots,' he said, flipping one of the photographs across the table for the little man to peruse. It was completely fogged.

'I think you must have had a faulty batch of film,' the man speculated blandly. 'I'd send a sharp note to your suppliers, if I were you.'

Tilson showed him another item. 'Your fingerprints. We took your fingerprints, too.'

'Ah yes.' The little man beamed. 'To send to Interpol, no doubt, to check that I'm not some mad international Anarchist bomber wanted for the shocking murder of the Queen and several corgis or some such.'

'Interpol, uh, yeah,' said Tilson, uncertainly. It was as if the word had been stored in some Section of his brain that was missing. He tried and failed to make some kind of mental connection with the word, and then simply forgot about it.

'Look at your prints,' he said, roughly pulling himself together and sliding the card across the table. The little man peered at the fingerprint smudges impassively, as though he couldn't plainly see that they were simple blobs of ink, with none of the whorls and sutures fingerprints commonly have.

'What sort of man has no fingerprints, is what I'm thinking,' Tilson said. 'The sort of man who takes them off with acid or sandpaper, I'm thinking. The sort of man who has something to hide…'

'I beg your pardon,' said the little man. 'I wasn't thinking at the time.'

'What?' said Tilson, suspiciously.

'I mean that I pressed down too hard. Nerves, you know. Do you mind if I borrow this for a moment?'

Tilson's steel-cased ballpoint pen, presented to him at the inaugural Annual Sons of the Frontier Dinner some years ago, was suddenly in the little man's hand. Tilson, who had simply pulled on overcoat over his pyjamas on being woken up an hour before, had been completely unaware of even having it on him – although he now seemed to remember putting it in his overcoat pocket some while ago.

The little man, meanwhile, was industriously rubbing the nib of the pen over a finger, which he then pressed with theatrical lightness against a corner of the fingerprint card. He held the card up and, without even looking closely, Tilson could see a perfectly ordinary print.

'Now I'll be quite happy to supply new ones,' said the little man, 'and even pose for another photograph, if you can find some film that hasn't been contaminated. But I really think there is no reason whatsoever to keep me or my young friends here a minute longer. Other than the fact that we're strangers and you don't like strangers. Don't you agree, Chief Tilson?'

Tilson tried to remember if he had ever, as such, told the little man his name. The crack about *strangers* also rankled. Whatever else he was, he wasn't some slack-jawed yokel who pulled out a twelve-gauge shotgun and blasted off a face he didn't know. But then again... there was a *wrongness* about the little man in front of him, a sense that he shouldn't be here. It was like that show he had seen on the Discovery Channel, about how baboons or some kind of monkey killed other monkeys who were not a part of their troop, or the feeling you get in a room when someone walks in who is not welcome.

Thinking about it, he could see how things could get out of hand. All these recent murders had tensions in the South Street Precinct running high. The papers and the TV news hadn't made the connection between them yet, merely reporting each case as and when it occurred, but within the police department itself there was a sense that people were looking for somebody to blame when the big story finally broke. Tilson was not the most perceptive of men but even he could see how the two patrolmen, Billy-Joe Wijikwaski and Johnny-Bob Garcia, could have instantly and blankly suspected a group of strangers, simply for the fact that they were strangers out at night…

'Murders?' the little man said, sharply. Tilson must have muttered something out loud. 'What's this about murders?' There was something in his tone that cut through all the police chief's layers of suspicion to hit some automatic and reflexive core, like the little man was a teacher, snapping out a question that you had to answer instantly. 'I think you'd better tell me all about it.'

And to his great surprise, Chief Tilson found himself doing just that.

Chapter Eight
Partial Definitions of Disorder

'Millennia ago,' proclaimed the splendidly berobed if largely insubstantial member of the Gallifreyan High Council, 'when Rassilon wrestled with the Great Beast, and struck off its head from which to take the branching golden tree of its metathalmus, wherein did lay the First Secret of Chrononambulatory Egress…'

'Yes, we all know the Legends from the Dawn of Time Travel,' said the Doctor, 'and very poetical and edifying they are to be sure, if needlessly messianic and containing about as much relation to the truth as a toboggan does to a small tub of weasel cheese. We also know for a *fact* that Rassilon came upon the great and glorious secrets of Time by way of pinching one of the translation belts of that species who attacked us in the Time Wars, in retaliation for the things we did to them before we'd even heard of them in the first place…'

'The Time Wars,' thundered the High Councilman, 'did not happen.'

The Doctor glared at him. 'Now, by "did not happen" do you mean that Gallifrey is doing a spot of cultural revision and would prefer to forget all about such things?' he said. 'Or do you mean that you've been doing some *actual* revising of the time lines?' His face clouded. 'If so, you'll have a difficult time doing it. I was there as an eyewitness, I seem to recall, and I think you'll have a hard job trying to paint me out.'

'The Time Wars did not happen,' repeated the High Councilman.

'Ah, well, yes,' said the Doctor. 'That clears things up immediately.'

Romana, meanwhile, had been peering closely at the High Councilman. 'I remember you, don't I? You're one of that new traditionalist faction that was skulking around just before I went away. Done well for yourself while I've been gone, have you? Isn't your name Wblk?'

'Wblk?' said the Doctor, interested despite himself. 'Bit of a short name for a Time Lord.'

'And what of it?' sniffed Wblk the High Councilman, trying for a lofty *hauteur* but failing to disguise the fact that this remark had cut him deeply.

'They're the ones to watch out for, I've learnt,' said Romana. 'They always seem to try and overcompensate.'

'Well, if the convention still holds that a Time Lord's name grows in length by his stature, reputation and deeds of note,' said the Doctor, cheerfully, 'all that means is our friend Wblk's acts of greatness are before him.' He turned back to the Councilman's apparition. 'Why don't you tell us all about it, Wblk? Sticking to the facts if possible.'

The High Councilman seemed a little deflated by the Doctor and Romana's derision. He fussed with his splendid semi-transparent robes, and continued in slightly less portentous tones...

* * *

In the UNIT barracks, Katharine Delbane found herself going through one of those dizzying moments where the very nature of the world around you changes, and changes again, and then changes yet *again* as your recognition lags behind the actual events.

She'd thought the weight barrelling into her had been one of the shadowy and half-glimpsed invading enemy forces, and made ready to kick and scratch in a desperate fight for her life – and then looked at the earnest, sweating face on the stumbling form and realised it was familiar. It was Sergeant Benton.

Her next thought was that he had been shot, that the hand clutched to his stomach was attempting to prevent his guts spilling out on the gravel... and then she realised that there was no blood, no obvious injury other than his lurching weakness.

Delbane sat herself up as he keeled the rest of the way over on to his hands and knees, both of them approaching the same general height but from different directions. Benton was shaking, his face pale and his jaws clenched in the manner of one fighting against unconsciousness.

'Been shot...' he slurred. 'Anaesthetic spray. Think it was supposed to knock me out but didn't work right. Year back I was exposed to... to...'

He looked at her owlishly and Delbane just *knew* he was trying to come up with something like the attempts at misdirection she'd been given before, like a drunkard trying to come up with excuses.

There was no time for this.

'You were exposed to something at some point that's counteracting it, right?' she said.

Benton nodded gratefully. 'I can keep it off. For a while.' He glared around blearily at the fallen soldiers who were still visible. 'They came in and went right through us. I think they're after...'

For a moment his features went slack, as though every muscle in his face had been cut, and then reanimated; it was like watching some science-fiction movie with a robot whose power is cut and then restored. 'We have to get to the Brigadier,' he said. 'The things he knows... we can't let him...'

Then his features went slack, again, and for the final time. He relaxed into complete unconsciousness and his face smacked into the gravel.

Delbane considered her options. If this were a movie, the first thing to do would be to acquire a weapon and fade into the scenery, becoming an unanticipated loose cannon and picking off the invading forces one by one. This being reality, she decided that the first thing to do was locate a phone and call for help. The Provisional Department had its own dedicated Special Branch armed-response unit for such times when an armed response was necessary and, failing that, if the worst came to the worst, she could always just dial 999.

The phone lines to the barracks, though, had probably been cut – and getting out on the street to use a public call box simply wasn't a possibility. The enemy would be watching the gates and the paling fence was unscalable. Delbane's mind worked frantically on a solution... and threw up a recently-seen image: a battered field telephone hooked to bulky and unfamiliar-looking storage cells and what was supposedly a transmitter aerial, reminiscent of a Jackson Pollock painting fabricated from wire.

The field telephone was currently residing on a bench in Dr John Smith's abandoned workroom. It was worth a shot. Trying to make as little sound as possible on the gravel path, Delbane climbed to her feet and set off, watchfully, in the direction from which she had come.

* * *

It must be noted here that High Councilman Wblk's explanation of the matters currently affecting the entire universe was literally untranslatable: even word-for-word those words would lapse into long strings of vocal and tertiary-sensual gibberish as they dealt with concepts with which the non-paratemporally existing human mind is not equipped to cope.

The idea, for example, that an incident in ancient Babylon and the first Mars landing are in a certain sense happening *simultaneously*, are components of the same discrete paratemporal Event, can only catch the faintest breath of notions and perceptions that a Time Lord would understand in the bone. In such drastically reduced terms, however, the situation Wblk described was more or less this:

The first Gallifreyan attempts at time travel, millennia before what the non-paratemporally existing mind would think of as *now*, had not been a spectacular success. Rassilon himself, though having an innate sympathy for the basic physical processes, was at heart a tinkerer – the Embodiment of the Will of an entire planetary population, but a tinkerer nonetheless. (Wblk, at this point, gave a contemptuous little sniff at such a thoughtlessly cavalier attitude to the mysteries of time and space.)

As a result of this, the thrust towards temporal break-out was characterised not so much by a noble race elevating its thoughts in universal serenity, as by the entire population of a planet hitting things with spanners, skinning their knuckles on some intransigently bolted-together contrivance and cursing.

The Gallifreyan chronosphere was littered with failed attempts by the time, as it were, the Scientific Elders hit upon what was subsequently and retroactively called the Type-one TARDIS design. Some of these prototypes were merely ill-conceived and dangerous, some of them were ridiculous to boot... and some of them had minds of their own. Some of them escaped, breaking free of Gallifrey's temporal pull to slingshot through the space/time continuum at any number of seconds per second...

And, occasionally, space and time being rather smaller in practical terms than people tend to imagine, they hit things.

'A prototype mechanism impacted upon a hitherto stable singularity,' Wblk concluded, 'trapping itself within the physical and temporal atmosphere of a planet and knocking it out of dimensional alignment. This basic incompatibility is, effectively, causing the singularity to destabilise, collapse into a discontinuous state.'

'A discontinuity *within* a planetary atmosphere?' The Doctor frowned. 'The Brownian effect of air convection on it would alone be a recipe for disaster. What are the effects at this objective point?'

'Localised contamination of the time lines,' said Wblk. 'Secondary resonance from the focal point is infecting the planet itself with parareality – the perceived world is being overwritten with discrete contextual event-packets of a higher order. The local population is adapting, of course...'

'Are you saying that this planet is *populated?*' said the Doctor incredulously.

'Lower-order sentients,' said Wblk dismissively. 'They're hardly aware that anything's going on. Even those in direct contact with the singularity have no idea what it truly means. The planet and its population are neither here nor there.'

'What a remarkably admirable sense of detachment you do have,' said the Doctor. 'What's the problem so far as *you're* concerned?'

There was a bleeping from the TARDIS console. A small red light began to flash insistently.

'The transdimensional stresses are increasing exponentially,' said Wblk, his tone rather pointedly oblivious to the Doctor's sarcasm. 'If left unchecked they could split the space/time continuum apart and open up a conduit to...' At this point Wblk's apparition pointed a finger in a dimensionally complex direction that, to a human observer, would appear to be receding no matter where it was seen from. '... To over there.'

'Oh dear,' said the Doctor, worriedly, his eyes boggling a little with concern. 'Oh dear me. That puts a more serious complexion on things, indeed.'

'Precisely,' said Wblk with a slight resurgence of pompous confidence. 'The only proper way to deal with this is to...'

He belatedly realised that the Doctor's worried reaction had nothing to do with the matters of which he was speaking.

'What are you doing? Get those out of me!'

The Doctor had walked over to the console and was activating a display. Because of its position, this had necessitated plunging his hands directly through Wblk's apparition.

'What's happening?' asked Romana, joining him.

'A friend of mine,' the Doctor said, working the display controls with rapid urgency. 'An old friend I knew... several times. I gave him the means to contact me, should he ever need my services and now... it looks as though he's in trouble...'

'Pardon me?' said Wblk the High Councilman, affronted at finding himself suddenly ignored. 'I *am* talking about an unstable space/time discontinuity set to tear reality apart like a rotten walrus, you know.'

'Yes, well,' said the Doctor. 'There's always one of *those* to deal with, and this one can damned well sort itself out for a change. This is far more important.'

Delbane slammed the handset of the field telephone down in its cradle with a terse but entirely heartfelt expletive. The phone had appeared to work and the battery cells seemed to have retained their charge – at least, the lights had come on when she had flipped the power switch – but the earpiece had relayed nothing but dead air.

On the off chance, she had cranked the archaic-looking mechanical handle with its little tin-plate label saying FOR EMERGENCY USE ONLY, and the result had been a randomly oscillating whine layered over static, from which occasionally broke crackling wails of foreign-sounding music and strings of distorted gabbling that might or might not have been words.

Either the field telephone was malfunctioning, or whatever had been set up to receive and return its transmissions was long gone. Either way, it was useless. Delbane had shouted into the handset that she was at the UNIT barracks and needed assistance, purely for the sake of the one in several million chance that there was anybody to pick up her voice.

Now she set about formulating other plans. Either the workroom had not figured in the enemy forces' plan of attack, or they had simply not got around to searching it yet. If the latter, then they must be getting around to it any second now. In any event, Delbane thought, action was better than inaction: it was time to leave. This decision was helped by her memory of Benton, a mental re-examination of her image of the fallen UNIT troops and her recollection of the lack of spilled blood. When resolving to walk into a possible shooting it does wonders to know that one is more likely to be shot with anaesthetic than bullets.

Benton's words implied that the Brigadier was in danger, and that made sense. If the attack had been intended for some terrorist or military objective, merely rendering the opposing troops unconscious rather defeated the issue. The enemy was obviously after something, or someone, and the Brigadier fitted the bill. If she headed for his office there was at least some chance that she'd learn more of what was going on, and whether she was able to do anything about it. Delbane fingered the flap on the holster of her service revolver and:

You do not need a pistol to defeat these Minions. You simply need your Word of Power.

Now where the hell had *that* thought come from?

It had popped into her head, fully formed, with seemingly no connection to even her subconscious mind. It didn't so much as *sound* like her, or like anyone else who had mastered the art of the common apostrophe in everyday use.

Delbane recalled a conversation she'd had once, nothing important, just the sort of general rambling discussion one has with a friend. She had wondered aloud why paranoid schizophrenics, whose malfunctioning brains should throw up utterly random delusions, like thinking gerbils were cheese and so forth, shared the remarkably common delusion that the government, or whoever, was beaming control signals into their heads. Her friend had pointed out that this 'delusion' was in fact the *sane* part of their minds, desperately trying to come up with relatively sane and logical explanations for thoughts they could not possibly have had.

The memory was vaguely disquieting and of no use whatsoever. Delbane set it aside, drew her service revolver and headed purposefully for the workroom door.

Which swung back to reveal a black-clad figure.

Even at this first direct sight of an enemy representative, Delbane saw that there was something very wrong about the shape of it. The sort of pattern-recognition processes that allow one to pull a familiar face from a crowd saw tiny variances of posture, of movement when it moved, that set it very slightly but entirely definitively outside the range of the human form. Consciously, as the figure lunged towards her bringing up a weapon obviously designed to deliver a gas discharge or liquid spray rather than a live round, her only thought was that the man looked *wrong*.

Later, when she tried to think about it, Delbane could find no explanation for what she did next. It was as though something – possibly the same something that had so recently put an alien thought into her head – had taken over her body and was operating it by remote control. It was as though she were possessed.

As the black-clad figure flung itself towards her she felt her hand drop the revolver it was carrying – throw it to the ground on purpose – and then reach up with a calm and easy motion to pluck the concealing hood from its head.

The scream she tried to give at the misshapen form that was revealed seemed to have been short-circuited. Instead, as the thing hit her with its anaesthetic spray and she felt her legs falling from under her, she felt her lips attempting to mouth words, form sounds of their own accord: '*Amarathma ne da* somon *rakthra moli damon su la tomanakath…*'

Chapter Nine
Sins of the Various Flesh

A mind was abroad in Lychburg – or more properly, a Mind. A disembodied intelligence that could not, in all justice, be termed as greater or lesser than human. It was different, it was Other, on levels which the human mind, being for the most part singular in nature rather than multiple and cumulative, cannot properly conceive.

The Mind flicked Its attention at random through sleeping heads, through the heads of small boys dreaming of egging the cars of their elementary school principal, through the head of that same principal dreaming of finally being rid of his aged mother; through the heads of cops dreaming of doughnuts, factory workers dreaming of beer, spinsters dreaming of husbands, housewives dreaming of detergent, teenagers dreaming of panty raids, lackeys dreaming of plutocrats, plutocrats dreaming of wealth undreamt of, convenience-store clerks dreaming of their registers, priests dreaming of their God... and all the while, as It flicked Its attention back and forth through the world that It had formed around Itself and defined, the Mind was aware that something was very, very wrong.

Something new had appeared in the world, something that was causing the carefully established order around It to fragment. The effects, at this point, were minor, in the same way that the first activated cells of a cancer are minor – but the Mind could see that this disruption, if left unchecked, might hurt It, hurt It badly. Possibly even kill It.

The disruption seemed to be centred upon the three tiny, individual minds who had come from the new thing when it first appeared. The Mind had tried to get inside them directly, tried to destroy them out of hand, but Its influence had glanced off them without their so much as noticing. They were protected, it seemed, by some Power almost matching that of the Mind's own. It would have to find some new method of attack.

For the moment, though, the Mind decided It was hungry. It was hungry for a particular kind of sustenance. Dealing with the individual mind that had been first affected by the appearance of the new phenomenon – the creature which had called itself Norman Manley – had only whetted Its abstract appetite.

The Mind now searched the confines of the world for individual minds that were still awake enough to give It what It needed.

Ah, yes. There was one. The Mind had made use of it several times before. It was like an old friend...

Michael Newbegin put his body through the postures and motions again: ten-second sweep of the room, catch and hold an eye for five and smile, forcing both sides of the mouth up simultaneously. Lopsided grins look cool on Elvis and on louses with a heart of gold in the movies; in real life they just look like the smile is a lie. Looking at thirty from the wrong end and feeling every minute of it, Michael was, he reflected, getting too old for this. The darkly handsome, slightly dangerous-looking face reflected back at him from the mirrored panes behind the bar was looking just that little too lined and desperate, the eyes just a little too red-rimmed and hollow. He could remember when this had been fun.

The Blue Lagoon was crowded, more for its legal status as a *club*, which had it staying open and serving after two until six, than for its attractions as a bar. It was a place for people to get toasted and hook up without braving the doormen and prices of a nightclub that wasn't one in name only. They definitely didn't come here for the ambience, for the ratty remains of Hawaiian flora crawling on the walls of the stand that hadn't seen a band in years.

Off to one side of the scarred copper counter, under a malfunctioning, flickering UV-strip, a demure-looking girl in a minidress of sporadically blazing white inclined her hips and simpered at a guy in a tired-looking executive-type suit. Probably one of the wannabe-but-never-wills from one of the companies over in the business quarter, out on a bender to forget his sorry excuse for a life, totally out of place down here on the Lychburg Wharf and trying not to look pathetically glad that somebody was taking an interest.

Good luck there, guy, Michael thought, recognising the girl. Lorna something. Into hippy crap like crystal bioaura massage and people keeping their actual hands to themselves. He remembered the riveting night he had spent with Lorna something, hearing at great length about how love was a beautiful, sharing, spiritual and above all *conceptual* thing. He remembered catching a glimpse of her bed through the crack in a door on his way out: piled with throw-rugs and a heap of stuffed, fluffy toys. There had been something odd about them, something about the way their various fur-covered limbs had been carefully positioned, but he had not quite been able to fix it in his mind.

Michael always seemed to attract girls like that. A lot of it might have been to do with the fact that he had attracted them in the Blue Lagoon, which by its run-down nature tended to attract the freaks, the dangerous and the crazy. The problem was, increasingly he was tending to attract the girls who were dangerous and crazy without being any *fun*. He ordered another hit of bourbon from Moe the bartender, dropped the bills on the counter and turned away – to find himself staring briefly into the narrowed and somewhat predatory eyes of a tall electric blonde in something tight, black and synthetic. Oh jeez, he thought, recognising and remembering her, she's on the loose again. She's gonna land on some poor sap with both six-inch spikes.

Something special, Michael thought, the bourbon finally taking hold and turning him more maudlin. *Someone* special. Someone, he added to himself, catching sight of a chick dressed up in a real-life approximation of Morticia from *The Addams Family*, who doesn't consider a surreptitious attempt to inject you with her own blood a basic and unremarkable part of foreplay…

'Excuse me?'

Michael realised that he'd been staring glumly into nothing but his empty glass for quite a while. He turned towards the sudden presence by his side. Plain black two-piece suit, worn with simple and unaccessorised elegance. Mid-twenties, ash-blonde hair swept back in a ponytail. Level, steady, sympathetic eyes. Just general sympathy, as a person, not sympathy for any loser she might be looking at.

'Listen,' she said, her tone casual, the most natural thing in the world as she glanced around at the Blue Lagoon. 'I know the men are supposed to talk to the women, but you looked sorta lost and nice and better than this. Do you want to ask if you can buy me a drink?'

The public hall of the precinct house was filthy and smelt decidedly overused in several senses, Victoria thought, but at least it was a definite improvement over the cage-like cell in which she had spent a large part of the night. The other occupants, not to put too fine a point upon it, had been rather more uncouth than otherwise. And several of the young – she hesitated to even think the word 'ladies' – had been quite frightfully immodest and familiar, in dress, word and manner of comportment.

At length, though, a burly female officer had removed her and told her that she was free to go, though warning her that neither she nor her friends would be allowed to leave town. The officer's demeanour had bordered on the insulting, but Victoria had wisely counted her blessings and decided not to make a deal of it.

The Doctor was standing by a telephone apparatus affixed to the wall and thumbing through a thick yellow gazetteer of addresses and numbers. Jamie was with him, sporting a new bruise under his left eye, but other than that seemed to be in much the same physical state as when she had seen him last.

'Yon lads had it in their minds to try a bit of monkey business,' he told her, 'but they thought better of it when I showed 'em my dirk.'

Victoria looked at him. 'You did say *dirk*, didn't you?'

'Ochaway, girl. I had it concealed about my person, no bother. It's amazing how some people take away from searching too close on what they think is a man in a dress.'

'That's the place for us!' the Doctor said, suddenly, jabbing a finger at an entry in the gazetteer. 'I'll order us a cab.'

He frowned with a slight air of puzzlement for a moment, as though trying to work out what he had forgotten, or at least got in the wrong order. Then he looked up to regard Victoria warmly.

'I'm glad you're all right,' he said seriously. 'And now, I think we all deserve somewhere safe and comfortable to spend the rest of the night.'

Her name was Susan Barquentine and she was a legal executive in a business quarter law firm, which amounted, so she said, to being a glorified secretary and coffee-bringer. She wasn't a regular on the singles scene – or at least, the singles scene so far as it was encompassed by the environs of the Blue Lagoon – but she was heartily sick of the bar downstairs from the offices in which she worked, where all the lawyers gathered and attempted karaoke after a hard day's high-paid legalistic bitching.

She was funny in a way that didn't take its own sense of humour seriously. It was just fun to talk.

'I had years with this kind of ideal guy in my head, you know,' she told Michael some time later, sipping a horrid concoction with fruit, little plastic flamingos and a name which would have been hard pushed to dignify itself as a *single* entendre. 'I could see him in my head, like he was there before me. I could see him all the time and measure every man I met against him.' She shrugged. 'I still see him in people, flashes of him, sometimes. The shape of his ears, the way his hair falls. I mean your eyes...'

She reached out and laid a finger, lightly, against his temple. 'You have wonderful eyes.'

The cab drove away after the driver had spent an inordinately long time checking the rumpled notes and change the Doctor had produced – after some ferreting around in his pockets to give him the exact fare.

Victoria looked at the establishment in front of her, which appeared to be a collection of tumbledown huts in which the occasional light burned, revealing signs of nocturnal activity even this late in the night. She looked up at the shabby, illuminated sign overhead.

'The Shangri La Fantasy Motel,' she read aloud. 'Fifty-three Themed Rooms for You to Live Out Your Wildest Dreams. Maid Service on Request. Major Credit Cards Accepted.'

'Well, it sounded nicer in the telephone book,' said the Doctor, a little dispiritedly.

The tenement block was on the bad side of town; garbage on the street, the occasional shell of an abandoned car, a number of ominously dark windows in the sides of otherwise inhabited and lit buildings.

'*This* is where you live?' Michael asked.

'I know,' Susan said, answering the unspoken rather than the spoken question as they picked their way through warren-corridors, almost entirely unlit by such infrequent, fizzing neon utility-tubes as remained within their lag-bolted wire cages. 'It's pretty bad. I don't live here all the time. It was arranged for me by Continuity, and I had to take what I could get.'

'What?' said Michael, an uneasy chill running through him from some source he could not name. 'Continuity ..?'

He realised that she had fallen, slightly and silently, behind him.

'Susan?' he said. 'I said what –'

A slim, dry hand clamped itself over his mouth with surprising force and violence. A warm, soft body pressed itself close to him, and then he was wrenched around. He felt the muscles straining in his neck.

He found himself looking into eyes in which something had appeared – no, in which something had gone, in the way that to *add* a negative number is the same as to subtract, leaving dead black holes that sucked his mind and consciousness, quietly and without fuss, into oblivion.

Victoria looked around at the various devices and… *accoutrements* that bedecked the cabin. They were reminiscent, from what she could only surmise, of the goings-on in a scandal from her own time concerning a house in Cleveland Street, and of certain rather puzzling passages in a periodical called *The Pearl*, which she had once found in her father's dresser drawer.

All of a sudden, certain comments made by the concierge as the Doctor had booked them bed and board for the night became clear. Victoria blushed furiously and choked; she thought for an instant she might expire on the spot from apoplectic seizure.

Jamie, for his part, was casting about with a kind of fearful, white-faced snarl.

He came from a time, Victoria supposed, when... fixtures of this nature were used in extremely businesslike and ultimately fatal ways. The fact that this room had been 'themed' to resemble what was thought of as a medieval castle, though in fact it was more akin to a Jacobean one, could hardly help matters.

'Why did you ..?' Words failed her. Victoria swallowed hard and tried again. 'Why did you only arrange one room?'

'I'm sorry?' The Doctor had been puttering around and peering amiably at the various items on display, as though admiring the handiwork and ingenuity without having the first clue of what all that effort had been for. 'Why one room?'

'And you could at the very least,' said Victoria pointedly, anger to some extent overriding her embarrassment, 'when the gentleman asked, not have said that yes, of course we were going to make full use of the facilities, share and share alike, and we'd let him know if we needed an extra hand...'

The Doctor looked at her, genuinely and absolutely at a loss as to her meaning. 'I thought it would be best if we all stayed together, until morning at least,' he said. 'I learnt some quite distressing things during our short stay with the police.' He turned his gaze to the window, over which had been affixed a set of stout-looking medieval bars. 'There's something out there, something dangerous. Something, I think, that might be very nasty indeed.'

'Michael?'

Formless shapes spun in front of his eyes: grey and black and white and skin-tone pink.

'Michael?'

The spinning forms cohered. A relieved Susan Barquentine smiled down at him, sweetly, like a happy child. Her eyes were dead.

'Hello, Michael,' she said. 'Are you feeling better now? I thought you'd died. I was worried, for a while.'

Michael Newbegin tried to speak and failed. His mouth was filled with something globular and rubbery secured, by the slip-tacky feel of it, with coils of electrical flex.

His head was free enough to move – if he didn't mind the sharp agony in the tendons of his neck – and as he moved it he got a sense of his surroundings. A cramped but scrupulously neat one-room apartment bare of any ornamentation, such furnishings as there were arranged with absolute, Euclidian precision, their straight lines parallel or perpendicular to all else. He was on his back, slightly reclined, secured to a surprisingly comfortable and expensive reclining chair by electrical flex that was presumably a match for the stuff securing the ball-gag in his mouth.

He was naked. The clammy feel down his back and thighs told him, without his having to strain his throbbing neck to look, that the surface of the chair itself was covered with polythene sheeting.

'I only did it so you'd stay, Michael.' Susan Barquentine was by the narrow, single bed off to one side, rooting absently through a large holdall in which things clattered and clunked. 'You have to believe that.' There was something bulky on the bed, covered by a quilt. 'I didn't think you'd understand. It was your eyes, you see. Your eyes are, ah...'

She selected an implement from the holdall, regarded it critically for a moment and then set it aside for later. She turned her vacant, smiling face to Michael again, gesturing with a hand towards a thing on the bed. 'I made it myself, in the way that Continuity said it had to be made. It was quite difficult. Look.'

Her hand pulled the quilt aside with a dramatic flourish, like the hand of a conjuror performing a trick. A bloated thing lay there, stitched together from any number of other bodies. A scar across its abdomen had burst the stitching and its mouth hung open, filled with a crusted fluid of corruption, but all things considered it seemed to be holding up relatively well.

'Isn't he beautiful?' Susan said. 'He's just like I imagined him. I made him. I can't make him move and some of him has rotted, but that's OK. I can make that better…

'When he can *see* me, Continuity will wake him up. He can wake up and love me when he has eyes.'

Chapter Ten
Cheating the Reader

... trapped and caught and falling head over heels with my heart in my mouth and juju shadow bogeymen are clutching at me with jagged claws the light behind their ragged eyes burning like the... hurts to breathe and blood and sick slick mucus on the walls and I think that
   something
is happening to
   my...

she was falling through what seemed to be a cavern of pale marble, its walls shot through with rose and glittering quartz deposits. The effect was that, although the cavern walls were patently rock, they seemed organic, with veins and capillaries. There were vast cracks in the walls and in the darkness within, as she fell, she thought that she could make out clusters of ghost-like, insubstantial faces.

Her stomach freefall-yawned inside her as she fell... and something seemed to be happening to her flesh: skin, muscle and viscera seemingly turned loose and painlessly gelid, sloughing and transforming into something metallic and mercurial, streaming from her bones like –

She hit the cavern floor and shattered it. She felt the force of the blow in its entirety but, once again, the sensation was strangely painless. Dazed and completely disorientated, the consciousness that had once been Katharine Delbane rolled her shining metal body over and hauled itself to its hands and knees.

Human hands burst from the cavern floor, sprouting through the cracks of impact like fungus flowers. The hands moved in a unified tangle, clutching for her, grasping at her with a blind and cloying intimacy.

The consciousness that had once been Katharine Delbane made her mouth scream:

'Amarathma ne da somon rakthra moli damon *su la tomankath…'*

And a light came out of her, a ball of white-hot plasma lashing out from her like a reflex-sting, blasting the human hands away and burning them to fractured, scattered bone.

For a while the consciousness that had been Katharine Delbane just sat there in the smoking pool of solidifying grease and bone, looking around at the glittering vastness of the rose-shot cavern. Slightly later she realised that, without somehow quite noticing, she had transferred her postures of attention to her hands which she was holding up in front of her face. They were of perfectly natural, perfectly sculpted mirror-bright chrome, as was, she realised, the rest of her body.

She transferred her attention again, became aware that her reflex-sting explosion of plasma (she had no idea how she'd done that but, then again, she could not have sat down and explained, precisely, how she made a hand move to pick something up) had knocked a new hole in the cavern wall.

There was something behind it.

The consciousness that had once been Katharine Delbane made her bright and shiny new body rise and, although she wasn't aware of it, her feet not touching the ground, she drifted towards the opening.

Beyond it, as she moved closer, was a gulf shot through with a single, crystalline structure of massive complexity, a mechanism the nature of which the mind, by its very nature, could not so much as begin to comprehend. As she drew closer to it, however, as the interplay of it became more distinct, she began in some small part to see how it might –

* * *

'Are you all right?'

Katharine Delbane looked up into the muzzle of an automatic rifle and at the dark shape beyond it. Her first thought was that she had been momentarily stunned, that the monstrous figure who had attacked her was now going for the definitively terminal kill. Then she saw the peaked, checked-band cap and the word POLICE printed in white across the bulletproof vest. The minor variations from the standard Metropolitan Police uniform told her that he was one of the department's Special Branch unit.

Delbane sat up with a groan. Her head was pounding with a hangover from the anaesthetic and her skin felt slightly numb, as though it wasn't properly connecting with the world. The hallucinations she had experienced while under the influence were already fading: something about hands and spider webs? She couldn't quite remember.

There was no sign of the black-clad man (she was positive, now, that it had been a man, her recollections having obviously been disrupted by the anaesthetic spray) who had attacked her. On the floor where he had been was a fine mass of ash, of the sort you got from burning paper. It certainly didn't look anything like a human outline, and nothing at all like those occasional 'strange but true' photographs of spontaneous human combustion, so why couldn't she shake the automatic impression that her attacker had burnt up explosively, like a Hollywood vampire with a stake through its heart?

Delbane looked around her, and saw that the filing cabinets in Dr John Smith's workroom were no longer in the positions in which she distinctly remembered leaving them. By the door, she saw the upturned metal wastepaper basket from which the ash had spilled. She clapped a hand to her uniform jacket and groaned again, this time not out of pain. Her zip-locked folder of appropriated notes was missing.

'I've found another one,' the Special Branch man was saying into his hand-held radio set. 'Female, just coming round. She still looks like she's out of it.' He frowned at the tinny and indecipherable voice from the other end. 'Well, yes, I suppose so.'

Delbane realised that, from the Special Branch man's point of view, she had been staring around dumbly. She decided to take charge of the situation, get to her feet and start eliciting some solid facts, but her legs didn't seem to be working properly at the moment.

'I'll be all right,' she said. Her tongue felt thick and useless. She realised that the Special Branch man hadn't understood a word and was leaning down to hear her more clearly.

Just then, two new figures bounded through the door, jostling each other in their eagerness to get through it. Both were in their early thirties, but both wore leather trousers of the sort more common to pathetic old dads who decide at the age of forty-five to grow a beard and buy a Porsche. The one with curly hair was wearing a brown leather jacket and a kipper tie with a picture of a cocktail waitress on it. The one with close-cropped hair wore a shiny pale-blue jacket with the sleeves rolled up to the elbows and a turtleneck. Both were quite extraordinarily well endowed in the gold Rolex and chain department, and the cumulatively bilateral effect was, as objective observers like Delbane had on a number of occasions remarked, that of a pair of complete and utter tossers.

'Don't worry, love,' the curly-headed one was saying. 'You'll be all right, the *Provisionals* are here now...'

They looked at Delbane and their faces fell.

'Oh, it's you, Delbane,' the short-haired one said. 'We thought there was some tasty soldier bird down in here.'

'Yes, well, life's just full of disappointments,' said Delbane, dislike giving her full use of her vocal cords again. 'Hello, Slater. Hello, McCrae.'

* * *

'Well I must admit,' Romana said as the TARDIS once again wheeled through the fluid chaos of the Vortex, 'that was rather unexpected.'

'What, how I extricated us from being trapped out of time without having to wait for Wblk the High Councilman to release us?' asked the Doctor, hanging on to the edge of the console as another quantum shock wave hit them as a result of their entirely unorthodox method of egress. 'It's just a notion I've been working on.'

'You must have been working on it for a while,' Romana said. 'I don't think *I'd* have hit upon such a complicated, ingenious and downright audacious idea in...' She thought for a moment. 'Two hundred and fifty-seven years. Two hundred and fifty-eight, possibly.'

The Doctor beamed proudly.

'I have to admit that I sometimes have my *on* days. On the other hand, Wblk's sure to tell all his friends precisely how I achieved the feat – I very much doubt if they'll ever let me use it again. They'll have safeguards well in place for the next time.'

Romana frowned pensively. 'Well, I just hope it's worth it. And I really wish it was in aid of going somewhere other than Earth. I loathe Earth in that century. All those world wars and extermination camps. Things like that are always so miserable and depressing. This friend of yours must be very important to you.'

'Well, you know how it is,' the Doctor said. 'Or possibly you wouldn't. You haven't been out in the galaxy at large long enough to form the sort of attachments I have.' He peered at a display, worriedly. 'It's been a while since we got the signal, what with the transit lag.' He turned to look out of the page at the reader with no small amount of concern. 'I just hope we can get there in time without doing something completely stupid.'

* * *

The attack on the barracks had resulted in no casualties – or at least, none could be immediately verified. When the Special Branch and Provisional Department operatives had arrived on the scene in force, they had found the UNIT personnel mostly on the point of waking up. There appeared to be no permanent physical damage to them, as was subsequently confirmed by the reawakened MO and his staff, but more extensive medical tests would obviously take some time.

Nothing of importance appeared to be missing – save for the one thing of paramount importance which could not properly be called a 'thing' at all. Brigadier Lethbridge-Stewart had disappeared without trace, along with any trace of those who had, presumably, abducted him.

Delbane finally arrived at the Brigadier's office to find a familiar figure already there: a craggy man in early middle age wearing a crumpled raincoat he never seemed to take off under any conditions whatsoever. The commander of DISTO(P)IA himself, Crowley, sitting behind the desk and fussing with the paperwork and pen set with the air of one trying such things for size before ordering them to his own liking. It seemed that the Provisional Spymaster was moving in.

'Making yourself at home?' Delbane said, more or less purely on the basis of something to say.

'I've had my eye,' said Crowley, 'on this office for a while now. In a sense.'

He picked up and absently toyed with a smallish, greenish cube of a substance that appeared to be lucite and to have been used by the Brigadier as a paperweight. 'You don't imagine we'd leave you here without keeping an Eye on you?'

That explained the swift response from department forces, whether Delbane had actually managed to call them in or not. 'Not Slater and McCrae, surely?' she said. 'I'd have spotted them a mile off if they were hanging around.'

'We have other means and methods, to be sure.' Crowley smiled slightly. Without it ever being stated overtly, Delbane knew that he shared her opinion of Slater and McCrae. The pair were a couple of incompetent louts, forever blasting around in a souped-up Ford Sierra, beating up anybody they thought they could get away with beating up and copping a feel of anything female they came into contact with, whether they thought they could get away with it or not. God alone knew why Crowley kept them on – Delbane was of the opinion that their primary function was that of decoys. They blundered around making a noise while the department itself quietly got on with the business in hand.

'Well, if you had other methods and means,' she said, a little bad-temperedly, 'why did you need *me* here in the first place.'

'You were our man, as it were, on the inside.' Crowley set down the little cube he had been toying with and leant forward on the desk, steepling his fingers. 'The woman on the ground, let us say. I understand you came into close contact with the attackers. Is there anything you can tell me about that?'

'I...' Delbane paused for a moment, uncertainly. 'I don't know. What I saw – what I thought I saw – was so strange that it had to be...'

'Strangeness,' said Crowley, 'is what I'm looking for. Has it not occurred to you that *strangeness* is precisely the matter with which UNIT is supposed to deal? What the tabloid papers call the paranormal?'

It quite simply hadn't, not to Delbane, in the same way that it hadn't occurred to her to wonder if UNIT's big secret was that they were all angels of God with their wings hidden under their uniforms, or comic-book heroes with superpowers, tights under their trousers and secret identities. It was quite simply unthinkable, in any real world, to the point where it would not even cross her mind to be dismissed.

Only now, with the idea in her head, did she see how it could be made to fit: all those requisitions in the files for industrial-strength garlic concentrate and caesium bullets...

'You can't be serious,' she said, as her mind flatly rebelled. 'A UN-funded taskforce for dealing with flying saucers, the beast of Bodmin Moor and the fairies at the bottom of the garden?'

'Not precisely,' Crowley said, a hint of impatience making itself felt beneath his veneer of urbanity. 'The true facts of the matter are rather more esoteric than that, but the fact remains that such forces exist and UNIT has the remit to deal with them. Had, I should say. This latest debacle, I think, together with your own reports, should be enough to make the case for the Provisional Department stepping in. Our function is to protect the country from the forces of *subversion*, after all – and what is the paranormal, when you come right down to it, but a subversion of our very reality?'

Delbane frowned. 'So let me get this straight. What I've really been doing for the last month is helping to give you the opportunity to extend your brief?'

'Not at all,' Crowley said smoothly. 'Although I'll be the first to admit that I have every intention of capitalising upon that opportunity now it's been presented. The Berlin Wall can't last for ever, and the intelligence community is going to have to acquire new interests – and fairies at the bottom of the garden, if I may say so, are always going to be with us. Clause 28 notwithstanding.'

'And the hunt for the Brigadier?' asked Delbane. She didn't quite know what she should be feeling. She was quite prepared to be used, even lied to and manipulated towards some greater good – that being after all a basic part of her job. She just wasn't sure that an interfactional tussle for administrative power and influence was what could be called the greater good. The unworthy thought crossed her mind that Crowley *himself* could have in some way orchestrated the attack on the UNIT barracks in the first place. 'What about the Brigadier?' she said again. 'Are we going to look for him or what?'

'Of course,' said Crowley sternly. 'The Metropolitan Police, Interpol, Customs and Excise and all the other appropriate forces of authority have been informed and mobilised. As have the press. An extensive manhunt, I gather, is already under way. There'll be no brushing of this matter under the carpet if *I* have anything to do with it. Lethbridge-Stewart is far too valuable an asset to leave in the hands of a person or persons unknown. And besides...' he smiled slightly. 'I'd like him back to see his face when I tell him the new terms under which the British arm of his taskforce is going to be run.'

He regarded Delbane with frank seriousness. She found herself wondering if he ever actually blinked.

'None of this concerns you at the moment,' he said. 'I merely bring it up to impress upon you that I want to hear the details of what you saw when the enemy attacked, however unlikely they might appear. So please, Delbane, do go on.'

The mannerly but firm tones of command were now entirely evident. Delbane groped for words to describe what she'd seen, when her her body had of its own volition plucked the hood from the figure that had advanced on her:

'It wasn't human,' she said at last. 'I mean, it *looked* man-shaped but there were things wrong with it. Let's call it a creature. It was some sort of human-looking creature. Its face, when I saw it, kept shifting – I don't mean moving around... I mean as though it was a face on a television screen, switching between channels, but in three dimensions...'

'Like a hologrammatic projection, I believe they're called?' asked Crowley. 'I gather the Americans are doing some quite impressive things with portable lasers at the moment.'

'No. This was solid. Forming and reforming into things I almost recognised. Insects, jackal heads...' Delbane's voice trailed off as she remembered how the creature's features had just seemed *wrong* – she could spend an hour detailing the specifics and still be no closer to explaining why. In the way that a situation or person can anger you in such different ways and on so many levels that the only release is a single and violent expletive, there was only one description for the thing.

'It was a monster,' she said, somewhat lamely.

Crowley had been following her attempts at explanation with thoughtful interest, nodding occasionally and seemingly recognising her reactions even if he wasn't taking in her exact words.

'Did it have a mark?' he asked, tapping his forehead with his thumb. 'Did it have a mark here?'

Delbane was about to say no – and then realised that wasn't true. As she had looked into that shifting wrongness there had been... *something* imprinted on it. It wasn't any kind of pigment, any kind of visual thing that she could draw on a sheet of paper, but it had been a... well, a mark. Something perceived in a way that was unrelated to the usual senses, impossible to describe in their terms, but something distinct and recognisable. She would recognise it if she saw it again.

'Yes,' she said. 'There was a mark.'

'Oh dear.' Crowley seemed to have taken her meaning. Worry surfaced from the urbanity and etched lines on his face. 'If what you're telling me is true, then I'm rather afraid that...'

There was a knock on the office door; an urgent knock, the exigency of which was confirmed when the knocker entered the room without waiting for an invitation. It was one of the Special Branch men. He seemed flustered.

'Mr Crowley, sir,' he said. 'I really think you need to see this. There's been a development.'

Dr John Smith's workroom was more or less as Delbane had left it. The exceptions were a rather large number of armed

Special Branch reinforcements, and the object they were pointing those arms at.

Slater and McCrae were still there. Slater, in particular, seemed to be in a bad way, as though he had recently experienced a profound shock. 'I was looking at it and it was *there*,' he was saying. 'I mean, the wall. No I don't. I mean I was looking at the wall and *it* was there...' He had obviously been propounding variations on this theme for a while now, caught in a minor mental and verbal loop.

It was a battered-looking oblongatic blue box, occupying the space where Delbane had previously surmised a missing cabinet – in fact, this assumption had fixed itself in her head so that her first impression was that she was looking at a big filing cabinet. Then she realised her mistake: it was an old-style police telephone box, probably dating from the 1960s and her reaction to its incongruity was rapidly blurred as she imagined all the hypothetical mental ways in which somebody could find it and haul it inside...

Past armed and watchful Special Branch men? And Slater, if you could believe him, was saying that it had appeared out of thin air.

'Well, I suppose this is a development of some kind,' said Crowley beside her, in the tones of one who had never been in this place before and so was completely underwhelmed by any transformation that might or might not have occurred. 'Though I fail to see how it might prove useful.'

It was at that point that the door of the police telephone box drew back with a slightly unprepossessing clunk, and a voice spoke from the darkness beyond.

'Come along, Romana, a quick poke around and we'll soon see what's what...'

A lanky man in bulky, horrendously mismatched clothing and a long knitted scarf stepped from the box, followed closely by a tall and beautiful woman with the bored-looking bearing of a high-fashion model, with raven hair and wearing a Chinese silk and brocade gown.

The man goggled at the massed ranks of Special Branch men in a sudden and slightly overplayed double take. 'Well, it appears that we have some visitors to our humble abode. This *is* nice.'

He turned to the woman and stage whispered to her out of the corner of his mouth. 'I'm afraid the old place seems to have gone rather downhill since I left it last.'

Chapter Eleven
A Small Tour of the Perimeters

Victoria woke to the sound of a coaching horn giving obstreperous voice outside, repeatedly, to the tune of what she recognised as 'Dixie' – the anthem, as had been, of the Confederate South. It was coming from the direction of the window of the Shangri La Fantasy Motel cabin, as was the new sunlight of morning. She clambered off what, for the sake of propriety, she insisted on calling the bed and, yawning, padded across the unpleasantly surfaced floor.

Jamie was sleeping on the floor by the wall in a curled-up posture that suggested he was missing the additional warmth and company of the family hounds. He stirred and opened his eyes, muttering a wordless, half-awake question.

'I think it's time we were up and about,' Victoria told him. There was another blast of mechanical 'Dixie' from outside. '*Someone* seems to think so, in any case.'

Through the window they saw the Doctor sitting in an enormous automobile, his smaller than average form all but lost in it. The car was a violent and highly polished fire-engine red, with white-walled tyres and a canopy that was currently folded back, giving the vehicle the aspect of a massive, slightly flattened, shiny brick. Mirror-bright chrome gleamed on the grille and bumpers, and swept-back projections on the rear reminded Victoria of the engine pods of the suborbital rocket ships she had seen on a visit to the twenty-second century, though here these seemed quite obviously for show.

'Time's wasting,' the Doctor said as they left the cabin to meet him. They didn't need to waste time dressing because Victoria, for one, would not have removed a single item of clothing in their present surroundings for all the coffee in Aribaca. 'And it doesn't do to waste time.'

Jamie was examining the automobile with the guarded enthusiasm common to men the universe over when confronted by a big, good-looking machine that they know they should be regarding as functionally useless. 'Where did you get this, Doctor? Last night you said we'd used up the last of our money.'

'Well, I was out for my morning stroll,' said the Doctor, 'and I happened across this place that was buying blood. I can't imagine *what* they want to use it for. I thought I'd better stop selling it when I had enough to rent a car, though. They seemed to be getting a little bit nervous when they realised my body wasn't going to run out of the stuff.'

'What do we need an automobile for?' asked Victoria. The acquiring of such an expensive possession, even on a rental basis, did not bode well for the Doctor's hopes of their leaving any time soon.

The Doctor beamed. 'Only bums walk around these parts, apparently. Which puzzles me a bit because I thought that people usually used their legs. On the other hand, I rarely get a chance to drive in this life. Hop in. I want to show you something interesting.'

They drove through streets packed with people who were dressed in a variety of outlandish styles and going about business the nature of which could sometimes only be guessed. On street corners, ratty-looking youths in leather jackets leant on lamp-posts and toyed with switchblade knives, wolf whistling at spandex-clad girls as they swept by on rollerblades. Newspaper boys in cloth caps declaimed the wares on their wire-frame stands. Men with sharp suits and ponytails held urgent conversations with their mobile telephonic devices. A policeman idly twirled his night stick.

An ice-truck driver wandered from a Kwik-Shop convenience store towards his horse-drawn conveyance, munching on a microwaved breakfast burrito.

At length they drew into the car park of the imposing steel-and-glass edifice of the Mercy Hill General Hospital. The hospital had a sign outside it reading: ASK ABOUT OUR GENEROUS MALPRACTICE SETTLEMENTS!!

'This isn't it,' said the Doctor. 'This isn't what I wanted to show you, but it's on the way.'

They walked through corridors and wards lined with beds. Many of the patients were in full body casts, engendering some doubt as to whether anyone was actually alive inside them. Orderlies and nurses shuttled about tending to the patients generally but never quite, if you looked at them and paid attention, doing anything specific. The Doctor led Victoria and Jamie through the maze of corridors, occasionally sniffing the air in a refined sort of way, occasionally cocking his head as if to listen to something no one else could hear.

Eventually they came to a small private room, in which lay the girl they had encountered out in the woodlands. Her head had been bandaged. An intravenous drip had been plugged into her arm and monitoring machines flashed and bleeped. A jolly-looking medical doctor was tending to her, chuckling to himself in a way that suggested that chuckling was his natural state.

'Is the young lady allowed visitors?' the Doctor asked, making to tip his hat and then looking disappointedly at his fingers when they failed to find one.

'Are you immediate family?' the jolly doctor asked them.

'I think we're more like friends,' said the Doctor.

'Well...' The doctor sucked his teeth consideringly. 'Ordinarily, I'd say that only immediate family were allowed, but what the hell. He he he...'

'And what's your diagnosis, doctor?' the Doctor asked, peering at the unconscious girl as she rested peacefully.

'My diagnosis,' said the jolly doctor, 'is a nasty bump on the noggin, causing temporary unconsciousness and amnesia.'

Jamie and Victoria looked at each other. They had become quite accustomed by now to the way in which the Doctor had the knack of getting what he wanted from people – not so much through some mesmeric influence but by somehow managing to do and say precisely the right thing. This was slightly different. The jolly doctor just seemed to be mad, hopefully in a harmless sense, doing and saying things that had no connection with what people did and said in real life.

'That doesn't sound very medically specific,' said the Doctor dubiously. 'If it's all the same to you, I'd appreciate a second opinion.'

Another doctor stuck his head through the door. 'Hello, everybody.'

'Hello, Dr Rick,' said the jolly doctor.

'I'd like to hear a second opinion on this patient,' said the Doctor. It was as if, thought Victoria, he was playing along with some common script.

'A second opinion?' Dr Rick scuttled into the room, rubbing his hands and exuding greasy untrustworthiness from every pore. He glanced at the unconscious girl. 'Hmm. Massive trauma, severe angioplepsy, diploid prolapsation and a suspected hairline fracture of the skull. It'll take months of intensive and expensive treatment to cure her, or my name's not Dr Rick.'

'Fair enough,' said the Doctor. 'Doesn't bother us, since we are not the people who will pay the bills.'

'Oh,' said Dr Rick. 'In that case, it's a bump on the head causing temporary unconsciousness and amnesia. She should be coming out of it, right about now.'

As if on cue, the girl stirred. She opened her eyes and groaned. 'What happened to me?' she murmured, running a frail hand across her brow. 'Where am I...?'

110

'You're quite safe. Don't worry,' said the Doctor soothingly. 'Can you tell me what happened?'

'I...' The girl looked around, startled. 'I can't remember anything at all! I can't remember who I am. I can't even remember my own *name*...'

'Now just what,' said the Doctor, back in the automobile and driving it with an inept recklessness that nonetheless seemed to have them avoiding certain disaster time and time again, 'did we learn from all that?'

'They were lying,' Jamie said from the back seat, shortly, his direct nature angered by those who resorted to subterfuge. 'They were putting on an act.'

'I'm not sure if that was entirely the case,' said Victoria, thoughtfully.

'Oh yes?' said the Doctor. 'And what do you think?'

'Well...' Victoria groped for the words to define some rather abstract concepts. 'If it *were* an act, I didn't form the impression that they were aware of it. It's something like the way that actors become the character they play, but more extreme than that. It looked wrong to us, but to them it was natural and real...'

'Well done, Victoria,' said the Doctor happily, turning the car sharply so that it narrowly missed an unexpected and frantically clanging trolley bus. 'The lies, I think, are being told by someone or something else.'

He took one hand from the steering wheel and gestured grandly to take in the world in general, the streets and buildings and people. 'Is there anything about this that strikes you as strange?'

'If you're asking me,' said Jamie, who had first met the Doctor in the battle of Culloden, and whose basic idea of a glittering metropolis was a lowland market settlement, 'it just looks strange, like all the other strange places you've taken me.'

'Well, I suppose you don't have too much basis for direct comparison,' the Doctor allowed. 'But take it from me, there are things happening here that simply aren't right. Everywhere we look, we see things that shouldn't be coexisting. Ice-trucks and mobile phones and trolley buses. Do you see all those automobiles parked outside that shopping mall, for example? The cars are from the fifties and sixties, the mall itself is classic nineteen-nineties... it's as though someone's just dropped all these things here, thinking they're what make up a town, without any regard to their proper context in time.'

'You said these things would happen if we were on Earth,' Victoria said thoughtfully. 'Do you mean we're not on the Earth?'

The Doctor frowned. 'I suppose we could be but, well... it's a bit difficult to explain. I think I'd be happier showing rather than telling.'

The Doctor's driving might have been erratic, but it covered the ground with efficiency, as well as with things spilled by other drivers as they swerved to avoid him.

Soon they were out past the city limits, with nothing to see but scrubby woodland and the occasional gas station. Victoria couldn't be sure, but she thought they were driving in the opposite direction from which they had first entered Lychburg, squashed up in the back of a police patrol car the previous night.

That meant they were travelling ever further from the TARDIS which, currently inaccessible or not, served as an odd kind of home base in this strange and futuristic world. It wasn't that this was particularly worrying, but her awareness of it settled in her mind like an itch she might at some point decide to scratch.

After a while, at the point where both Victoria and Jamie were assuming that the plan was to drive on into some other town than Lychburg, the Doctor said, 'We're getting close now, I think.'

A track led off from the road to what appeared to be, through the occasional bit of obscuring vegetation, a big open space in which was a huge, flat structure like a giant-sized magic lantern screen. A sign on a scaffold arch that had been erected where the track led into the space read DRIVE-O-RAMA, and on a hoarding to one side were the words: 'Showing Tonite: It Came from the Hell Planet Beyond Time!'

'Is that it?' Jamie said from the back of the car. 'Is that what we've come all this way to see?'

'In a sense, Jamie,' said the Doctor, driving the car straight past the Drive-o-Rama. 'Now, if you'd both like to hold on tight to something... I'm not quite sure what's going to happen next...'

Absolutely nothing happened next, save that the car sped on along the road. The Doctor seemed a little disappointed.

'I was sure we'd have felt *some* effect at least,' he said, crestfallen. 'By my reckoning we should all have exploded, or turned ourselves inside out, or something of that nature and... ah, well, never mind, here we are again.'

Without changing their direction of travel, they were coming back up the track leading off into the Drive-o-Rama. Everything was precisely as they had seen it so recently, save that they were approaching the space from the opposite direction and the track led off the other way.

'It's like the TARDIS,' said Victoria, worriedly, as she realised what had happened. 'Only it's happening...' She tried and failed to come up with something not quite as nonsensical as: 'outside in, rather than inside out.'

The Doctor nodded. 'It seems our travel plans are thwarted in every... well, in every direction we turn. We're trapped here, I think, like insects in a killing bottle.'

Chapter Twelve
An Assemblage of Small Mementoes

'Well of *course* I'm Dr Smith,' the new arrival exclaimed indignantly from his cell. 'Who else would I be?' Through the spyhole Delbane saw him rummage around in his coat pockets, then stop when he realised that one of the Special Branch guards in the cell with him was on the point of doing something rash with his weapon.

'I was merely trying to lay my hand on my affidavits,' he said hastily, holding his hands where the guard could plainly see them. 'I was even going to offer round the jelly babies, or toffee creams, or possibly a pickled egg, but now I rather think I won't.' He sat down on the bunk, which gave a dejected creak of old springs.

The Special Branch guards remained impassive, as they had since the man had been brought here to the UNIT glasshouse, which was inordinately large and extensive, contained cells that could be pressurised and gave off more of the general impression of being some high-technological *containment facility* rather than anything else.

It wasn't the job of the guards to talk or think, it was their job to keep the prisoner secure and, should it come to it, shoot him without a qualm. As a result, with the cell door unlocked – the new arrival ostensibly being held merely until his identity was confirmed – the situation was more dangerous than if he had been locked up for committing a crime.

'And I completely fail to see,' he said to Delbane, as she walked through the door, 'what the point is of segregating me from my companion.' He seemed entirely unsurprised to see her, and it was as though he were simply picking up some previously interrupted conversation. 'We arrived together, if you remember, so don't you think we'd have done all our nefarious plotting and collusion beforehand?'

Delbane ignored the question as one of the guards went out and brought her an incredibly uncomfortable canvas and tubular steel chair. The way this man had arrived, in addition to all the other strangeness she had so recently experienced, had left her feeling a little unbalanced inside. She wondered if she was entirely in her right mind.

She decided to stick to simple, solid procedure:

'You claim to be Dr John Smith,' she said. 'How can you prove that?' She waggled a file at him meaningfully. 'There are no verified photographs of you anywhere on record. Not one. How do we know you're who you say you are?'

The man shrugged. 'I'm afraid I don't photograph very well. Sometimes they come out and it's like looking at a completely different man. I suppose I could point at a mirror and go "that's me", but that's an incredibly tedious old joke, and I think we've had quite enough of them for a while.'

He beamed suddenly, with the air of someone holding the other person in a conversation up to complete and utter ridicule. 'I'll tell you what. Why don't you have one of my old UNIT friends vouch for me? Or more than one? Or every single one of them? That should go some way to convincing you on the law of averages if nothing else.'

'That's already in hand,' said Delbane. 'There are other matters to clear up first. For one thing, how did you manage to break in without people seeing you?'

'I haven't broken anything,' said the putative Smith. 'I have a perfect right to be here, and I defy you to prove I've broken anything at all, at least in that sense.'

'Our man Slater,' said Delbane, 'is swearing that you appeared out of thin air, right before his eyes. Or rather, that thing you came out of did. That's clearly impossible...' She quashed the thought that Slater, whom you couldn't honestly think of as a recruit from the brightest and the best, was not the ideal person to bear witness to an impossibility.

She decided to just cut to the chase: '... so just what the hell is happening here? What are you playing at?'

'Slater?' said the possible Smith. 'Was he the chap who looked like he was having a small but rather neatly formed nervous breakdown?' He snorted. 'Things must have gone downhill if people are put out just by things appearing out of thin air. Happened all the time in my day. If that day still, in fact, existed.'

'What do you mean by that?' said Delbane.

'Dr Smith' ignored her question. 'It just so happens,' he said, 'that I am something of an amateur illusionist, with a small sideline in conjury, sleight of hand and prestidigitation. You people happened to come upon me just as I and my lovely young assistant were practising our magic cabinet trick for the UNIT Christmas Ball.'

'Christmas Ball?' Delbane looked at him. 'It's the middle of July.'

'I did say I was something of an *amateur* illusionist,' said Dr Smith blandly. 'I sometimes need a lot of practice to get it right.'

There was a knock on the cell door and another Special Branch man came in with a familiar figure in tow. It was Benton. He looked haggard and slightly dazed, but at least 300 per cent better than when Delbane had last seen him. She found she was glad about that, strangely enough, and wondered what would happen to him and others like him if Crowley's plans for the administrative annexing of UNIT came to fruition. Would he, and they, be kept on in some toothless, showcase capacity or would they simply be heaved out?

'Corporal Benton!' Dr John Smith bounded from the bunk in galvanised delight, heedless of the threat of what now amounted to three armed Special Branch men. 'Or is it Sergeant now?'

'It's Sergeant, Doc.'

Benton, though more restrained, seemed as delighted to see Smith as the other was to see him. It was like watching years fall away from the man.

'That's nice to know,' said Smith. 'Sometimes you can only tell what time it *is* by the internal references.'

'I was worried you might have... uh... changed so much I wouldn't even recognise you,' said Benton.

'No chance of that. Not for a while, anyway.'

Benton's face now seemed to collapse in on itself slightly, in the manner of a man reduced to tears but fundamentally unable to cry. 'You have to *help*,' he blurted out. 'The Brigadier's been taken and these people...' He looked around at the Special Branch men and Delbane with conflicting emotions, the conflict being which degree and sort of dislike would gain the upper hand. 'Well, look at them. These people...'

'Never fear, Sergeant Benton,' said Doctor John Smith blithely. 'We'll put things right. All will be well, and well, and all manner of things shall be well, as I remember remarking to Francis Bacon one night as, for reasons of his own, he was trying to stuff snow up a chicken...'

He turned to beam happily at Delbane. 'I think you'll agree this clears up almost any question that I'm not *precisely* who I say I am – and, if you'll recall that dossier of yours, that means I have quite a bit of seniority around here.'

He looked at her again with steady, perfectly clear eyes, and something in his expression sent a shudder through her. It wasn't a threat – because a threat, whatever else it does, limits the possibilities of what might happen. Continue to impede me much longer, Smith's eyes said, and anything – literally *anything* – could happen.

'Now if we can just organise the release of my lovely young assistant,' he said, lightly. 'We can make a start at finding out what's *really* going on.'

Two hours later, the workroom of Dr John Smith – or just the Doctor, as he insisted on being called, since that was the name his friends used and they were all going to be such good friends – was entirely more recognisable. As opposed to *un*recognisable. That was because it looked even more like itself than before: a confusing, otherworldly mess.

After his release and that of his so-called assistant the Doctor had caused several more bulky items of old junk to be taken out of storage and had appropriated several of Delbane's prized computer units, with the Special Branch men doing the heavy lifting for the most part. It was amazing, really. With his credentials accepted it was suddenly as if he owned the place, getting others to perform his bidding by the simple act of asking them with the air of one to whom a refusal was unthinkable.

The computers and other items of an arcane electrical nature had now been wired together with a tangle of serial leads, telephone flex and even in cases a chain of paper clips. A number of thick tubes ran from this insane cluster to disappear inside the police box, the Doctor's so-called 'magic cabinet', which he had forbidden anyone to so much as touch on pain of being drummed out of the Magic Circle. 'And I mean,' the Doctor had said, 'an entirely different concern than the likes of Ali Bongo.'

Classified equipment, so he said, of such a nature that it would take a rewriting of various unnamed but apparently fundamental laws to divulge it, was kept in there. The tubes themselves varied from vulcanised rubber in which something seemed to pulse, to what might or might not have been the fleshy tendrils of an alien tentacle-monster from some old American pulp science-fiction magazine. Delbane had tried to trace where these tubes actually led, and how they connected to whatever it was they were connected to, but she had lost them in the tangle.

Other leads were hooked to modem-cradles for phone handsets, one linking via British Telecom to a bulletin-board server, one apparently to a timeshare on a NORAD satellite and one to the field telephone Delbane had tried to use earlier. There were banks of oscilloscopes, each set to a different and apparently random waveform; there was a collection of police and military walkie-talkies, each babbling away and blasting with static; there was a wide-band radio, connected to the barracks' high-powered amplified mast, with a complicated clockwork device over the tuning knob to cycle it through the range of every available waveband and back again.

There was a collection of television sets, four of them set to the main channels and the rest to the local variations that made it some way through the static to the Greater London area. A Sanyo VHS video recorder had been scrounged from the officers' mess and hooked up to another set – although, instead of a video cassette, the Doctor had inserted an item that appeared to be a heavy, densely packed and almost infinitely complex multiple sandwich of electronics. The output from the video recorder looked like nothing on Earth.

The cacophony of voices and white noise, the flickering images, faces and erratically scrolling blocks of text were like some scene from a chamber in one of the more technologically advanced circles of utter screaming hell. And within it stood the Doctor – if 'standing' can be stretched to mean puttering around it with a kind of amiable abstraction, suddenly pausing stock-still with a look of absolute and frantic concentration, bounding into frenetic action and typing so frantically on a keyboard that it broke, muttering half-heard gibberish all the while, looking raptly at the result on one of the myriad cathode-ray tubes, running over to intently check another display, cursing and running back to hit some item of equipment with what looked like a spanner but one with wires and quartz crystals sprouting from it, standing stock-still again, then scribbling excitedly on a notepad, reading the result, scowling and tearing the sheet out to crumple it violently into a little ball and then throw it negligently over his shoulder...

Katharine Delbane, with her technical experience, had been one of the people who had helped the Doctor throw this demented mess together – in the sense that she had been one of the people whom the Doctor had asked to do something, had done it and had only later started wondering *why*. Now, she stood on the periphery of this preposterous display with Romana, and the adverb for enquiring about cause, reason or purpose was occurring to her seriously.

'What the hell is this supposed to achieve?' she asked. 'It doesn't really do anything, does it?'

Romana looked down her nose at Delbane. 'Don't ask me. I have little to no experience at all with this so-called technology of yours.'

In the short time since she had met her, Delbane had conceived a dislike for Romana – the Lady Romana, as the woman had said, correcting her – that bordered upon active hatred.

Delbane came from an army family, a number of whom were quite senior in its various branches, and throughout her life this had led her into contact with what might be called the British upper crust – the families who still provided most of the country's generals and admirals, as they had since the time of the Norman Conquest. The families who had, in the Crimean and Napoleonic wars, bought their sons commissions which had them playing an inept and lethal game of soldiers with real men.

The difference between these families and Delbane's was that their *primary* function was to fill the House of Lords; they sent those members who were surplus to requirements into the military, in much the same way that third sons of the nobility were once sent into the Church. And such people regarded the likes of Delbane and her family as little more than jumped-up middle-class tradesmen.

Discrimination, basically, works in bands: those occupying one become nearly invisible to those more than a couple of bandwidths away – in either direction. In objective terms, Katharine Delbane might not come from people who lived six-to-a-room in a council flat, dependent on a giro after being made redundant from a canning factory, but in the class-structure terms of the world in which she actually lived she was the lowest point on the totem pole, the target for contempt, and she knew it. She remembered meeting the grandfather of a captain she had once been dating, and he… just what had his name been? She couldn't recall. In any case, her treatment by him had been just another of the incidents that had left her thoroughly disillusioned with regular army life.

Now, she was getting that contempt in spades from the Lady Romana. The woman might look like a superannuated hippie chick, but her manner was straight out of the features pages of *Horse and Hound*. As she stood there, half a head taller than Delbane, she seemed to broadcast a sense of flat disdain as though she had seen what Katharine Delbane's world had to offer and was, frankly, not impressed. Delbane couldn't think of anything she'd done to engender this rudeness from Romana – other than being one of the people who had shut her up in a cell for a while, of course.

'If the Brigadier still had the little, ah, transmitter unit he used to contact me on him, finding him would be simplicity itself. As it is, we're having to improvise.'

Lost in bad-tempered musing on the class struggle, Delbane realised that she had forgotten about the Doctor and his insane activities. Now he was standing before her, grinning with pride and eager to talk. Delbane wondered if this was intended as a direct compensation for the stony aloofness of Romana.

'The enemy will have covered their overt tracks,' explained the Doctor, 'so any *clues* we have as such are worthless. We have to take more of an holistic approach to our detective work.'

He gestured grandly at the flashing screens, the stuttering and roaring speakers. 'Any event, no matter how small, impacts upon the world and changes it – and a sequence of events changes the world in a particular way. If you accumulate enough data, enough to produce a conceptual... well a conceptual data field, you can step back and watch the patterns occurring within it. If you can pull out the particular pattern you're interested in and identify it, you can extrapolate from the known variables and...'

He caught sight of Delbane's expression and his enthusiasm collapsed slightly.

'It's not a particularly difficult thing, you know, any more than the mental processes that allow you to identify both Great Danes and whippets as species of dog. It's simply a knack. The systems that control London's traffic work on the same basic principle, factoring anomalies through the known variables of people getting up in the morning and going to work, going out to lunch and so forth. And speaking of which... I'm not sure I added the factor of *lunchtime* into my calculations...'

The phrase *out to lunch*, Delbane thought, was having some decidedly apposite connotations at this point. The Doctor, meanwhile, had bounded over to an Apple keyboard and was typing frantically. He hit the Enter key, stared at the resulting display on the monitor and then bounded back triumphantly.

'Do you want the long answer or the short answer?' he said.

'How long is the long answer, precisely?' asked Romana. It was the first time she'd spoken save to snub Delbane.

'Well, if I detail all the factors and the basis for the fuzzy-logic processes that allow a reasonably corroborative gestalt,' said the Doctor, 'fifteen years, give or take a couple of weeks.'

'I'm game,' said Romana. Then she turned to Delbane and sniffed. 'Though I suppose, under the circumstances, it might be better to go for the short answer.'

'You can't be taking this seriously!' Delbane exclaimed to Crowley. They were in the Brigadier's office, poring over a London street map which was spread over the desk and so large that several sections flopped over the side. The Doctor was tracing the route he had in his head as the one that the kidnappers had taken, marking points of interest with a big Magic Marker, while the Lady Romana stood off to one side watching with cool uninvolvement.

'Would it help if I said satellite-surveillance tracking was involved?' the Doctor asked. 'I used data from several orbital satellites in my calculations.'

'I have to admit,' Crowley said to Delbane, 'from what you say, it sounds a little preposterous. However...' He frowned, thoughtfully. 'From what I gather about the Doctor, from the records you transcribed, it seems that he's well known for his unorthodox methods – and those methods, from the documentary evidence, seem to work. You're absolutely positive that this is where the trail leads?'

This last was to the Doctor. Crowley was pointing at a spot on the map where the scientific advisor had drawn a quite definitive-looking cross.

'Within the limits of an imperfect world, yes.' The Doctor tapped the map. 'At least, that's where the trail stops with no indication of where it might lead on. The forces that were here are there, or were there until very recently. It's a point of transitional importance if nothing else.'

Delbane snorted. 'There are police APAs out, there are Special Branch units combing the city and the railway stations, ports and airports are being watched. Do you really want to waste resources on a wild-goose chase like this?'

'All the same,' said Crowley, 'it can't hurt to have a look.'

'Well, I'm not doing it,' said Delbane.

Crowley smiled slightly, and a little nastily. 'I was thinking of perhaps Slater and McCrae?'

'Those chaps who seemed so disconcerted to see us when we arrived?' the Doctor said. 'Marvellous. It'll give them a spot of occupational therapy and bring them out of themselves. I trust that they have all the skills your, ah, Provisional Department expects of its men?'

'You could say that, yes,' said Delbane, avoiding Crowley's eye.

'Splendid.' The Doctor turned to the Lady Romana. 'I'd like you to go with them. Let me know what you find.'

'A little outing with the aboriginals,' said Romana, sourly. 'How perfectly lovely.'

Chapter Thirteen
A Sunny Afternoon in Central Park

As the sun through the alders dappled the well-kept grass of Lychburg Central Park, turning the flow from the ornamental fountain to a rainbow spray and the bronze statue of the city's founder, Zebedia Lynchall (with a silent 'n') golden in its light, Artie Bunson set his big, heavy holdall down on the ground and himself down on a bench.

His brown paper bag of lunch was on his knees – though as he was coming off his shift as an orderly in Mercy Hill it was more the equivalent of his main meal of the day. Peanut butter and jelly in Wonder bread, which his mother seemed to think was enough for anyone.

Gang-markers and obscenities had been cut into and spraybombed over the vinylised steel of the bench but Artie remained oblivious to them, not being able to understand the one and his mind automatically shying away from contemplating the other. His mother, when he was a child, had rapped his hands with an old steel-edged ruler which she kept for that special purpose, if he had even so much as *looked* like he was thinking a Bad Word. Or, pretty much, for any other reason.

There was a rummy asleep on the bench beside him, head thrown back and snoring, relatively clean but sloppy and smelling like he had been drinking something stronger than beer even this early in the day. Artie looked at the sleeping form with distaste... and found himself wondering, without thinking or caring about it either way, what would happen if he took his finger and shoved it deep and hard into the man's eye.

It wasn't just as if he could see it happening in front of him, it was as though he could feel himself doing it, his hand moving and the slippery sensation on his finger, the sounds and jerking as the body went into spasm...

And then, quite without feeling anything either way, Artie didn't do anything at all. There was no conscious decision involved; it was like someone else was doing his thinking for him. He simply sat there, nothing in particular in his mind, his eyes resting on the little man and his two companions who had spread a checked cloth on the ground some yards away and were eating a picnic lunch from a wicker hamper, and listening to what they were saying.

'I'd already intimated something of the kind,' said the Doctor around a Cajun-fried chicken leg, into which he was tucking with relish. 'My people have a... well, we're rather sensitive to the *shape* the world makes, if you see what I mean. I'd hoped my feelings were just the result of whatever it was that was affecting the TARDIS itself, but it seems they were not. I do beg your pardon. I shouldn't be speaking with my mouth full. Here, let me dab that off with a napkin. It seems,' he continued, rather less messily, 'that we're trapped here in more senses than one. We can only hope that the next murder we see won't be our own...'

'Murder?' said Jamie, pausing with a devilled egg halfway to his mouth. 'What's this about murder?'

'Oh, I'm sure I mentioned the murders,' said the Doctor. 'Didn't I mention the murders?'

'No,' said Victoria, who was suddenly feeling that no matter how bad she might have thought things were, they were suddenly going to get a lot worse. 'You didn't mention any murders at all.'

'I'm sure I must have,' said the Doctor. 'I can't imagine me not mentioning something as important as murders.'

'Nothing at all,' said Jamie.

'Well, surely I must have said *something* about murders when I…'

'Doctor,' said Victoria, with a sense of huge but slightly worn patience. 'Possibly it would be simpler if we all pretended that you *had* told us, but we've forgotten, so you'll have to tell us all over again.'

'Oh. Yes. Right-oh.' The Doctor waggled his eyebrows seriously, preparing to tell a tale that would make mere mortal men shake in their boots with crawling terror. 'Are those mushy peas?' he said suddenly, spoiling the effect and dipping a finger in a little pot to have a taste. 'Oh.' His face fell. 'It appears to be some kind of avocado dip. Anyway, according to Police Chief Tilson there have been a number of suspicious and rather gruesome deaths. The methods and circumstances are variable but there's a taste – to use Tilson's rather fulsome terms – of them being the work of the same individual. He started talking about splash patterns and disposition or some such, but I'm afraid I found the whole thing quite distressing and didn't listen to that bit very closely. The interesting thing, I gather, is that the timing and positioning of these murders – or at least, the circumstances that can be pieced together, as it were, when the remains come to light – means that they cannot possibly be the work of one person. Two or three have been known to happen, apparently, on different sides of town within minutes of each other.'

'So there's more than one killer,' said Jamie. 'That's simple enough.'

'Quite possibly,' said the Doctor. 'The other thing is that possible killers have been caught – or at least, suspects and material witnesses have been identified and questioned. The trouble is that none of them have any motive, or any recollection of their whereabouts at the time the murders were committed – and other people keep turning up out of the blue, it seems, to furnish them with cast-iron alibis. Then vital forensic evidence vanishes without trace, other spurious leads crop up from nowhere and before any of it can even be begun to be sorted out, there's another run of murders that put them right back to square one again. The police department here isn't really up to dealing with something on this scale, and it has them running around in a bit of a flap. Also, I feel, the police, or anyone else, are not exactly in their right minds at this point.'

'Well, if the local police aren't up to it,' said Victoria, 'why don't they just send a... telegraph message or similar to – oh.'

'Exactly,' said the Doctor. 'There's nowhere they can send a telegraph message or similar *to*. The city is isolated.'

'But how could people not notice that?' Victoria asked. 'And how would they get things like food? It would run out, surely?'

'Nobody would have to be any the wiser,' the Doctor said. 'If there's nowhere to go outside the city limits, as we proved, it would never occur to people to do so because it would be a basic impossibility – to even *think* such a thing would be madness, plain and simple. Or possibly, people *think* there's a world out there, and occasionally make plans to travel to it, but something always comes up – the world itself conspires against them by its own laws of cause and effect. And as for food and suchlike...' The Doctor waved the issue away dismissively. 'Food appears on your plate because the waiter brought it. And the waiter got it from the chef, and the chef got it from the market, and the market got it from its suppliers... it doesn't have to *come* from anywhere, originally, so far as any one link in the chain is concerned.'

'But it would have to start from somewhere...' Victoria began. She was getting a megrimous fatigue from trying to keep all this straight.

'Doesn't have to,' said the Doctor. 'Our own universe works on a process of expansion and contraction, from Big Bang to

Gnab Gib, and a single point where it *started* isn't necessary. And besides, as I said, this place seems to have its own laws of cause and effect.

'Anyway, wherever this place is in terms of the rest of the universe, and whether it was created artificially or not, there's no way for anything to get out. I think this entire town is in the centre of a killing-bottle for something. Or possibly a larder, though what might actually be feeding is anyone's guess. And speaking of food...' The Doctor perused the remainder of the picnic. 'Has everyone finished? Good. We're off back to the Mercy Hill hospital.'

'We're going back there again?' asked Jamie.

'Yes. I want to see the body the young lady so conveniently forgot being near to when it died in the flames... hopefully before it gets mysteriously spirited away.' The Doctor started packing the last of the food away in his wicker hamper. 'I'd have gone back to the hospital earlier, but it's always best to see the hideously charred and horribly mutilated remains of a dead body on a full stomach.' He thought for a moment. 'Or should that have been *empty* stomach? Oh well. Never mind.'

It was quite strange, all things considered, that in an establishment as large as Mercy Hill the first person of any note they ran into was the jolly-looking doctor they had encountered earlier. His name, it transpired, was Dibley, and at the moment he was looking distinctly less jolly. This was almost entirely due to the Doctor's manner.

In her time spent travelling with the Doctor Victoria had found herself constantly surprised at him, not so much by the way in which his entire manner could change almost from one minute to another, but by the way he seemed to inhabit that manner so completely that on some deep level you were shocked when he changed it once again. Ordinarily, he took the part – *was* the part – of a silly little hobo (as she believed the Americans called it) drifting wherever the fancy took him and amiably allowing himself to be taken along with the circumstances in which he found himself. Indeed, he seemed to be most happy in that persona and took pains to preserve it when at all possible.

When danger threatened, however – being trapped in a town elided from the universe of space and time and with a killer on the loose, for example – it was as if he put the clown aside and transformed himself into a man of action, fearlessly hunting down the particulars of the case like a bantam-sized Sherlock Holmes... a man whom, in the face of all probability, he claimed to have met.

Already, in the past few hours, Victoria had seen him display a fine (if, it must be said, rather condescending) scientific mind, and now she saw him display something new – a patrician sternness that, it seemed, would brook no demand on its forbearance.

'You can't come in here...' Dr Dibley was spluttering as the Doctor stormed through the Mercy Hill morgue. He attempted to clutch at the intruder with the intention of restraining him, but the little man seemed to be always out of his grasp. The general effect was of a large and portly shape skipping and fluttering about the Doctor with all the effectiveness of a moth around an angry gaslight.

'I think you'll find I have the authority to go where I like,' the Doctor told him, seeming to loom over the hapless medic despite being a full head shorter, and carefully leaving any particular authority he had unspecific. That was a part of it, Victoria thought: if the Doctor had named the authority on which he was acting, it would have probably been the Order and Garter of Advanced Busybodiness, Second Class.

The two men had fetched up against the stainless steel doors behind which the bodies, presumably, were kept to avoid them cluttering up the corridors. The Doctor perused them with a look of disdain. 'These are your post-mortem storage facilities? There hardly, if you don't mind my saying so, seem to be enough, unless you have an extraordinarily quick turnover. I'm looking for the body of a man who died last night in suspicious circumstances.'

'This is a big town,' said Dr Dibley. 'There would be more than one –'

'But not that many burnt alive in a car wreck,' said the Doctor. 'Well, man?' he continued, in a clipped and rather military-sounding voice which he had no doubt picked up on his travels and squirrelled away for later use. 'Which one is it? You wouldn't want me opening doors at random. Who knows what I might find?'

Loath as he was to go around showing bodies to people who were, after all, complete strangers, albeit complete strangers with a commanding manner, Dr Dibley couldn't help but turn his eyes to a stainless steel door off to one side.

'Thank you so much.' The Doctor stalked over to the door and opened it with a flourish. 'Now, then, we'll soon see... Oh dear.'

The overwhelming sense of authority suddenly left him and he craned his neck disappointedly inside, just to make sure he hadn't been mistaken the first time. 'It seems we're too late after all.'

Artie Bunson opened the door of the tenement apartment he called home and crept inside as silently as he could. If his mother heard him she would no doubt insist that he tell her all about his day, make her a calamine tea, have him do her corns with a paring knife and yet again leaf through the family album, telling him how he had been such a beautiful baby and his poor dear father would have died of disappointment in him now, had he been alive.

From the door of Mother's room, he heard a gurgling snore. That was good. As she grew older Mother tended to sleep more and more. Artie, while awake, dreamed of the day she would never wake up.

In his room, the same room in which he had slept as a child, he was free to work on what he thought of as his 'hobby'. Artie couldn't quite remember when it had started, but at some point years ago he had discovered an impulse in himself to acquire little human figures and put them into poses. In a cupboard – the one thing he had ever stood up to Mother about, telling her that she could not look in there on pain of, well, pain of never waking up – was a collection of little girls' dolls and GI Joes, little men and women moulded out of clay and Silly Putty. Each one was very carefully twisted and positioned by refined increments into shapes that spoke to something deep inside him.

Artie looked at the little men and women for a while, then carefully took them from the cupboard and lay them on his bed. He was going to have to find somewhere else to store them, now; he had to make room for his new project.

He wondered, idly, why he had never thought of this before. All the pieces, as it were, had been there but only today, as he was going off shift, had the idea occurred, fully formed, as though someone or something bigger and brighter than him had for a moment been doing his thinking. Now that the idea had occurred, however, he could see possibilities for developing it.

Artie Bunson unzipped his big, heavy holdall and started taking out the charred skeletal remains of what had once been a boy called Norman Manley. He started piecing them together on the floor, ordering them by careful increments of refinement into something of his liking.

Chapter Fourteen
Reversals Without Transition

'Are you all right?' Jim McCrae flipped his cigarette butt from the Sierra. 'I thought you'd gone completely tonto on me for a while, son.'

They were parked in the parade ground that served as the UNIT, and now the Special Branch, car park waiting for the Doctor's assistant to come out.

'I'm fine,' Danny Slater said. He was already going through that mental healing process common to those exposed to the physically impossible; the mind papering over the sudden holes in its world-view with false memory perceptions. 'It just gave me a bit of a start, that Doctor guy doing his magic trick and all. Threw me a bit.' Slater thought for a moment. 'I can see how it was done now, of course. You get this big sheet of mirror, right, and you put a flap in the back...'

'That Romana bird, though,' said McCrae. 'She was a bit of all right.'

'You're not wrong there,' Slater replied. 'I'd look for a hand grenade down her vest any day of the week.'

'And you'd probably find one.' McCrae lit another Rothmans with his gold-plated Zippo and scrunched around in the Leatherette passenger seat to shove the lighter back in his leather trousers. 'More of a side to her than somewhat, I thought. Nice pair on her, though.'

Danny Slater shrugged. 'I don't know about that. I don't like it when they hang down all dangly like that.'

'I suppose they could get caught on things if you're not careful,' McCrae said gnomically. 'You couldn't operate heavy machinery.'

'Yeah,' said Slater. 'I've always preferred plain gold earrings on a woman, myself. Or possibly a couple of studs.'

Katharine Delbane's opinion of the pair was well-founded. The mistake would be to assume that Slater or McCrae were not perfectly aware of this, or could bring themselves to basically give a toss. Their work for the Provisional Department bordered on complete incompetence – but it was the incompetence of any man who was ever asked to do the washing-up. Do it badly enough, for long enough, and nobody expects any better. Meanwhile, you can put your feet up while somebody else does it for you – exasperatedly, three times out of five.

Slater and McCrae were, quite simply, a couple of lads who had lucked into working for the Provisional Department, having been palmed off on it after their original stints in the army and police.

TV and movie ideas of covert-operations work notwithstanding, the life of a department operative was remarkably safe in reality, so long as you took steps to make it so and avoided the sort of unfortunate assignment where you had to protect some defector or whatever with a price on his head and assassins after him.

House surveillance was merely an opportunity to catch up on your kip out of the rain. Shadowing a target was a chance to go shopping. And the joy of it was that the work was in any case so nebulous that you were covered. Slater and McCrae knew precisely what their purpose was in life; it was to be a voice on the radio saying, 'Control, the suspect has given us the slip,' and then going off to get a kebab.

The door of a barracks hut swung open and Romana came through it, heading for the car with a determined stride, her skirts swishing about her.

'That's quite a walk she's got on her,' said McCrae.

'Yeah,' said Slater. 'I have a bad feeling about this.'

'You're not wrong there,' said McCrae. 'This does not bode well. I have the nasty feeling that we're going to be expected to do some actual work.'

Outside the wire a number of unkempt-looking women were linking arms and singing something about universal sisterhood. Amongst the pink triangles, labris-axes and CND badges they sported, Haasterman noticed a number of high-level Wiccan symbols and suppressed a small smile. If only they knew.

The energy these people generated, in thaumaturgic terms, was barely enough to power a minor Circle of Protection, but every little helped. In fact, the existence of the women's camp had been the deciding factor in Section Eight deciding to use this particular base, as opposed to one further west; supersonic transport-technology made the difference of an extra couple of hundred miles from US soil completely and utterly meaningless.

'Look at 'em,' Lieutenant Major Derricks jerked a thumb towards the tents and teepees of the camp itself, where a news crew were interviewing a collection of protesters. 'You know what they're saying, don't you? How us Yanks are gearing up to kill their precious kids.' He snorted. 'Bunch of dykes. What do they care?'

There were so many contradictions in that statement – the most obvious of which being that several of the interviewees were sporting children and babies in arms – that Haasterman decided to leave it alone. Life was too short. Derricks was one of the regular base personnel, its security officer, which basically meant that he was the on-site representative of the CIA. A muscular and sweaty man with problems of a certain psychological kind. This was par for the course, in Haasterman's experience. Servicemen based overseas were generally screened to be utterly trustworthy in some respects but in others were the sort of men and women that the people back home were damned glad to see the back of.

A thin drizzle flecked at Haasterman's uniform jacket from the miserable grey sky. It seemed that this damn country was determined to reinforce every common prejudice about it, every time he arrived.

When Section Eight had come in with their request for use of the facilities – a request that was, effectively, an order that could not be refused without running for president and winning – the base commander had cleared out a hangar for them. Interestingly enough it was listed in the map records as Hangar 18. Haasterman headed back to it, dodging across the taxiways, occasionally returning the salutes from base personnel that his uniform required and wishing it looked less like the barely-worn-in fancy-dress get-up it effectively was.

Within the hangar, some technicians were wiring up the sensor and data systems while others were going over the transport, which included two out of the three prototypical Snark IV cargocopters that the Section had brought in.

A squad of black-clad ground-force troops, provided by the Section's point man in the UK, were in evidence, seated around a number of trestle-tables off to one side, playing cards and drinking coffee through the mouth slits of their knitted Balaclava hoods.

Haasterman knew that, in the interests of security, it was standard operational procedure for them never to remove these if there was a chance of them being seen and recognised, but the sight of all those masked and faceless men was a little disquieting all the same.

The sigils of Protection were already in place about the walls and activated, but the concentric circles that bound a pentagram drawn in powdered chalk and pig's blood on a cleared area of the hangar floor were broken, and the final lines still had to be drawn. Haasterman walked past it to where a technician was plugging leads into a portable scrambler switchboard-pack.

'Do we have a secure international line?' he asked. *Secure* meant something several orders of magnitude higher than anything available on the base itself, even the lines of communication step-connecting its missiles to the nuclear football.

'Go right ahead.' The technician gestured to a handset. Haasterman picked it up and punched in the direct code for Dr Sohn in Lychburg. It was time for his hourly reality-check.

With the general decline of commercial shipping in the latter half of the twentieth century, London Docklands had become redundant; real estate ripe for the clearing and property developing that in very real terms embodied the Spirit of the Age. In other words: a collection of uninhabitable, partially completed architectural white elephants built on the cheap by money-grabbing jackals.

'There you go, sweetheart,' Slater said as he pulled the Sierra into the shadow of Pyramid Wharf, the half-built tower block that would one day be seen from every point in London, much as those who saw it might wish they couldn't. 'That's the place this Doctor of yours told us about.'

'Very nice,' said Romana, brushing at some errant cigarette ash that had found its way on to her gown. She had cracked a window on the drive to avoid breathing in the fug of smoke coming from McCrae but, in any case, what with the general air pollutants of this primitive society in any case, she'd had to shut down two-thirds of her lung capacity completely. She could feel the pollution doing her harm.

Slater peered through the windscreen at the block. The superstructure was up, but only the first fifteen floors had so far been installed in some module-based building process. There didn't seem to be any actual work going on, for all it was a weekday, and the only vehicles in evidence were dormant earth movers. There was no sign of any conveyance that might have served the dangerous agents of some mysterious enemy force – and this, so far as one Daniel Michael Slater was concerned, was all to the good.

'Now, what I think we should do, darling,' said McCrae, speaking Slater's mind for him, 'is scout out the area for a while. Sit tight and wait for developments…'

He realised that he was talking to thin air. Romana had left the car, slammed the door behind her and was storming for the block; the way she moved showing that her attitude could have been summed up in two words. And they weren't 'bless you'.

'Oh, bollocks,' said Slater, as visions of a tranquil afternoon spent smoking in the car and drinking tea from a Thermos went out of the window. 'That's torn it. I suppose we'd better show a bit of willing.'

'I suppose we'd better had.' McCrae sighed. 'Oh well, by the looks of it, if there ever *was* anybody here, they're long gone.'

'There is that,' said Slater. 'I suppose.'

McCrae started fumbling in the glove compartment, for the department-issue automatics that had hardly ever seen the light of day and never once been fired.

'I told you I had a bad feeling about this,' he said.

They set off after Romana's rapidly diminishing form and followed her into the block.

The ground-floor reception area was actually nearing completion. As their footsteps rang around fake marble walls and floor, both Slater and McCrae felt decidedly uneasy. It was the feeling one could imagine having upon entering some brooding gothic pile in the middle of a thunderstorm, with cobwebbed suits of armour seeming to look at you and something hiding in the grandfather clock. The feeling didn't seem to fit these ostensibly stylish and well-designed surroundings at all.

In fact, what the pair were feeling was the perfectly natural terror of an animal taken from its natural habitat. Subconsciously they thought the docklands should be mouldering old warehouses and derelict shipping cranes, and this ersatz finery dumped on top of it just seemed fundamentally wrong. They hurried on to catch Romana up, more for the comfort of the fact that she was another living being in this place than they would ever care to admit.

'There's nothing here,' McCrae said, in the tones of someone hoping this was true. 'Whatever we're supposed to be looking for, it's gone.'

'There's something,' Romana said, in tones of irritated concentration. 'I can feel it. There's something left here for us to find...'

Finding things or not, however, rapidly became academic – because the things that had been left here suddenly found *them*. A number of doorways on the ground level had yet to be filled and had been sealed with grubby plastic sheets. Now, they split open with a sound like tearing skin and things came through them, black-clad semi-humanoid things, more than a dozen of them.

They engulfed Slater, McCrae and Romana, and bore them down to the artificial marble floor before they even knew what was happening.

In the UNIT barracks, Katharine Delbane was finding herself at something of a loose end. In police-procedural TV shows this was the sort of time that is conveyed by shots of customs officials carefully checking man-sized crates at an airport, uniformed bobbies looking around derelict factories with torches, tracker dogs straining on their leashes as handlers lead them around woodland areas for no good reason, and so forth. Such things were of course happening, somewhere, in the general sense, but the reality of the situation so far as she,

Delbane, was concerned was that she was simply hanging around with nothing to do and nobody to talk to.

The Special Branch men had long left to go about their business. Crowley was sequestered in the Brigadier's office and the few other Provisional Department operatives he had brought in were busily examining this and itemising that as though they were pricing things for a clearance sale. The UNIT troops, to a man or woman, regarded her with cold blank disgust now that her true identity and purpose for being here were revealed. Sergeant Benton had turned his back on her in the canteen and continued his lecture to the other NCOs on the subject of how they had to hold things together until the Brig was back and these Provisional bastards were sorted out. Strangely, the prospect of a change in the administration of UNIT seemed more important and deplorable than semi-men in black coming into their barracks and shooting them.

The upshot was that Delbane had more than enough time on her hands to think, and she was thinking that she'd made a big mistake. Not in any particular way, but in the vague sense that everything in her life and world was a mistake. Without realising it, she now saw that in the weeks of working here she had soaked up something of the UNIT family atmosphere, the sense of people working together for something genuinely fine and good. A sense of... well, the sense of working for something greater and more noble than one's petty individual interests.

Now that atmosphere had been spoilt, and Delbane had been instrumental in spoiling it. It made her feel... not dirty, exactly, but shoddy. Worthless inside.

To take her mind off things she found herself following the Doctor, telling herself all the while that she was simply keeping an eye on him. There was still no absolutely positive identification and vetting on him, after all. The Doctor, for his part, just seemed to be generally and good-humouredly pottering around, reacquainting himself with the surroundings, chatting with old friends in the ranks (who studiously ignored Delbane) and taking in changes after a long time of absence. He seemed absentmindedly unaware of Delbane's presence, but at least he didn't actively shun her.

It was his good humour, in the end, that got to her.

'Don't you care about your friend?' she asked him, as he was happily scanning a notice board, in one of the dormitory huts, that detailed, amongst duty rosters and the like, a raffle in aid of the London Lighthouse and a sign-up for a rounders team.

'Pardon me?' The Doctor turned and regarded her with a friendly smile that, in the present circumstances, had her sternly stopping herself from bursting into tears.

'I mean,' she said quickly, to cover this up, 'your friend the Brigadier. He's been gone for hours and all you've done is... well, I suppose you've tried to find him, but now you're doing nothing. The people who took him could be doing *anything* to him.'

'Oh, I think that's unlikely,' the Doctor said, a little complacently Delbane thought. 'Though I don't expect you to believe me, I know for a *fact* that certain things will happen. Or have happened. Or will have happened.' He paused, as if trying to work out that last statement in his own head, and then gave up. 'Just take it from me that barring some deep and fundamental manipulation or disruption of, or in the very nature of, the...'

It was as though his ears had suddenly caught up with what his mouth was saying. His face fell.

'Oh dear,' he said.

Haasterman put down the receiver that had connected him to Dr Sohn and regarded it broodingly. Things were bad, very bad; it seemed that his role for the foreseeable future was to be picking up the phone and hearing how things were very bad, and getting worse.

As if it had in some way read his mind, another phone began to bleep: the scrambler-phone hooked to the British Telecom system. Haasterman picked it up and spoke his name.

It was Section Eight's man in the UK. 'Things are in motion,' he said without preamble. 'The girl is in our custody and she should be arriving with you imminently.'

'Very well,' Haasterman said. 'Move into phase three of the operation. Remember to be careful – don't let anything slip until we have the target under secure conditions. It could ruin everything if you gave the game away right now.'

'What's happening is this,' said the Doctor, some forty minutes after his latest brainstorm.

He was back in his workroom, trotting rapidly back and forth between the screens and consoles while Delbane watched him dubiously. 'I was simply trying to interpret the data and come up with a meaningful pattern. I never anticipated that someone else might have been actively, consciously *manipulating* the data and imposing a pattern of their own...'

'So how the hell would somebody do that?' Delbane asked. 'Manipulate chaos. Are you saying somebody made a school bus half an hour late, purely to jam up traffic at a certain time and throw your crazy calculations off?'

'Essentially, yes,' said the Doctor worriedly, seemingly oblivious to sarcasm. 'If that someone knew precisely what he or she were doing and had some insight into my methods, they could lay a trail for me that led straight into a trap.' He typed on a console, and the sounds and flickering lights that filled the workroom suddenly changed their tone – Delbane had no idea what it meant, but the shifting of the composite was noticeable.

'See here...' said the Doctor. 'Well, no, of course you can't – but if you remove the falsely imposed trail, another becomes evident, leading somewhere completely different. The enemy didn't leave here with the Brigadier and go to the London Docklands, they went to –'

'Precisely, Doctor.'

There was a moment of shock that seemed to turn the thunderous noise and light around them to silence. Then Delbane and the Doctor turned to see the voice's source.

It was Crowley. His face seemed subtly different from the one with which Delbane had come to be familiar; harder, and shedding its patina of urbanity. His eyes were very cold. In one hand he was toying with the little Lucite paperweight that Delbane had noticed earlier in the Brigadier's office. In the other he held a massive American-made automatic pistol, of the gas-primed sort that could blow a hole through two-inch armour plate.

'Bravo, Doctor!' he said. 'I knew you'd find the place eventually – if you were indeed the man you purported to be. The man whom, in one sense, this entire operation has been set up to snare.'

Chapter Fifteen
Making Different Plans

'Well, I have to admit,' said the Doctor, 'it hasn't been much of a day for stopping the unstoppable forces of Evil. I have to admit I'm a bit stumped.'

They were back in the car again, driving on what, Victoria gathered, was a freeway. A number of people in other cars had fired pistols at them, but they seemed to have been aiming to miss.

'Do we really have to stop it?' said Victoria, carefully, as if trying on a new idea for size.

'Why, Victoria.' The Doctor looked at her. 'Whatever can you mean?'

'It's just that, well, this monster, or whatever it is, is preying on the people here in some way and that's very sad and so forth, but it hasn't really done anything to *us*, has it? You said that this wasn't our world and doesn't work by the same rules – so what if this state of affairs is perfectly natural for this world? What if there *is* no way to stop it, and all we'd achieve by trying is to be killed?'

Victoria hoped she didn't sound like a coward, because she really didn't mean it in that way. The monster here, if such existed, seemed to kill in more intangible and distinctly more nastily messy ways than she had thus far encountered on her adventures with the Doctor, it was true... but, more than that, she had the feeling of being caught up in something complicated and vast. Something too big for her to comprehend in anything other than the most peripheral of ways; something with which she could simply not imagine herself, Jamie and even the Doctor being able to cope.

'In your own world,' said the Doctor, 'on the Earth, it's the natural order of things for the strong to crush the weak, for predators to eat prey, for time itself to bring nothing but misery, death and decay. And in certain senses, in the long term, that's perfectly right. But in human terms, what is *right* is fighting such things even to the death. If we didn't, we might as well kill ourselves the moment we're old enough to be aware of the world. Riding out the shocks the flesh is heir to, kicking against the pricks, that's what being human is basically all about.' He thought for a moment. 'Or so I'm told. Besides,' he continued, in slightly less inflated tones, 'if our chap hasn't come for us yet, that's just because he, or indeed she or it, hasn't quite worked out what to do with us. It'll come for us, sooner or later. These things always do. And I, for one, would like to deal with it before it does. We have to find it before it finds us.'

'And how do you propose to do that?' Jamie asked. 'From what you say, this thing is a...'

'An Entity, I suppose you'd call it,' said the Doctor. 'Piezoelectromagnetically-based autonomic macroconstructs not really being my style at all.'

'... an Entity without a body to call its own. It could be anywhere. How are we ever going to find it?'

'It must have a... well, not a lair as such,' said the Doctor, 'but a point of convergence of some kind, a place of Power. Somewhere big and where people can congregate...'

It was at this point that the car chose to stall. It spluttered and choked and freewheeled some way to a halt on the hard shoulder.

'Now I wonder if that was an omen of some kind,' said the Doctor. He peered at the extensive collection of dials and switches on the dash. 'Oh. It seems that when I rented the car I forgot that it needed to be filled with petrol. Oh well. It looks like we're on foot again. Is there anything around within strolling distance?'

Victoria and Jamie looked at each other, forbearing to comment, and then both pointed wordlessly to the huge building that lay beyond the nearest exit ramp.

'That'll do,' said the Doctor, looking at it. 'It's a place to start, anyway.'

The Shady Pines Shopping Mall declared itself to be the Biggest in the World – and in the special circumstances of Lychburg this was literally true. With more than three thousand discrete businesses on a complexly variable number of levels, fifteen hundred of them actually in stores, it was inevitable that three unwary travellers would get separated from each other and lost within minutes.

The Mind that lived, in one sense at least, in the very heart of the world and, in another sense, was the very world itself, had by now had time to think – if the term 'thinking' can be applied to conceptual processes that had all the relation to those of a human that an evil whelk has to an ice-cream stand. These three individuals were indeed different (the Mind thought) and quite unlike any other in the world. The Mind could not find a single way inside; It could not find a way to feed off them at all.

The sustenance of the Mind had about the same relation to the chemical and physical energy transitions that characterise the feeding processes of almost all other lifeforms – from carbon-based biological to what are misnomerically termed 'energy beings' – as the data-stream linkages between two computer networks have to a toaster plugged into a power outlet or the crude power supplies of the individual computers that make up the networks. The Mind was an Abstract Entity; the food that sustained It was the interplay of action and reaction and consequence, the constant exercise of Its own definition of Itself. Thus It would take control of an individual mind and set it to kill another, imbuing and subduing the victim with Its essence, becoming in a very real sense both the murderer and the murdered. There were other forms of interaction between individual minds and their bodies, to be sure, but none so intense as murder. Besides, in the end, the Mind just liked to do it.

So far as the Mind had an actual name, in the sense that one might think of oneself as identifiable other than simply as 'me', the Mind called Itself Continuity. Because that, apart from being just Itself, was what It ultimately was – perfect, self-referring and eternal.

Now, that Continuity had been broken by the three strange individuals and the thing that had carried them. For years, the Mind had quite simply been unable to think in terms of any other outside world from the one It now inhabited, purely because there had been nothing to remind It that such worlds had or ever would exist. Now, It was beginning to remember – although Its processes of memory were as similar to that of human recollection as the sound of a tuba is similar to a monkey in a little hat.

The Mind remembered that It had once lived Somewhere Else. There was another world, Somewhere Else, and these three new individual minds held the key to it. The Mind was aware of them now, three points of unknown blankness in the world, delineated by the holes they made in it and the ripples of their passing through it. The Mind considered matters for a while. If It couldn't subsume them directly, as yet, then It would just have to achieve Its end by other means.

In the Shady Pines mall several hundred people, more or less at random, wondered what it would be like to brutally and horribly murder those nearby to them in the crowd. A second later, most of them forgot about this and started thinking about other things, like wondering why they suddenly had an impulse to buy a children's doll, or something of that nature, and twist it into interesting shapes.

Chapter Sixteen
The Festival of Masks

The helicopter, though big enough to be a cargo craft, was sleek and black and packed with cutting-edge prototypical stealth technology – the technology that would be released to the public some decades later as state of the art. The fact was that, here and now, there was an orbital transcontinental shuttle service for those who knew about it, and man had set foot on Mars more than five years before. Admittedly, man hadn't set foot on Mars *again*, on account of what he had found there. However, the fact remained that, with the exception of the occasional Airfix kit that got a bit too enthusiastic, and aside from computer-based informational technology which by its nature grows up in public, the basic technological level of Planet Earth was far in advance of anything dreamed of by the vast majority of those who populated it.

Romana thought the helicopter looked quaintly baroque and archaic.

When the black-clad, hooded figures had fallen upon herself and the two human men, Slater and McCrae, they had injected the three of them with an anaesthetic compound – much as, she understood, they had done previously to the soldiers in the UNIT barracks. The two Provisional Department men had of course succumbed, but due to her Gallifreyan biology Romana had merely felt a slight sense of disconnection. She had decided, however, to play dead (or at least unconscious) and let these people take her where they wished. The Doctor had after all told her to learn all she could, and this appeared to be the most direct available route to do so. She had no doubt that she could deal with anything humans might be able to throw at her, should the need arise.

Her supposedly unresponsive body had been dumped, along with those of Slater and McCrae, in the belly of the 'copter. The interior had been fitted with luxurious and roomy seats obviously designed for the transportation of passengers, and passengers of some importance at that. By sheer coincidence, Romana had been left with her head against one of the portholes, so she could see out. This might have been of some actual use had she the first notion of the geography of this planetary landmass.

As it was, she saw the grubby concrete and redbrick sprawl of the conurbation devolve into a green and gold patchwork of crop fields, bounded by hedgerows and scattered with woodland and small settlements, linked by a meandering system of paved roads. We are all of us – human, Time Lady or flesh-eating slime-marmoset from Squaxis Beta – bound by the circumstances of our upbringing. Those circumstances fix for us the basis of normality no matter how much we realise, in later life, that they aren't particularly normal. Accustomed to self-enclosed, hermetically controlled citadels and synthetic methods of food production, Romana thought this aerial view of an idyllic country scene was unconscionably sloppy and wasteful.

Now they seemed to be coming upon an installation of some kind, an airfield by the look of it – Romana was vaguely aware that stratospheric transport on Earth commonly involved the taking off from, and landing on, long, space-wasting 'runways'.

As the 'copter descended towards the hangar buildings of the installation proper, she saw a haphazard collection of tents and shelters bivouacked outside protective fences. Camp followers? The provisioners, armourers, common-law wives and prostitutes who trailed along with the military in their various campaigns? She assumed so; the time frame was about right.

The 'copter grounded by the hangars and Romana closed her eyes. She heard the sounds of what, presumably, were black-clad men hauling out the unconscious bodies of Slater and McCrae. Hands took hold of her and she let herself go limp, noting with some slight degree of amusement that her relatively dense Gallifreyan dead weight was causing a degree of consternation, and the eventual necessity for three pairs of hands to convolutely heave her from her seat and lift her up.

She was carried, with bellicose grunts of exertion from her porters, out into the open air and then inside again. Some time later she was unceremoniously dumped on a padded surface and felt the sting of a needle in the side of her neck. Her finely tuned senses felt the foreign compound enter her bloodstream and she realised it was a stimulant, no doubt intended to counteract the effects of the anaesthetic. It would probably have no effect on her in any case, but she diverted it away from her paracerebellum and directly into waste-processing organs that were the equivalent of kidneys, just to be on the safe side.

The men left, shutting and locking what sounded like a heavy steel door behind them. Romana opened her eyes and sat up. She was on a bunk in a cell which was of similar dimensions to the one in which she had been held in the UNIT barracks. Its construction seemed subtly different, however, as though minds of a completely different set had determined its construction: bare and solid breeze-block walls as opposed to painted brick. There was no window, barred or otherwise, but harsh fluorescent lighting and chilly, recycled-smelling air blasting from a grille. A pristine stainless-steel object was bolted to the concrete floor in a corner and plumbed in, possibly intended for the disposal of bodily waste, but Romana, on the whole, decided that she'd rather exert bodily control.

The cell was also occupied. A middle-aged man in shirtsleeves and a pair of trousers that appeared to reach no further than his calves, where they were tucked into thick woollen socks, had left the bunk he had obviously been occupying against the far wall and was hovering over her uncertainly, unsure whether or not it might be needlessly forward to offer some physical assistance.

'Are you all right, my dear?' he asked.

Romana would be hard-pressed to think of herself as anybody's 'dear', but one of the advantages of being better travelled than most, and highly intelligent to boot, is the ability to extract true meanings and motivations from words. The man was simply and genuinely trying to help a fellow creature in distress.

'I'm fine,' Romana told him, rubbing a finger over the puncture wound in her neck. It was healing faster than it would with a human biology and starting to itch. 'What is this place? Where are we?'

'It's American, I think,' the man said. 'Other than those combat-armoured johnnies, I've seen a couple of USAF uniforms, and the man who... questioned me had an American accent. Baltimore, I think, though I can't be sure.'

The acronym meant nothing to Romana. She noticed that, though he seemed physically intact and in reasonably good health, there was bruising around the man's face. Somebody or something had hit him solidly, two or three times.

'As for where we *are*,' he said, 'I couldn't tell you. I remember being in my office and feeling rather tired, and the next thing I knew I was waking up here. I assume they knocked me out with gas or the like. And the uniforms and accents might be purely for the purposes of misinformation, after all...' He paused and looked at Romana thoughtfully. 'Please don't think me rude, my dear, but there's the possibility that you might have been placed here as a part of the interrogation process.

Opening up to a friendly face, and all that. I hope you'll forgive me if I restrict my conversation to subjects of a nonsensitive nature? I don't mean name, rank and serial number and suchlike nonsense, but...'

'I understand,' Romana said, and she did. There was a sense of forthright decency about this man, a basic inability to automatically think the worst of someone even under the circumstances of possible interrogation, that she found herself responding to, and warming towards, despite their short acquaintance. She wondered how his decency, and he, had ever managed to survive. 'We won't talk about, ah...' She groped around in her depressingly thin knowledge of this place and time: 'Invasion plans and rocket bombs. I'm the Lady Romana.'

'Delighted to meet you,' said the man. 'Lethbridge-Stewart, Brigadier, with a serial number that's neither here nor there for all the good it does anybody these days. I've always wondered why you seem to be expected to give it...'

'Brigadier?' said Romana. 'So *you're* the Doctor's friend.'

'The Doctor?' Instantly the Brigadier's face and manner were transformed. It was as though a switch, somewhere, had been thrown and a light had come on inside him. 'The Doctor is here?' he said, forgetting in his enthusiasm that he was intending to keep a rein on his mouth.

'Well, not so much *here*, exactly,' said Romana, 'as around, generally.'

'I never so much as dared hope that he might be. What brought him back, here and now?'

'I thought you'd contacted him.' Romana was slightly puzzled. 'He said you had a way of contacting him.'

'I did,' said the Brigadier, 'but I never got the chance. I wonder how he knew?'

Romana, for her part, was wondering the precise same thing. If the Brigadier hadn't contacted the TARDIS to bring them to

157

Earth in the first place, then who or what had? She had little time to consider this, however, because at that point she heard the sounds of the cell door being unlocked. She motioned the Brigadier away from her and lay back on her bunk, where she began stirring and blinking dazedly in the manner of one slowly surfacing from a healthy dose of anaesthetic.

The door opened and a man came through wearing a greenish, slightly sloppy uniform, possibly one of the USAF uniforms of which the Brigadier had spoken.

He was unshaven and muscular, and Romana disliked him on sight. There was a certain set to his eyes which looked innately hurt and angry, with the kind of anger that wants to take itself out on the world. He was naturally, constantly sweaty and there was an air about him of a man constantly keeping himself in check.

A pair of similarly uniformed, though neater and less decorated, men appeared at the doorway behind him, one levelling his automatic projectile weapon at the Brigadier, the other levelling his at Romana, just in case either of them tried anything. It seemed that this behaviour was going to be the defining characteristic of almost everybody she met on this planet and Romana, for one, was getting diploid-heartily sick of it.

'You,' the first man said, taking hold of Romana by the shoulder to shake her. 'You should be awake by now. We need to question you. We want to know what you know.'

'Oh, you'd be surprised at what I know,' Crowley said, back in the UNIT barracks, aiming his gun directly at the Doctor. 'For one thing, I know that you have two hearts – which is why I chose a weapon quite capable of blowing both of them out of your chest in an instant. Armour-piercing rounds, which I suspect would break through even such a notoriously thick skin as yours.'

The Doctor held up his hands in the generally accepted manner for the circumstances. 'If you know so much,' he said, waggling his fingers, 'then why bother with this charade? I gather from what people are saying...' he nodded his head towards the suddenly dumbfounded Delbane '... that the young lady here was sent in specifically to root out the things it seems you already know.'

'Miss Delbane had her uses,' Crowley said airily. 'She provided me with what we might call *supplementary* information. Every little helps. Her primary function, of course, was merely to provide the excuse for my personal interest in UNIT. So far as the powers that be were concerned, one of my operatives was in danger so of *course* my department had to step in and deal with things. My people, the people I ultimately work for, have been aware of you and your activities for years. It's simply that we've never felt the need to acquire your... services until now.'

His aim still unwavering, Crowley held up the glittering cube in his other hand. 'It's a pretty little thing, isn't it? We've been aware of its existence for a long time. It was a simple matter, in the end, to disable Lethbridge-Stewart and appropriate it for our own ends...'

'So it was you who contacted me?' The Doctor nodded to himself, as though certain things that had been opaque had now become clear. 'I have to admit, there was something slightly wrong about the particularity of it, but it was so vague, at that point, that I couldn't quite pin it down at the time.' He frowned, and then actively scowled at Crowley. 'You know, if you – or the people you ultimately work for – wanted my help with something, you'd only have to ask. I'm quite easy to find at any time and place one might need to find me, after all.'

'This is too important to leave to chance,' said Crowley. 'Or to your noted intransigence. The situation is such, Doctor, that time is of the very...'

Delbane, meanwhile, had been taking all this in with the sense that her very world was falling apart around her ears. Identity, in the end, is a fragile thing; you build your life around the idea that who you are and what you do is important and will make a difference to the world, and it's a blow to realise that the world, quite simply, does not care if you live or die. For all the moral ambiguity of her work, which in a certain sense devolved to nothing more than lying and sneaking around, Katharine Delbane had thought of herself as performing it in what was ultimately the public interest. Over the past few hours her mental picture of her role had been devalued, and now Crowley had devalued it again: player to disposable pawn in three easy steps.

'You're not doing this with government sanction?' she asked him angrily. 'The Prime Minister herself sent me here…'

'Oh, it's easy to manipulate a rabid old trout like the Prime Minister,' said Crowley, absently, still watching the Doctor like a hawk. 'Play on her clinical paranoia in the right way and you could have her going after GCHQ. This is the woman who started a small war over a couple of Argentinian scrap-metal merchants.'

'But we're a government department,' Delbane said. In her own mind, she knew exactly what she meant. She believed, fundamentally, that the government was the democratically elected representative of the people. She really *did* believe in her oath to serve them; she really and wholeheartedly believed that she was fighting for the principles of truth and democracy, and was willing to sacrifice and debase herself to those ends. It was starting to dawn on her that not everybody thought that way.

'You stupid girl,' Crowley said to her. 'Do you really think the government of this tinpot little island has any real say in anything?'

It was the 'stupid girl' that got to her, in the end. You spend an entire life building yourself up, and being good, and doing the right thing, and a single piece of rudeness and contempt can make you realise it was all for nothing; it can knock you down with the force of a physical assault. In her conflicted state, Delbane found herself in the grip of a mindless, white-hot rage that had her wanting nothing more than to pull out her service revolver and shoot Crowley stone-cold dead.

What we really want deep inside being seldom what we get, she pulled it out in that smooth way that telegraphs no threat and aimed it squarely at her departmental superior. Crowley's focus of attention and gun were on the Doctor, and he simply didn't notice until it was too late.

'Give up the gun,' Delbane told him. 'I'm technically an officer in the Provisional Department of Special Branch, and well within my rights to arrest you. We can sort out the charges and make the deals later. For now, you just give it up.'

Crowley turned his head to look at her. 'I don't think I want to do that.'

Something ignited in his eyes. They blazed with a shifting, pulsing light.

Delbane's arms dropped loosely as though every tendon had been cut. The revolver clattered to the floor. The second time this afternoon, she thought, dimly. She looked into Crowley's burning eyes and felt the will draining out of her as though it were an actual, tangible substance, like a liquid. She had once, a year and a half ago, on some other and not strictly relevant case, passed out through loss of blood. This felt similar, the sense of something slipping away, but she remained bright and alert and in control of herself, waiting for someone to tell that self what to do...

'Go and stand over there,' Crowley told her.

Delbane went and stood over there.

'I think we'll take you along with us,' Crowley said musingly. 'It would be a crime to leave you here in this state, and we could always do with an extra pair of willing hands. And now, Doctor...' He jerked the barrel of his gun towards the police box in the corner of the workroom. 'I think we've had quite enough of these irrelevancies. We have your friend the Brigadier. We have your young assistant, by now. And for what it's worth, I have an additional hostage in Delbane here. I can tell her heart to stop, and I don't think you'd like that. It's time we left.'

'And where are we actually leaving for?' asked the Doctor, who had turned to look at Delbane with some degree of concern.

'I'll show you,' said Crowley, 'never fear. And when we arrive, the masks shall come off and all shall stand at last revealed in Glory.'

'It would make a change,' said the Doctor, shortly. 'And tell me, have you ever thought of seeing a specialist about that needlessly self-important and messianic tone?'

Chapter Seventeen
The Spirit of Free Enterprise

Victoria leaned over the chrome-steel rail of the balcony and tried to spot the Doctor or Jamie in the crowd below. There was no sign of them. Losing them hadn't been her fault, she told herself; it had merely been a question of the fact that in a series of adventures through space and time involving, in some peripheral part, the use of elevators, ramps and levitating platforms, she had never happened to encounter a moving staircase.

On her travels with the Doctor she had learnt to her cost that it was essentially small and inconsequential things like this that sometimes caught you on the wrong foot – an electrical device rather than a towel to dry your hair, fluoridated toothpaste and a little brush rather than astringent and a finger – and one had to consciously learn to recognise them and use them for the first time. She had been two floors up (this being a moving staircase that traversed three floors at a time in the interests, she supposed, of efficiency for those patrons who knew how many floors they wanted to go) before she had shaken off the startlement of a mind that insisted that a flight of stairs that moved was flatly impossible. Victoria had told her mind, sternly, that if it could cope with time-travelling boxes being bigger on the inside than out, metal men who walked and people living in crystal bubbles beneath the sea, then it could da- it could very well deal with something as simple as that.

It occurred to her that separated like this from the Doctor and Jamie, she would be easy pickings for any monster with a mind to commit horrible and beastly murder. On the other hand, this was a public place, a place of commerce. Victoria found it hard to conceive, unless the world had gone completely mad, of anyone or anything walking into a place like this and killing people. She was safe enough for the moment.

This floor seemed to be the domain of a number of haberdashers. There was the entrance to an establishment by the name of Bloomingdales nearby leading into a store which, looking through the window front, appeared to comprise several floors of the entire precinct. The gowns and trouser suits on display in the window looked quite stylish, but then Victoria caught sight of a number of photographic representations of women wearing them and realised that all the women were old enough to be her mother. She walked on along the shiny marble floor of the balcony to a store in which the images depicted young men and ladies more her own age. It was called, for some obscure reason, GAP.

Inside, over some method of gramophonic reproduction, a rather frightening-sounding man was shouting angrily about how he wanted to shoot his bitch with his mother's funny gun to the accompaniment of what sounded like people hitting a number of galvanised rubbish bins. Victoria knew enough to realise that this was probably a variety of music around these parts, but found herself wondering what the dog had done to need shooting, and just what it was about the matriarchal weapon that was so particularly humorous.

Victoria steeled herself to tell the shopkeeper that she was merely browsing rather than intending to purchase, but the wares of GAP were displayed on serried racks from which you seemed to be expected to help yourself. The clothing on display seemed to be of a sort suitable for a labourer, and all of it in a grand total of three colours. All the same, by comparison, Victoria was becoming uncomfortably aware that her own clothes, after her recent exertions and a night spent in them, were not exactly fresh. She was also in dire need of new footwear – preferably, she thought, without heels.

She noticed, at the counter, that a young woman was paying for her purchases with an oblong card reminiscent of the credit-chip she had amongst the personal possessions in her pockets – acquired during a visit to the NovaLon Hypercities in the twenty-second century several weeks ago, if that actually made any sense. Victoria decided it was worth a try, and walked over to the counter. 'Can I use this to pay for something?'

The shopgirl, a rather rough-looking young lady with a shaven head, a ring through one nostril and a contraption in her ear which buzzed tinnily, examined the card dubiously. 'We don't take, uh, New Fiduciary Treasury of the PractiBrantic Apostates.' She thought for a moment. 'You can use it as photo ID, though, maybe.'

'Photoidee?' said Victoria. The word was unfamiliar to her.

'For sure.' The girl slid a card and a ballpoint pen across the counter. 'Fill that in, yeah? We can run a credit-check right now.'

Victoria filled in the card, using the address of an aunt, twice removed, who had lived in Boston almost a century before. The girl took it and began typing on a sleek-looking item reminiscent of a mechanical typewriter, humming tunelessly, though whether it was along to the sound in her ear or the angry man who didn't like dogs it was difficult to say. After a while she turned back to Victoria with a smile. 'You're cleared for up to five hundred dollars store credit. Bring your stuff back here when you're done, yeah?'

Victoria was surprised at how easy it had been. She had a shrewd idea that, had this been anywhere but here where interactions between people seemed to involve a large degree of play-acting, it would have been rather harder to acquire credit of such an astronomical sum. Then again, looking at the big pasteboard price tags, now that actually buying what they were affixed to was a possibility, the sum didn't seem quite so astronomical after all. Either the GAP emporium was extortionately expensive or the currency extremely inflated.

In the end, Victoria selected a pair of heavy khaki trousers and a yellow vest, a bulky padded jacket in bright orange and a pair of brightly coloured, thick-soled plimsolls. She took her potential purchases into a changing cubicle to try them on – feeling rather daring even though she knew that, here and now, doing so was seen as unremarkable in spite of such public surroundings where there were even *men* around.

As she was pulling on the trousers something twitched at the curtain hanging across the cubicle door. There was a little strangled sound, as though somebody had been meaning to shout something and had bitten the exclamation back.

'Ah, hello?' Victoria said, as the first seeds of apprehension planted themselves in her mind. 'Is there anybody…?'

The curtain was torn back, partially ripped from the rod that supported it. Standing in front of Victoria was a woman, possibly in her mid-twenties and rather overweight. She wore panties and a vest on which was printed the words Hard Rock Café. Around her ankles hung a new pair of short trousers with a price tag still attached – she had obviously been in the process of putting them on when she had suddenly and simply forgotten all about them.

The features of the woman's face were slack. Her eyes were dead and blank, nothing living inside them, so far as human beings define life.

Jamie, strangely enough, did not find crowds frightening although for the most part of his life he had never experienced them. In fact, that was a large part of why he wasn't frightened; where somebody like Victoria had fundamental expectations of what life in a city was supposed to be like, to Jamie it was just something new. He didn't feel the kind of vertiginous culture shock that is similar to putting your foot on a step and finding it isn't there, or, indeed, that it is moving.

Instead he had become diverted by, and lost in, the new sights: the wonderful colours, impossible to produce in his own time, that still fascinated him; the fantastical contraptions, even the purposes of which he could sometimes barely guess, leave alone the processes by which they operated; the mysterious smells of food made from the flesh of beasts and fruits that might as well have been the hypogriffs and mandrakes of myth and legend for all they related to his world. The Doctor had explained to him, once, the difference between magical and physical matters, and Jamie had nodded intelligently; he could see the distinction – but deep inside he always found the later eras to which the Doctor had taken him magical, in feeling if not in fact.

Jamie didn't mind that he had become separated from the Doctor. He had absolute confidence, borne of long experience, that should some life-threatening event occur the man would come running to the rescue before you could say Jack Robinson. For the moment he decided to continue with the Doctor's plan, if it could be called such, and search for anything that might denote some invisible murdering fiend living nearby. Of course, though, the distinguishing feature of an *invisible* fiend was that you couldn't see the laddie in the first place.

On the other hand, the best place to start looking for anything in a strange place, anything the locals themselves might find out of the ordinary, was to ask around in a tavern. The Doctor had given him some of the remaining money he had received from selling vast quantities of blood, and the sums printed on the promissory notes seemed more than enough for a round of drinks that might loosen a few tongues.

Besides, thought Jamie, at this point a small dram for himself would be welcome indeed. He looked about him and spotted an establishment that seemed to fit the bill nicely – if the sign outside, showing a collection of happy men with tall hats and tankards was any indication.

Steps led down into a room of oak panelling, the grain too regular and repetitive to be natural, and brass fixtures. The dim and flickering lighting was not candlelight, as Jamie had first thought, but came from a number of galvanistical contrivances in the shape of candles that mimicked it. A few afternoon patrons sat around the bar counter or in little booths, all of them drinking some kind of yellow liquid that Jamie assumed was the local beer – anything else it might be didn't bear thinking about, at least not without a stiff drink inside you beforehand.

The atmosphere seemed not exactly sullen, but subdued; people about drinking at this time of day, here, seemed to be keep themselves to themselves. This did not bode well for the purposes of eliciting information.

Mindful of the fact that he should be keeping a clear head, Jamie put down his collection of promissory notes and asked the landlord for a flagon of small ale.

'We got Heineken or Schlitz,' said the landlord, who seemed dressed rather splendidly for a tavern, in a bow tie and waistcoat.

All things considered, Jamie decided to go with the Heineken.

'You English?' asked the landlord, pulling what appeared to be an imperial pint of the yellow stuff from an engine that gurgled and hissed quite alarmingly.

'I'm a Celt,' said Jamie shortly, with a depth of feeling seldom heard in the twentieth century even at a football match.

'I like the English,' said the landlord, all oblivious. 'All very polite and *thenkyew-very-much*.' The nasal tone he used had

Jamie actually siding, momentarily, with the English – if the other side were Americans saying *thenkyew-very-much*.

'Always wanted to go to, uh, England,' the landlord continued. 'For a... you know...' His voice trailed off, as though his mind had completely forgotten what his mouth was saying.

It was at that point that a portly man walked down the steps. The landlord and patrons, every single one of them, turned their faces to him and shouted, 'Dan!'

'What would you say to a beer, Dan?' the landlord said, already sliding a full glass over to the portly man.

'I'd say, have you brought a friend?' said Dan, downing the liquid with a single swallow.

'And how's the wife?' asked the landlord, pulling him another.

'Don't talk to me about the wife,' said Dan, gloomily. 'I had to brutally murder her last night.'

'Women, eh?' said one of the patrons, a distinguished-looking gentleman with a balding pate. 'I had one argument with my wife about the maid overstarching my socks, and she stormed off back to brutally murder her mother, stepfather, half-sister and a neighbour who happened to be calling. I had to brutally murder the maid myself.'

'It's the same all over,' agreed the landlord, refilling a bowl with salted nuts. 'You remember how I had to brutally murder my fiancée, Father Grobegobbler, the organist and half the choir on our wedding day...?'

All of a sudden, the conversation stopped. Every eye in the room, two to a face, now turned towards Jamie who – not being born yesterday by quite some while – had been very quietly making his way towards the door.

Chapter Eighteen
The Best Laid Plans

The Tollsham USAF airbase, situated some sixty miles northeast of London, was originally the base of operations for Tornados and F-111s set and ready to beat off the godless Soviet hordes if they ever, somehow, made it past the buffer zone of half the European continent and tried to make the UK a first-strike staging post for any possible attack on the US. Conventional warfare on the European continent being notable by its absence, the Tollsham base had been more or less restricted to manoeuvres, sonic booms that wrecked the sleep of those for miles around and the occasional summer open day and air display when base personnel sold cans of badly iced Budweiser, let schoolchildren sit in cockpits and a Tornado, or possibly an F-111, occasionally crashed.

Then certain people in Her Majesty's Government got the idea in their heads that, far from being a post-manufacturing banana economy without the bananas, that was functionally distinct from a tinpot Third World nation state only by way of having not so nice a climate, Great Britain was still in fact a world power and a force to be reckoned with in international affairs. One hasty re-cementing of a 'special relationship' later, the UK's rickety old submarine-based Polaris nuclear deterrent was in the process of being dismantled, orders were in for a spanky set of Tridents and, at some point, they would arrive. For the moment, though, the practical upshot was that US Tomahawk self-guiding, fission-armed missiles were allowed in bases like Tollsham.

This had two main effects. The first was that any number of extra Soviet guidance-control systems were locked solidly on to heavy population centres, as opposed to the North Sea, a patch of the Atlantic or a collection of relatively isolated submarine pens in the Scottish Hebrides. The secondary effect was that the proximity of these population centres made it not too uncomfortable for politically aware Britons to go to the bases, camp outside them and protest.

Lieutenant Major Ernest Derricks didn't think in terms of cause and effect at all. He just thought that the women outside were ungrateful bitches, spitting on the protection he and his fellow countrymen were providing from the forces of Communism. It was an insult to the US of A and, by extension, a direct insult to himself. Well, he'd show them, one of these days. One of these days he'd show them all.

In fact, in the past, he already had.

There were a number of unsolved bar-girl murders from Saigon more than fifteen years ago, when Ernie had been in the business of airlifting troops before his reassignment into Air America and then Security – the US Military Police had other things on their mind at the time. Since then, such easy opportunities had not presented themselves and he had sublimated furiously, but the fact remained that Lieutenant Major Ernest Derricks was a man with certain 'issues' – which might or might not have stemmed back to a mother, in his native Maryland, who liked the occasional bottle of Jack Daniels and administered punishment by way of a cheese-grater.

Now he had taken it upon himself to question the girl brought in by the Section Eight intruders on the base that was his responsibility. He had been told by Haasterman to simply hold her and the other detainees, to just keep them incommunicado, but this whole set-up stank to the Lord God Almighty in his Heaven. Neither Derricks nor his men had been allowed to set foot in the hangar that the Section Eight people had taken over, and this rankled him. He was determined to find out something of what was going on.

If you had asked him why he had chosen the girl to interrogate, rather than any of the men – particularly the senior British officer who might be expected to have the most information to be extracted – Derricks would have told you that it was simple procedure to pick the subject who was most likely crack in the minimum amount of time, and would have been puzzled that you even felt the need to ask.

'And the purpose of this is supposed to be?' the girl said as Derricks's men handcuffed her to a chair bolted to the floor of what, with some slight degree of euphemism, was called the debriefing room. Her accent and attitude were what Derricks thought of as quintessentially English, which is to say snotty and oh-so-superior in a way that set his teeth on edge. He remembered the retainer he had worn as a child to prevent him from grinding them together, before he had learned to control himself.

He controlled himself now, without thinking about it, intent on preparing the pentathol needle; Derricks made a point of carefully administering such things himself.

'Just relax,' he told her. 'I just want answers. If you give them to me, you won't be hurt.'

In Hangar 18, amongst the now-installed sensor and display consoles, Haasterman was once again in contact with Dr Sohn in Lychburg.

'It's building exponentially,' she was saying, over a line that hazed in and out through static underlain with a kind of half-heard gabbling that put Haasterman in mind of the voices of the damned, screaming and pleading in Hell.

'The flares are starting to run together and there's...' Another burst of static. '... behind it, if you get what I mean, Colonel. Something forming. It's like the feeling you get when you see and recognise something – just the feeling, without actually *seeing* anything.'

This was not the sort of statement that would look good in a congressional report come budget time – assuming anyone or anything survived the next few hours to have an interest in a report. And from the sense of fear in Sohn's voice, and the sounds in the background, Haasterman had the idea that the operational lifetime of the Lychburg Installation could be judged in minutes, if that, rather than hours.

'I think it's time you fell back,' he told Sohn. 'Can you send across your latest data before you do?'

'We could do a modem-to-modem transfer,' Sohn said, her relief at being given permission to withdraw evident. Haasterman found himself strangely pleased that, given their not particularly friendly working relationship, it had not occurred to her to pack up and move without his say-so. 'Problem is,' Sohn continued, 'with the level of redundancy we'd have to use because of the scrambling protocols, it would take more than an hour.' She paused for a moment. 'I could simply upload the raw data to an unsecured BBS…'

'What the hell,' said Haasterman. 'Somebody intercepts it and can make any sense of it in the time we have, that somebody could probably solve all our problems by waving a magic wand or time-travelling. Do it.'

He dropped the handset in its cradle and cast his eye across the technicians as they operated their consoles. The overall effect was reminiscent of the ground-control facilities used in the NASA space shuttle and rather more classified HOTOL programmes. The difference was this equipment registered something other than *space* and, like the installation back in Lychburg, contained a rather more esoteric mix of basic technologies. An ancient stock-ticker linked to Lloyds of London chattered away, for example, while an operator fed the figures into her console verbatim. Another operator seemed to be doing nothing more than playing a computerised game of poker. Another threw hand after hand of yarrow stalks, transcribing the interpreted results.

It was the closest they could come to gauging the fluctuations of reality and even this far from Lychburg those fluctuations were evident. It was an ugly feeling, thought Haasterman, to know that the world was invisibly changing around him, elements of one order of reality supplanting another, on levels that those who would be affected were unequipped to perceive.

Oh well, he thought, at least it meant that if all else failed, the world wouldn't *feel* the final change that simply switched reality off.

He hoped to God that the Section's man here was right – not in this solution being the only one viable, but in it being a solution at all. Coming here to Britain and setting long-laid plans in motion seemed to… well, they seemed increasingly to Haasterman to be acts of desperation. Clutching madly at yarrow straws, the signs you read within them merely leading you further to the darkness.

For more than forty years Haasterman had lived in a world of duplicity, but he had tried to retain some measure of honourable conduct, managing to avoid the out-of-hand black-bag and wetwork so beloved of more conventional intelligence concerns. The kidnapping of a high-ranking officer of a friendly power and, from what he gathered, some completely innocent and uninvolved woman, merely to use them as bargaining chips, rankled. It was not, quite simply, the act of the man he thought himself to be. It was not as if, he reassured himself, there was any intention of actively *harming* them if things went well, but…

But what if things did not go well? One step leads to another, one compromise of principle to another. What if the lever of mere threat didn't work? What then?

Ah, well, at least that was a question for some future point. For the moment the detainees, and Haasterman's slightly shaky principles, were entirely safe.

* * *

'You must be feeling tired,' said Lieutenant Major Derricks, 'after all you've been through.'

'Not particularly,' said Romana. 'And will you please stop fiddling with that pocket watch. It's becoming inexpressibly annoying.'

Derricks put the watch back in his pocket. He tried to do it smoothly but Romana saw a slight, embarrassed hastiness in the movement, like a small boy caught doing something he shouldn't. She had not for one moment taken this man's threatening manner seriously, but now it occurred to her that on some level he couldn't quite believe in it himself.

'Now you come to mention it,' she said, 'I *am* feeling a bit worse for the wear. I didn't notice it before, but now I –'

Derricks glared at her suspiciously as her voice broke off and she stared straight ahead, completely immobile, her eyes wide and her pupils dilated. He waved a hand in front of her face. Her eyes remained still and unblinking.

'Some kind of allergic reaction...' he muttered to himself.

'Reaction,' said Romana, precisely but tonelessly. Only her mouth moved: it was as if every other nerve impulse in her body had been physically cut.

Derricks relaxed slightly. 'You are feeling happy and relaxed. You are feeling warm.'

'Warm,' said Romana.

'You are with a friend,' he said, sinking to a crouch until their heads were level with each other. 'I am your friend and you are with me and we are talking.'

'Friend,' said Romana. 'My friend.'

Lieutenant Major Derricks put his face close to hers. 'You are telling me about why you were brought here.'

'Here.'

'Why were you brought here? Why did Section Eight bring you here?'

'Well, it certainly wasn't to have you breathing all over me like that,' said Romana, reanimating her face. 'What *have* you been eating? And just what is this Section Eight you're telling me about?' She smiled brightly. 'Is it a secret?'

In Hangar 18, Haasterman turned to one of the technicians manning the comms link. 'Is it coming down?'

'It's coming.' The technician indicated a screen down which the hexadecimal gibberish of machine code crawled. The collected data had no immediate use, due to the time-lag of transferral, but it was useful to have a comprehensive backup copy should anything happen to Sohn and her team – now, hopefully, in the process of evacuating.

Haasterman watched the scrolling alphanumerics for a while. They were meaningless to the unaided eye, of course, but he couldn't shake the feeling that the visual rhythm had a kind of beat to it, and that the beat was accelerating, building up a sense of tension...

'Colonel Haasterman!' an operator called suddenly. It was the man throwing yarrow stalks. He was picking them up and throwing them, rapidly, over and over again. Even before Haasterman reached him, he saw that they were falling in the precise same pattern. Over and over again.

'Chapter twenty-four,' the technician told him worriedly. 'I remember because, uh, it's an old Pink Floyd song.' He quoted:

'*A movement is accomplished in six stages,*
And the seventh brings return...'

'Sir?' another operator said. 'Something's happening...'

On the computer screen, where she had apparently been playing random hands of poker, every single card was coming up a joker.

Haasterman realised that the sense of increasing pressure he was feeling wasn't psychosomatic, but physical – he had been thinking in abstract terms for so long he had forgotten to think in concrete ones. Now he felt the presssure resonating through him, smelt the tang of ozone in the air like an oncoming electrical storm.

'Take your positions!' he shouted to the hooded, armoured troops who were already mobilising, discarding their cards (Haasterman wondered if *they* had all somehow turned into jokers, like the virtual cards on the operator's screen) and reaching for their weapons. They ran for the chalk-and-pig's-blood pentagram inscribed on the hangar floor, as something appeared in its centre with a shock-smack of displaced air.

After the interrogation, Romana was taken to a different cell from the one to which she had first been brought and which had contained the Brigadier. She supposed this was because her captors had originally thought her unconscious, and now they did not want to take the chance of any collusion between the two of them.

After the failure of the drug he had administered, the officer – Romana simply thought of him as a soldier of some kind, being ignorant of the specific distinctions – had bombarded her with entirely vague questions on the level of who she was, where she had come from and why she was here. The non-specificity of the questions had left them open to any and all kinds of answers, which Romana had duly supplied until the man had tried to hit her. It was easy, with the pre-emptive reflexes of a Time Lady, to manoeuvre herself out of the way and the man had ended up injuring his hand quite nastily on the back of the interrogation chair.

By the time Romana had finished telling him precisely what she thought about people who seemed to feel the need to assay completely unprovoked physical assaults upon seemingly helpless females, the officer had been white-faced and shaking with an impotent mix of anger and humiliation at certain of her rather generalised personal comments, which had apparently hit home. Romana feared that he was in the process of some incipient nervous collapse. Fortunately, the man seemed to be under orders from his superiors not to harm her permanently. The fortune in this case was his; while Romana would never ordinarily countenance the use of superior Gallifreyan strength and ability in the form of violence against lower species, her patience had been wearing more than slightly thin.

In the end, the officer had called in two of his men to take her away, simply to get her out of his sight.

The feeling was mutual, so far as Romana was concerned. Local colour was all very well, but enough of a good thing was a healthy sufficiency.

The new cell was almost precisely similar to the old one, save that one of the bunks was folded up and stowed in a corner. The other had been freshly made and a neatly folded towel and a little paper-wrapped cake of soap lay on it. It was as if these people thought of this place as some hostelry, and she as a guest. The effect was defeated, however, by the fact that there was nowhere to wash except in the toilet bowl.

Romana wandered about the cell soaking in the structure of it – becoming, in a sense, one with it.

It wasn't a question of examining the hinges of the door and peering at the minute cracks between the breeze blocks: to her the cell was a temporally dynamic structure, from the processes that had gone into its building to the flow patterns of people coming in and going out and moving around. Rather like the Doctor's attempts at constructing a data field, Romana extended her senses to take in the cell as a gestalt, abstract whole, looking for any useful pattern that might emerge from that whole; some set of circumstances she might take advantage of, manipulating their dynamics in a manner that would ultimately result in her escape.

The problem was, the only viable dynamic pattern she could see at the moment was waiting until somebody else opened the door and let her out.

'There you are at last!' a voice snapped bad-temperedly. 'Time might have no meaning to such as us, but are you aware of how *long* it's taken to find you again?'

In her abstracted mental state Romana found that she was actively *surprised* by this intrusion, taking place as it did in a spatial dynamic which in conventional terms made it completely impossible.

She turned to see the hologrammatic apparition standing in the middle of the bunk so that its sour-faced, berobed form protruded up from its centre. It was, of course, Wblk from the Gallifreyan High Council.

'I've been incorporating and disincorporating across half of this benighted planet looking for you,' he said. 'And I must say, I haven't exactly been impressed by what I've seen. The locals seem particularly unevolved, I must say. I can't see what the attraction is to you people.'

'That's the Doctor,' said Romana, who was damned if she was going to make excuses for a planet that seemed to be entirely made up of incarceration facilities and people sticking needles in one, 'not me. He tells me it'll grow on me.' While having no particular reason to like Wblk the High Councilman, a brightening thought occurred to her. 'Have you come to take me out of here?'

Wblk looked at her, then rather pointedly stuck his hand through the wall and waved it around with no resistance. Romana's preternaturally acute hearing thought it could hear the horrified yelp of a cell inmate on the other side of the breeze block and soundproofing.

'Fair enough,' she said. 'Then why are you here?'

'When the Doctor and yourself left us so inconsiderately,' said Wblk, 'we could have pulled you back at any moment. We've known about that particular method of breaking free from null-time for centuries – we just never thought that somebody would be mad enough to try something so foolhardy and dangerous. We let you go because you were heading for the place and time in which we wanted you to be...'

'I had my suspicions,' said Romana. 'I know that there was *something* going on behind all this, something more than meets the eye. I just wish I knew what it was.'

'That's precisely why I'm here,' said Wblk the High Councilman. 'There are certain things, if reality as we know it has any hope at all, that it is imperative you know.'

And he began, at last, to explain.

Chapter Nineteen
Everything Must Go Before the Dark

The Mind looked at Its work and congratulated itself upon Its invention. It had been easy, simply by applying Its influence, the correct degree of redirection here and there, to split the three strangers up. Now it had two of them, and the third would surely soon follow. Detaching a number of pieces of Itself to deal with the taking of the captives to Its place of Power and make them ready for Conversion, the Mind returned the majority of Its attention to hunting the third.

This third individual was strangely elusive - the Mind, though not entirely comfortable with the distinctions between individuals other than Itself, had formed the impression that this particular individual was more powerful and far trickier than either of the other two - but the Mind was confident that this tricky individual would be found before the Darkness Time, when the Mind would, after years of somnambulic forgetfulness, unlock the doorways of the World.

The Doctor was enjoying himself. True, he was here looking for clues as to some intangible horror the like of which, effectively, would give the murders of Jack the Ripper a run for their money. True, his young companions seemed to be nowhere to be found, and might at this very moment have found themselves in dire and extreme peril... but it didn't do to let such things prey on your mind. If you simply lived in and enjoyed the moment, it left you confident and relaxed to deal with whatever it was that moment might bring.

The Doctor, in himself, was of course completely unaware of the levels of his mind that were, in themselves, *entirely* aware of the invisible tendrils with which some other Mind was probing, attempting to find a way around the shields and defences and get in. He couldn't afford to let himself be aware of it, he thought: his unawareness was the whole reason why the probing tendrils couldn't find a purchase, and slid off.

He had wandered down to one of the lowest areas of the mall, a cavernous but brightly lit basement space given over completely to an ice rink. For a while he had enjoyed the unconsciously collective ballet of skaters of varying degrees of proficiency skating together, the avoidances and near misses and occasional collisions. After a while he had tired of just watching, pinched a pair of skates from a young lady who was looking the other way, and taken to the ice himself.

After reducing the ice rink to complete and utter chaos, he had taken an elevator up several floors and wandered into a music emporium, where he had sat down at a miniaturised electronic piano and in the space of a few minutes found several Lost Chords – all of them, unfortunately, extremely cacophonous, the last one of which had shattered the store window and, by some abstruse means, fused all its lights.

Now he was standing outside a store called Fractured Planet. In the window were plastic replicas of monsters and robots and rows and columns of garishly coloured comic books, every single one of them depicting a mesomorphic man or extraordinarily pulchritudinous young woman in the sort of leotard that would have one arrested, like as not, if one wore it in real life. The Doctor recalled seeing super-hero books (he believed they were called) like this before, on his travels to the Earth, and had rather enjoyed the innocence and otherworldliness of them. He was therefore slightly dismayed to see that every single man and woman now had huge guns and were industriously blasting away at all and sundry.

Inside the store, a fat man with a beard was talking on the telephone behind the sales counter.

'Worst episode ever,' he was saying with lordly contempt. 'As we all know, Mr Enigma can only regrow parts of his body if more than half of him remains in one piece. So unless...' Here the fat, bearded man gave a snuffling laugh intended to convey to the world in general its utter and irredeemable stupidity. 'So unless there has been some cataclysmic change in the nature of space and time so that you can have more than 100 per cent of a thing, you can't have more than one Mr Enigma running around, let alone five or six. And the planet of the Bottersnikes was destroyed in the Replicant Wars – so how could it be destroyed again? And plus it was one of the Heathcoate Dwibbler Mr Enigmas, and we all know that the Heathcoate Dwibbler Mr Enigmas were utterly crap compared to the... excuse me? That is not a toy. That is a hand-painted scale replica of the *Evil* Lieutenant Whopley confronting her heroic twin with her sonically vibrating pulse-pump.'

This last was directed, pointedly, to the Doctor, who put down the model and smiled apologetically. 'I beg your pardon.'

The Doctor wandered over to the science fiction section of the store and scanned the collection of books, noting that there were any number of paperbacks concerning this Mr Enigma whom the clerk had been on about, from several publishers and with titles ranging from *Mr Enigma and the Creature of the Celestial Temple,* to *Mr Enigma Does Some Stuff,* to *Mr Enigma Travels Smugly Up Himself.* There were rather more books about the EarthFed Space Patrol, though there were fewer writers' names on the spines, and a smattering of generic books about dragons, unicorns, dolphins and sub-Tolkienesque fantasy lands of the sort that would have Baron Munchausen turning into a realist in disgust.

There were also a few science fiction anthology magazines. One of them was called *Astonishing Stories of Unmitigated*

Science!, which gave the Doctor a little thrill of recognition. He had once, in other times, been an *Astonishing!* subscriber, and even an occasional contributor under an assumed name, but he'd had no idea that the publication had survived past the 1950s – assuming that its appearance here was not, in fact, merely yet another example of the temporal mishmash that was Lychburg. He picked up the magazine and, after assuring himself that the fat clerk was looking the other way, utterly spoilt its resale value by actually opening it to read.

For the fraction of a second that, to a human observer, would be an odd little man simply rifling the pages of a magazine, the Doctor allowed himself the pleasure of entering a world where all the issues were simple, every problem could be solved by a jut-jawed man of iron will and technology was a friend that would have us all living in power-domes on Mars within the decade.

After a moment's happy nostalgia, however, he paused, opened the magazine to one page and watched it closely. 'Oh dear.'

Shifts in basic reality take a bit of time and acceleration until they become generally noticeable. Who cares whether, for example, one of the discrete molecules that make up an apple on a tree three miles away is present or missing? The short answer is that we all will care, a little later, when the universe unravels around us like a knitted scarf caught on a nail, but for the moment we don't. In the same way, a physical artefact like a book or a magazine will stay, in physical terms, pretty much the same. It is the *information* it contains, the words on the page, that change. Books, and their languages and attitudes, become meaningless not just through cultural and generational drift – they are a reflection of how the universe itself is changing all around us on the subatomic level.

Here, the change was visible to the naked eye. The Doctor looked at the words as they squirmed and transformed on the

Astonishing! page and came to a decision. Mental defences that have one acting and thinking as if one doesn't have a care in the world are all very well, but they assume the fact that the world will continue to be there not to have a care *in*, for the good and the monstrous evil alike.

'Look at this,' he said to the fat clerk, dropping his guards, speaking loudly and not in fact speaking to the clerk at all. 'Your world is collapsing around your ears – if you *have* ears in any proper sense – even as we speak. If something isn't done to stop it, we're all going to find ourselves disappearing up our own quantum packet.' He waved the magazine in front of the clerk's face. 'Something of you might survive in some form, I suppose, but I doubt it – and even if you do, what are you going to do then? You won't have anything to feed on. You'll just diminish until there's nothing left. Why don't you let me –'

The clerk's eyes, meanwhile, had glazed over and human animation had left his face. The thing that had taken control of him stared blankly and listened to the Doctor's ravings for a while – then simply lunged for him.

'Look, this isn't the way you should be doing things at all!' the Doctor exclaimed, jumping back. 'If you'll just listen to what I'm trying to tell you...'

He was answered by a fist swinging round in a bludgeoning arc, hard enough, he judged, to break human bone – in the clerk's hand and in the jaw of anyone it hit. The Doctor ducked under the fist, turned whilst still in a crouch and darted from the shop.

People outside turned instantly to look at him with that same blank stare. It had been a mistake, the Doctor realised, to open up his mind and attempt to talk about things reasonably. Even if he raised his mental shields again, the thing that could control these people had now fixed upon his position. First order of the day, at this point, was to try to give it and those it controlled the slip again. The Doctor ran down a marble-floored promenade, scattering shoppers as he went, vaulted onto a downward-going escalator and attempted to avoid the people on it by running down the moving handrail as though it were a tightrope. Centuries ago, he recalled, before catabolism had taken its toll upon his original body, he had been something of an acrobat and could have done this before breakfast while thinking six impossible thoughts. Unfortunately his new body, though resilient, was not entirely built for such feats.

He plummeted thirty feet, landing on his dignity and bruising it more than was entirely seemly. No time to worry about that, though; the Doctor bounced to his feet and sped on through what appeared to be a food hall filled with people eating repasts from various vending kiosks.

As he ran, every single one of them stood up and turned to face him.

Something arced between them, a form of crackling energy that for a moment was physically visible: a flickering, bluish nimbus around each individual, tendrils of that same blue stuff intangibly linking them to each other. The air crackled with tension and ozone, the building charge of an oncoming electrical storm.

Members of the crowd moved themselves in front of the Doctor's course of flight, cutting it off. He skidded to a halt on his heels, looked around wildly for a moment and then became calm.

'Now, I know for a fact that none of you really want to be doing this...' he began.

The blast of the discharge knocked him off his feet and set his clothes on fire. As the flames flickered around him and the alien energy crawled through him, the Doctor relaxed into a cavernous and insensate void.

* * *

The Mind did not breathe a sigh of relief – even if It could do anything with whatsoever feelings of relief It might have had in the first place. It did, however, feel that things had gone well. This individual had, indeed, been the more powerful of the three, and as such would surely prove to be the crucial component in the Mind's plans. The Mind now caused a certain number of those whom It controlled to take the quarry to join the other captives in Its place of Power.

The night was coming, now. Of course, the night could have come any time the Mind liked – Its intention and will being the physical law of Its World – but It knew that the individual creatures within the World functioned better with regular periods of darkness and light.

In any event, it was good that the night was coming now. The Dark Time was approaching and this time, in accordance with the plans of the Mind, the darkness would be ultimate. There was a new World coming, and a World which the Mind had long forgotten to be reclaimed.

Chapter Twenty
An Attendance to the Opening of Hell

The glowing, interlocking crystal column in the console in the centre of the chamber, ground to a halt with a sound like gears clashing in the engines of the universe itself. Katharine Delbane watched it dumbly; her body was still not under her control, her mind was in something akin to shock. Something appearing out of thin air, or being bigger on the inside than the outside, doesn't sound like much – if the appearing or being bigger doesn't happen directly in front of you.

The effect of flat impossibility on the psyche is remarkably similar to the physical effect of being hit by a truck: imagine it all you like, and work out strategies to cope, but when it actually happens you just go to pieces. It was as though her mind had shattered, was only able to think in small and disconnected fragments.

And underneath it all was... something else. It was like looking through a broken pane of mirrored glass that, previously, had reflected back nothing but the image of herself. Now, she thought she could glimpse what was beyond it. Something big, and dark, and moving, and alive. *This* had no problem at all with things being bigger in the inside. After all, it was able to fit itself into something as small as a human skull...

Delbane realised that the Doctor's head was in front of her, peering at her with a kind of barely restrained and murderous fury that... no, she thought, murderous was the wrong word. Without quite knowing how she knew, she realised that the Doctor was fundamentally incapable of murder as such, even if, like a veterinarian, he might sometimes find himself forced to put lives to sleep. Not murderous then, just toweringly, terribly angry.

He turned his head to glower at Crowley – whom Delbane could not see as he was beyond her direct line of sight.

'This is obscene,' the little man said. 'Stop it, stop it now.'

There was a chuckle off to one side. 'I'm surprised, Doctor,' said the voice of Crowley. 'Killing and kidnapping and quite possibly torture you seem to pass off lightly, yet you're disconcerted by the mere subsuming of a will to my Influence?'

'Killing and kidnapping and quite possibly torture can be borne,' said the Doctor, deadly serious. 'In a sense. This is a desecration of the very human quality that *allows* such things to be borne. And as I recall, you were once rather hot on the basic sanctity of that. "Do What Thou Wilt" and so forth...?'

There was a pause.

'Ah, Doctor,' said Crowley. 'It seems that you have intimated something of the truth of my nature...'

The Doctor shrugged. 'You never even bothered to cover your tracks. I never met you back then – or at least I haven't yet – but from what I know about you, you seem to have changed for the worst, no matter how well you've worn in other respects. I'd very much like to know how you managed to survive for so long.'

'Time,' said the voice of Crowley, 'has its effect. And there are... methods, let us say, for countering and even reversing its grosser physical effects.'

'Oh, I know all about that,' said the Doctor. He gestured towards Delbane, his face still burning with anger. 'You have what you want, to the extent that anybody does, and holding the poor girl like this simply serves no purpose. Let her go. Let her go now.'

The sound of a man sucking his teeth consideringly. 'Very well,' said the voice of Crowley. 'Although, I think, I'll leave her slightly, ah, *bemused* for a while, just in case she attempts something unfortunate.'

There was no transformation, no sense of something happening inside, but Delbane found that she was in control of her body again. She looked around, dazedly, at the white-walled room, at the complex octagonal console-array in its centre, at the Doctor and Crowley. Her feelings were too big for her even to *feel* properly. There was just an overwhelming, debilitating lassitude.

'What...?' she began, and couldn't think of anything to say after that.

'It's going to be all right,' said the Doctor, seriously, and she believed him – although a little voice inside her said that at this point, in this state, she'd believe anything, no matter who said it.

'Your confidence is heartening, Doctor,' said Crowley. He waved a hand towards a lever on the console-array. 'And now, I think we should be leaving. The good people outside must be wondering what's happening in here.'

'Well, this is very nice,' the Doctor said cheerfully, walking out of the TARDIS behind Crowley. 'Very intimate and friendly.' He took in the hooded troops levelling their weapons at him, peered enthusiastically at the signs and sigils on the walls – then stared at the sensor and data-processing consoles. He let go of a still-dazed Delbane, whom he had half-led out of the TARDIS and, without a thought to the high-velocity muzzles tracking him, bounded over to the consoles.

'Oh dear me,' he said. 'Oh dear, oh dear, oh me. You're attempting to manipulate reality with a cargo-cult set-up like *this?*'

'No, we're not,' said an ageing man in a US colonel's uniform, who seemed to be more or less in charge around these parts. 'This just allows us to gauge the fluctuations in the global state-vector. We're not manipulating it.'

'Oh yes you are,' said the Doctor, darkly. 'You just don't know it. I should have realised. I should have noticed – but idiocy on this scale was unthinkable even to me.'

'Now see here...' the colonel began, possibly affronted by the Time Lord's dismissal of his establishment.

'I rather think,' said the Doctor coldly, scanning the various readouts and displays with dismay, 'that seeing anything at all is going to be slightly academic, soon.' He turned back to glower at the colonel and Crowley, who now bore something of the aspect of shamefaced schoolboys. 'I think now might be the time for you to tell me exactly what it is you've done.'

Reliable sources of the time have it that Edward Alexander Crowley, otherwise known as Aleister, otherwise known as 'the wickedest man in the world' or the Great Beast, died in 1947, in the seaside town of Hastings. Reliable sources were wrong on several distinct counts. By the time of his rather boisterous funeral service in Brighton, he was happily ensconced several thousand miles away in a high-security research facility in the United States.

Which particular state remains classified, but it was the sort of area where you couldn't walk three steps from your house without stumbling over an ancient Indian burial ground, finding an entire town that had been mysteriously depopulated or falling down the shaft of a haunted mine. Such an area was rank with superstition and foreboding – the sort of place where horror stories, if not real horrors, grew with fecundity. The fact that ghosts, ghouls and things of a monstrous nature had about the same actual existence as the object of a medieval witch-hunt was neither here nor there – the psychic climate was perfect for Crowley's particular work.

The war had just ended, and the United States was busily appropriating everything it could from the remains of Nazi Germany. The relocation of rocket technicians and nuclear scientists was well known – it would in fact serve certain interests to have the global population living in fear of the well-documented A-bombs that were subsequently produced.

Other things, however, were appropriated, too. Certain discoveries made when the death camps were liberated were preserved, and such accumulated procedural data as remained was extrapolated and worked upon to produce, in the fullness of time, any number of results in the military and commercial fields, from mycotoxins used in germ warfare, to medical gene therapy, to a method for preserving the 'toasted freshness' in the contents of a box of cereal. Such things were kept secret on the basis that (a) germ warfare and the like are by their very nature classified, and (b) it's not exactly a winning marketing ploy to draw a through-line from your breakfast treat of choice to injecting a pair of twins with strychnine just to see which of them dies first.

On another level, the semi-science of propaganda developed explosively using Nazi methods – not just in the crude processes of commercial advertising, televisual programming or the rigging of political elections, but in the basic psychological processes capable of subsuming and transforming an entire culture and its mythologies over years instead of decades or centuries.

Under Nazi control the German people had believed in such unmitigated, hastily invented and reinvented tripe as Manifest Aryan Destiny, Pellucidor, the lost island of Mu and the World Ice Theory as sincerely as any tenth-century peasant had believed in the imminence of Judgement Day and the Divine Right of Kings.

It was this transformation of mythology that was of particular interest to certain sections of the US security services – an interest that dated back to the war itself, when the likes of Tolkien and his inkling ilk had written reams of bombastic and semi-coherent cod-legendary garbage under the direct instruction of the Allied command in an attempt to counter the Nazi world-view.

What interested them most, however, was the fact that Germany's leaders were documented proponents of the Black Arts – and that practising them appeared, from such evidence that survived (only to be immediately hushed up), in some strange sense to *work*. Such evidence included engineers' circuit diagrams designed to control V-2 rockets by summoning the *Vandertoten*, or 'roaming dead', to inhabit them; notes attributed to Albert Speer (though subsequently disavowed) on the practical functions of Sacred Geometry in State Architecture, and apparently genuine footage of Paul Joseph Goebbels using the fat of a ritually murdered Jewess to levitate a full three inches off the ground.

The possibility that magic might actually *work* defied all logic and reason – but the mere existence of that possibility was enough to merit further investigation. The atom had only recently been split and harnessed, and who knew what other, supposedly impossible phenomena might be fact rather than fiction? With the US economy shifting from a war footing there was money in the national coffers to spend on such possibilities, even something abstruse as this, purely on the off chance. Besides, intelligence reports from Stalin's Russia spoke of secret experiments involving the paranormal, based on findings in the Polish death camps – and the last thing the United States needed was for the Soviets to get ahead in what might effectively turn into a Charms Race.

The problem was, looking into this possibility was not like debriefing technicians and scientists who had worked on formulating jet propellants or refining heavy water. If magic had been used at all to obtain unnatural power it had been used by the inner circle of the National Socialist Party – by the people who had actually *got* that power – and now the vast majority of those people were dead. Those concerns interested in investigating the matter were forced to look further afield, to the sources from which those ideas had originally come…

'It was a godsend.' Crowley said, as the lights from displays flickered about him in Hangar 18. 'In a sense. My notoriety in England was starting to prove a positive hindrance by that time, and my new American friends allowed me a fresh start. Now I had the funding and resources to make the greatest leap in the Hermetic Arts since the age of John Dee…'

'To what end?' asked the Doctor, frowning at the various consoles with distaste. 'I'd be the first to agree that what you call Magic has its uses, but all of this doesn't exactly seem to be benign.'

'Well, I have to admit that the arrangement was that I find military applications for my work,' Crowley said, looking towards the US colonel, whose name was apparently Haasterman.

'The Soviets were loading for bear,' Haasterman said. 'Joe One had already been tested. Russia was a nuclear power, and sharing that technology with China back then. If there was something extra we could put in the hat, we went for it.' He seemed neither apologetic nor proud: he was simply stating how things had been.

'And the results were beneficial rather than otherwise,' Crowley said. 'The solution to the Cuban missile crisis – to take but one example – involved certain processes that you might find surprising, even now. Without going into irrelevant details, our work has saved the world as we know it from destruction more than several times.'

'A destruction,' said the Doctor, 'almost brought about by your Cold War mentality in the first place, I have no doubt. You won't justify yourselves that easily.'

'Well, be that as it may,' said Crowley. 'Great things were achieved.' His face fell a little. 'All in all, it made the failure of what was, perhaps, our greatest enterprise, more galling.'

'That always seems the way,' said the Doctor dismissively. 'I'm sure you'll tell me all about it, at great length.'

'The practice of Magic is,' said Crowley, with a slight sense of offended dignity, 'in its ultimate sense, the exercising of Belief. The words and protocols, the specifics of the actual rituals are meaningless in themselves, merely being tools to instil and direct a sense of absolute faith. The Nazi inner circle proved that. They basked in the unconditional faith of their subordinates, of their entire nation and its annexed states, feeding off this to turn their delusions into physical fact, transforming the very reality around them, for a time. The fact that they didn't know quite what they were doing, led in the end to a catastrophic loss of faith in themselves every bit as debilitating as their military collapse on the Eastern Front...'

'Our idea,' said Haasterman, who seemed to think that Crowley was meandering off into needless reminiscences, 'was to consciously utilise those so-called Magical processes, to open up a portal between our own world and another...'

The Doctor looked at him, aghast. 'Oh, did you really? And did it occur to you that the uncontrolled linking of two quantum state-vectors with distinctly different energy slopes would result in the massive exchange of energy, creating an explosion or implosion that would be devastating either way? What did you *call* this idea of yours, a Demon Bomb?'

'Well, uh...' Haasterman at least had the grace to look shamefaced. 'We provisionally nomenclaturised it as the Golgotha Project...'

'The place of skulls,' the Doctor said with a snort. 'You know, it never ceases to amaze me. You people pick up things faster than almost everybody else in the known universe – concepts and processes for which others strive for millennia before they so much as begin to grasp them – and then you just bang them together until they go boom.'

'You people...?' asked Haasterman, puzzled.

'Never mind.' The Doctor turned to Crowley, with what was almost a snarl. 'So just what did this "Golgotha Project" of yours entail?'

This was the early 1960s and the height of the Cold War, a time of fear-fuelled, low-grade mass hysteria that had had America rooting out so-called subversive elements with all the ferocity of an Inquisition, accumulating a weapons stockpile capable of cracking the planet open more than fifty times over – and would have it escalating a sabre-rattling police action in Asia into a land war that, for various logistical reasons, it had not a hope in hell of winning.

This was also a governmental system that, while ostensibly a form of democracy, was prone to having notions that seemed like a good idea at the time: like infecting Negro populations with syphilis and leaving them untreated, or knowingly exposing whole battalions of troops to dirty cobalt-bomb fallout without protection, just to see what happened. Life, if not cheap, was easily expendable by anyone who might manage to convince themselves that it was being spent in the interests of preserving Truth, Justice and the American Way.

So when the idea of the Golgotha Project was first mooted, and rather like it had been with the aforementioned dirty-fallout tests, it was relatively easy to squeak it past the congressional powers that be by producing actuarial tables to the effect that the possible deaths involved would be nothing compared with the deaths incurred if the Commies beat them to the punch. The town of Lychburg in the great state of [classified] was chosen as the first test site by the highly technical statistical process of sticking a needle (first sanctified with arcane guidance-rituals) into a map and picking a geographically self-contained and out-of-the-way population centre near where it ended up.

Section Eight specialists moved in and, under the guise of conducting a marketing survey, transformed the town to fit the necessary parameters; first by subliminal mass-conditioning and then by complete narcoleptic and operant-conditional brainwashing on an individual basis. Certain members of the body politic who proved intransigent at this stage, who took it into their heads to wander around shouting about how the town was being taken over by alien pod-people and the like, were summarily excised. The end result was an entire population that, as one, could be led, upon the application of certain stimuli, to act and think and Believe with all their hearts in ways, in ideas and in *things* at their controllers' will.

Thus far, thus good, and nothing out of the bounds of conventional physics. Rather like Germans believing in Aryan Supremacy, or Christian Fundamentalists believing in the coming of Judgement Day, any delusion imposed upon the population of Lychburg would effectively change reality within the confines of that population, because it would inform their very thoughts and acts whatever the literal truth of it. The problem was, of course, that while the entire population of Lychburg might believe that Demons had appeared, for example, summoned from the very Mouth of Hell to sweep down upon and destroy the enemies of their nation – and while they might think and act precisely as if that were the case – the number of demons appearing in the real and physical sense was, in actual fact, zippo.

The tertiary phase of the Golgotha project was to turn the *effective* into the *actual*.

While the processes and rituals of Magic were, at root, just tools in the mental kit that allowed the summoning and channelling of Power, they would have been nothing had that Power not existed, to some extent, in the first place. Scattered across the Earth and through its history were certain objects of a mystical nature, thought of in more credulous times as divine, devilish or sorcerous; in more contemporary, if not enlightened times, as alien – if not from another planet, then at the very least not of the world we know. Cursed burial treasures, pieces of the True Cross, mystic rune stones, brass bed-knobs and swords of invincibility lobbed at passing knights by a samite-wearing woman in a pond.

Many such items could be explained – or at least explained away – in the prosaic terms of technological innovation (of *course* King Arthur's sword made him invincible, or rather the prototypical steel swords of his men made them invincible when they fought against people armed with bronze), or mistranslation, or sly jokes aimed at the overly gullible (good luck in finding a *peacock's* egg). But the fact remains that a percentage of these items, in one sense or another, existed.

When Edward Alexander Crowley was recruited by Section Eight and brought over to America, he took several such items with him. The particular nature of one of these remains classified, as do records of its essential origin. It was simply codenamed the Arimathea Artefact.

It is unclear whether the artefact was intended as the equivalent of a primary trigger in a nuclear device or as its payload. In any event, its function was to serve as a focal point. Key individuals in the conditioned Lychburg populace were implanted with superconductive transceivers (a restricted technology that would not find its way on to the open market for several decades) that linked them directly to the artefact and served as channels for the force of the belief of those around them.

At last, after more than three years groundwork, the site was ready for preliminary testing. The Section Eight specialists were removed to what was thought to be a safe distance, and command-code images were streamed to the Lychburg population. The image consisted of something simple, easy and culturally familiar to the American Midwestern mind – the opening of the Gates of Hell.

The result was complete and utter disaster.

'This is mostly based on years of analysis by the number crunchers,' said Haasterman. 'I mean, what can we *really* know from dimensions that we can't even imagine...?'

'What indeed,' said the Doctor, shortly. He seemed to be barely restraining an utter sense of rage.

'Something opened up,' Haasterman continued, seemingly not noticing this, his eyes slightly vague as though lost in some private memory that was being replayed in front of them. 'The camera monitors showed nothing, just an area of blank phosphor, and then they went dead. The sensor-readouts showed a... a *rift* opening up, a conduit to some other dimension, somewhere else – and then things went haywire. From the analysis, it seems that something came from *another* somewhere else, another direction entirely. It impacted with the rift and it...' His voice trailed off as he tried and failed to come up with words to explain what had happened.

'I was there,' Crowley continued, taking up the story. 'In the control cabins before we were forced to decamp. It was like a dome of alchemical light – vitreous, gemlike and consuming. Something lived within it, screaming and writhing in the light. Something...' He frowned, as though in mild, quiet puzzlement. 'I have encountered wickedness in various forms – have been called wicked myself, if you'll recall – and I think I know something of evil. This thing gave off the impression of an Evil so pure that I cannot express the magnitude of it – utterly inimical to life, all life as we can possibly know it. The mere presence of it seemed to harbour... not death, precisely, but negation. The negation of life.

'It expanded at what I should say was a fast walking pace – easily slow enough for us to make our retreat from it, but there was a sense of unstoppability about it, chewing through the bedrock of the land, its apogee ever rising. I have no doubt that if left unchecked it would have eventually consumed the entire world. Fortunately, contingency plans – though I had not been aware of them myself at the time – were in place.'

'We had bombers overflying the area,' Haasterman said. 'We were able to deploy a nuclear strike.'

'Why does that not surprise me?' the Doctor said. 'Tactical nuclear strikes seem to be the fashion around these parts. And did such a crude attempt work?'

'Apparently so,' said Crowley. 'I and my cohorts were caught on the edge of the primary blast – but fortunately I have some small expertise in conjuring up, as it were, a degree of personal protection. Additionally, it seemed, the globe itself soaked up a large part of the energy expended and the resulting fallout. I was the only survivor, however. Later, when I and suitably protected staff returned to investigate the result, we found that the globe had contracted leaving a crater with a ball of some unidentified matter physically floating in its centre.'

'Unidentified matter?' the Doctor asked.

'We have carefully refrained from so much as touching it,' said Crowley. 'Who knows what the effect might be? Visually, it appears to be a perfect globe of some metallic and mirror-bright substance. *Appeared*, I should say...'

'From what the number crunchers say,' added Haasterman. 'The theory is that the strike knocked it out of dimensional alignment, causing it to collapse under reality as we know it. It's remained in that state for decades without changing...'

'One of the things you really ought to know about me,' said the Doctor, seemingly inconsequentially, 'is that in some ways I'm occasionally gifted with second sight. Or possibly hearing. Can you guess what I'm seeing, or possibly hearing, right now?'

Haasterman nodded. 'The globe's destabilising, changing in ways we can't predict – and we have no way of stopping it.'

The Doctor shrugged, rather scornfully. 'So heave another bomb at it, why don't you? You did it before, so why don't you do it again?'

'That remains, of course,' said Crowley, 'a last resort.'

The Doctor turned to stare at him anxiously. 'That was a joke. You *do* realise that was a joke, don't you?'

'Quite so.' Crowley became slightly more confident and expansive, in direct proportion to the Doctor's sudden apprehension. 'And this brings us to why we've gone to extraordinary lengths to bring you here. We've known for quite some time of your existence as an alien life form here on Earth...'

'Alien?' Haasterman was startled, suddenly suspicious. 'What's this about an alien? You told me he was –'

'Well, *I've* known of your nature for quite some time,' said Crowley, 'and of your access to technologies of which we can only dream. We intend to appropriate them, quite frankly, Doctor. Our need is, after all, far greater than yours.'

The Doctor regarded him blankly. 'I don't think so.' He reached out and shook Crowley's hand, then a slightly bemused Haasterman's, with a cheery mockery of civility that made his underlying feelings of pure loathing abundantly clear. 'Thank you so much for bringing the matter to my attention – though a little less of the circumlocution might be nice, next time. The matter will be dealt with momentarily. And now, if you'll excuse me...' He turned his back on both of them and started towards the TARDIS.

'Oh no,' said Crowley with his easy urbanity. 'I really don't think that will do at all. This is far too important to leave to what, I gather, is a notoriously cavalier and slipshod attitude. If you refuse to give us what we need, we'll have to use more direct means of persuasion.'

Haasterman, meanwhile, had picked up a telephone handset and was mumbling into it. Now he put the handset down again and nodded briefly to Crowley.

An access hatch in the big hangar doors swung open and a pair of figures trooped through under armed guard. The Doctor took one look at them and his face split into a sunny smile. 'Brigadier! Romana! I must admit I was getting slightly worried about you both. I'm so glad you're not dead.'

'That,' said Crowley, his voice hardening as the black-clad troops already gathered in the hangar turned their weapons on the new arrivals, 'can still be easily arranged.'

Chapter Twenty-One
Everything Merges in the Night

As night fell in Lychburg, every single one of its inhabitants – whether man, woman or child – decided they would like to go to a certain place. If you had asked them, they would have come up with perfectly natural and logical reasons why this was so, but if you had pressed them they would probably have become restive. If you had pointed out that it was a little strange that every single one of them had decided to go to a particular place that night, if you had pointed out that this was, not to put too fine a point upon it, the behaviour of people who were not in their right minds, the good people of Lychburg would no doubt have murdered you, horribly and brutally, on the spot.

Had it been possible to achieve an aerial view of this exodus, the levitating observer would have noticed something strange. It was not the fact that from this hypothetical height those on foot seemed to be keeping pace with those in vehicles, at what must have been an insane and ultimately enervating run. Nor was it the fact that over two hundred thousand living beings were managing to do this with the spontaneously regimented coordination of an army of soldier ants. It was the fact that these people were travelling in completely opposite directions, heading out from all points of the compass, but somehow ending up in exactly the same place.

When the Mind that lived within them all had taken control of any individual directly, It had left that individual with an unnamed and irrational desire to take or make some vaguely human form, and fashion it into new positions. Now that process was to be repeated on a larger scale.

* * *

The woman in the haberdashers had grasped Victoria by the throat and suffocated her into a swoon, despite her attempts to scratch and claw at her attacker. She had come back to herself in an office, handcuffed to a metal chair, where a man in a uniform with a peaked cap, a badge on his jacket reading SECSERVE SECURITY, had been holding a telephone apparatus to his ear. The man's eyes were as dead as those of the woman who had attacked her, and he had spoken no words at all, either into the telephone or to Victoria herself. She had the distinct impression that this was being done not to serve any function, but as a travesty of the procedures by which people ordinarily did such things.

Presently, a pair of policemen of the same sort that had apprehended herself, Jamie and the Doctor when they first arrived here, had come into the office and silently and implacably dragged an entirely unsilent and struggling Victoria to their automobile, where they had flung her into the luggage compartment in the rear and slammed it shut behind her.

After a knee-and-elbow-skinning drive, the automobile had stopped. Victoria had nothing with which to tell the time, so she was uncertain as to how long she had been left in the compartment, but through the crack in its hatch she had seen the light from outside fade. It seemed that it was now night.

Abruptly, the hatch swung upwards. Standing over her were the two policemen, their outlines dead black against the lightly starlit night sky. From within each of their eyes there issued a dim, bluish glow.

They dragged her out, and silently hauled her over to a dark shape that, from the look of it, was another, larger conveyance. Two more figures were there; a third was lying at their feet. The policemen flung Victoria painfully down beside it and it stirred and groaned. It was Jamie.

'The pack of them took me down,' he said, recognising her. 'Knocked seven shades of, uh, Sunday out of me and threw me out in the midden for dead.' He jerked his head toward the two figures standing by him, who had been joined by the policemen. All four were now standing still as statues, the lights in their eyes directed squarely on their captives, watching over them. 'Yon scunners came along and brought me here.'

'And where precisely *is* here?' Victoria asked him.

'Your guess is as good as mine,' he said.

Victoria cautiously climbed into a crouch and craned her neck around. Nothing but the night, the sound of things in trees, the distant murmur of the city. She stood up to take a better look around. Smoothly and without warning, one of the dark figures stepped forward and shoved her down. The hard earth stung at knees already the worse for wear, and she let out a hiss of pain.

'Are you all right?' Jamie asked her.

'I'm fine,' she managed, biting back an exclamation which would, if let out, have been rather stronger in nature than *bless me*. 'I thought I saw a set of lights coming,' she said when the urge to emit oaths like a guardsman had subsided. 'Of the sort they have on automobiles. Someone else is coming, I think.'

Later, when a number of varieties of dust had settled and Victoria was in a position to review events with some small degree of equanimity, she would admit that this was, in all probability, the greatest understatement she was ever likely to make.

For the moment, though, they both heard and saw the automobile Victoria had mentioned approaching. Four figures, as opposed to the two each guarding Victoria and Jamie, dragged out a fifth, instantly recognisable as the Doctor. Victoria's joy in seeing him was slightly marred by the fact that he seemed to be unconscious. His body sagged, supported by arms gripped on each side, and his head lolled bonelessly. When he was dropped to the ground next to Victoria and

Jamie, he landed in a twisted heap and steadfastly refused to move at all.

'I don't think he's getting up...' said Jamie, in the slightly worried tones of one who had been hoping that the reappearance of the Doctor might be the prelude to a dramatic and ingenious rescue, but was coming to the realisation that this was not to be the case. He got no further because at this point a certain number of important things, if not everything, changed.

There was a blaze of light off to one side as a huge, flat plane lit up with perfect and dazzling whiteness. Angular black shapes stuttered and jerked across it, flashing with a disturbing frequency that set the mind jerking along with them, made the body tremble as though with some form of telegraphic Saint Vitus's dance.

Then the shapes on the plane resolved themselves, darkening slightly. Colour burst across across it: a sky of such a deep and vivid blue as to seem entirely unnatural. A silvery disc hung against the sky, spinning slightly lopsidedly on a thin piece of wire. There was a ululating whine, which rose and fell like a theremin on a life raft, and the scratchy sound of martial music. Letters appeared on the screen, overlaying the sky and the silver disc:

IT CAME FROM THE HELL PLANET BEYOND TIME! A Ronaldo P Dementi Production.

The hands of one of her automaton-like guards heaved Victoria roughly to her feet. To one side, she saw, another was doing the same to Jamie and two more were lifting the insensible Doctor. From this slightly higher vantage point, in the light from the screen, she could now see the open, slightly inclined space of the Lychburg Drive-o-Rama.

And from the direction of the city of Lychburg itself, she saw and heard the first signs and sounds of vehicles and running feet approaching in their thousands.

Chapter Twenty-Two
The Doctrine of Opposites, and What It Really Means to You

The thing inside Katharine Delbane seemed to be growing; it was an almost physical sensation and not just in her mind, as though her skin were some kind of costume, inert and sloughing loose, with something greasy and tensile moving around inside. She felt remote, not simply dazed, as if her sense-receptors were disconnecting from the world.

(It's nothing. You have nothing to fear.)

Delbane felt a cold chill of fear. She constantly bolstered her self and identity by constant internal reassurance, but that particular internal, reassuring voice had nothing to do with her.

She had simply stood there in the hangar, watching and listening as Crowley and the US colonel talked complete and utter insanity to the Doctor. Unlike before, it wasn't so much Crowley's debilitating influence as simple bewilderment: insanity or not, she had no frame of reference for dealing with the matters being discussed, not the first idea of how to react.

Now she watched the figures that were being led in by a rather nervous-looking lieutenant major and a squad of armed servicemen.

She recognised them at once. The Lady Romana's velvet dress was looking decidedly crushed and rumpled, but she herself seemed physically unhurt, glancing around with vague interest as though she were out for nothing more potentially perilous than a country walk. The Brigadier seemed slightly more knocked around, but his bearing was dignified and military; whatever had been done to him, it had not even come close to breaking his spirit.

Behind them came Danny Slater and Jim McCrae. The two Provisionals seemed to have lost a bit of weight, the small amount some people lose when they have a nasty shock. They were looking around the hangar and at its complement of armed and obviously highly dangerous men with outright fear. Whatever they had signed on for in a life with the Provisionals, it certainly hadn't been this.

'Slater and McCrae?' Crowley was musing to himself. He turned to the colonel. 'I'd rather assumed that you'd simply had them killed, Haasterman, I confess.'

'That's not how things are done under my command,' said Haasterman shortly.

'Of course,' said Crowley. 'On the other hand, the more the merrier.' He turned to gesture towards Delbane. 'Have one of your people take her over to join them, will you? We might as well get some use out of her, untrustworthy though she has proved to be.'

Colonel Haasterman seemed to be going through a small crisis with his conscience. 'I don't like this part of things,' he muttered, whether to Crowley or to himself it was impossible to say with any great degree of alacrity.

'As neither do I, Colonel,' said Crowley, easily. 'However. We are on a certain course, now. Certain things simply have to be done.'

A black-hooded man grabbed hold of Delbane and hauled her over to the other detainees. In her detached state, by the time she'd decided that she was damned well going to make a fight of it, it was too late. The Lady Romana looked at her and gave her a slight smile that, strangely enough, seemed more friendly than otherwise.

'Can't say I think much of your planet,' she said. 'Some of the locals are perfectly frightful. However have you stood it?'

'What...?' Delbane began.

Romana became distant again. 'I wasn't talking to you.'

The hooded men had taken charge of the captives now, covering them with their weapons, and the servicemen who had brought them in were just hanging uncertainly about.

'Thank you, Derricks,' Colonel Haasterman said to their commander, dismissively. 'That's all we need you for right now.'

The commander, a big, rather unpleasant-looking man, looked as if he was going to make something of the colonel's tone on general principles, then snapped out irritable orders to his men and they headed for the door. Delbane got the impression of a bully who had quite recently suffered some kind of blow to his confidence and found himself demoted in the universal pecking order.

As this Derricks and his men left, the hooded troops moved in and one of them shoved Delbane to her knees. Standard execution posture.

She felt the cold muzzle of a gun touching the back of her neck with such a purity of sensation that she honestly couldn't work out if it was actually happening or if her imagination was anticipating the event. She stared at the floor, trying to think about absolutely nothing, noting from the corners of her eyes that the process was being repeated on the other detainees.

'And now, Doctor,' the voice of Crowley was saying off somewhere in the middle distance. 'We know you take great stock in the lives of your friends, and in life in general. If you do not give us what we want, if you still refuse to turn your technology over to us, I shall have – that is to say, Colonel Haasterman here shall have – his men terminate the lives of your friends, one after the other...'

'And if that doesn't work?' said the voice of the Doctor. He sounded worried. 'I ask, ah, purely for the purposes of information, you understand.'

'Then we shall have to become more extreme,' said the voice of Crowley.

'There's no need for any of this.'

This new voice, coming from beside her, was so unexpected that Delbane found herself turning to look at its source in surprise, regardless of the putative gun on the back of her neck.

The Lady Romana had climbed to her feet and turned to push the rifle of a hooded man away from her, in much the same manner that an adult might push away an unappetisingly half-sucked stick of barley sugar proffered by a particularly grubby child. She turned back to Crowley and Haasterman with a sardonic and perfectly calm little smile.

'You don't need the Doctor to give you access to the TARDIS,' she said brightly. 'I can do that, and I can show you everything you need to know about its operation.'

* * *

They were now inside what Romana had described as the console room of the TARDIS, together with Haasterman and Crowley and a large contingent of black-hooded troops. The Brigadier, Delbane and the two Provisional Department operatives, Slater and McCrae, had been brought along, too – as hostages, possibly, or simply to avoid them getting troublesome if left on their own.

'Oh, Romana,' the Doctor said dramatically, clapping the back of a hand to his forehead, 'how could you betray me like this?' It was hard to see how he could possibly think he could get away with such a bit of blatant overacting.

'Simple,' said Romana. 'Back in the Academy of Time, I remember, one of my tutors told me I had an uncommonly sensible head on my shoulders, and I'd rather like to keep it there, thank you very much.'

The thing inside Delbane seemed to be doing most of her thinking for her. It was noting with a kind of cool interest the various reactions of the people here to this physically impossible space, the walls of which had unobtrusively shuffled back to accommodate them. But this wasn't true, the shred of identity that was still Katharine Delbane thought. The walls hadn't moved, the room had always been this size – it had just, in a sense, only always been this size since comparatively recently.

The Doctor and the Lady Romana, of course, were completely unaffected, and the Brigadier only marginally more so – no more than anybody would normally be on walking into the space of someone other than themselves. Crowley and the hooded troops seemed merely oblivious to it. Haasterman, however, looked wild-eyed and frightened, and Slater and McCrae seemed utterly terrified.

'And besides,' Romana was saying as she tinkered with the complicated array of levers, switches and dials on the central console, 'I think I've had more than a sufficiency of your attitude of late – sending me off on fools' errands simply to pander to your entirely affected concern for these people. Let them get on with it and wipe themselves out, I say. I couldn't, quite frankly, care less.'

She turned to Haasterman and Crowley and smiled sweetly. 'Now as you can see, the basic principles are quite simple. The sublaminar processes are modulated by a stepped series of quantum-depolarised frabjastanic couplings, the resulting gravmetric packets being filtered through a reciprocating Brantis-Wankel ambulator to convert their subneutronic spin from anticlockwise to inside out, providing the basic template for the mesonic collapse of the interstitial mesh into what is rather colourfully, I'm afraid, called the Walrus Mode. With the pranantic waveform properly antifrated, it's just a matter of setting up the proper Boolean constraints to regulate the Planck-collapse whilst avoiding complete polyhelical overload on the macrotransablative level, and there you are. Of course, that's putting it in layman's terms. It's ultimately far more complicated than that.'

There was a moment's silence while Crowley and Haasterman looked at each other.

'I think,' said Crowley at last, a little uncertainly, 'a rather more practical demonstration might be in order.'

'Happy to oblige,' said Romana, and pulled a big red lever.

There was a blinding explosion of light from the central column. The floor heaved with a gargantuan shock, knocking the occupants of the console room off their feet and flinging them against the walls. Delbane found that the Doctor – who had somehow managed to retain his footing – was instantly beside her, pulling her up off the floor. She blinked at him through yellow and purple spots detonating in front of her eyes.

'Brigadier!' the Doctor was shouting, off to one side where the Lady Romana was helping the soldier to his feet, 'help us get those two young chaps out of here.' He pointed with his free hand, the one not supporting the groggy Delbane, to the collapsed and now actively gibbering Slater and McCrae. 'I don't think it would be safe for them if we left them.'

He looked about wildly and spotted a doorway that had opened up in the wall when the shock wave hit.

'Come on,' he said cheerfully to Delbane, 'let's get you to safety.' And with that he dragged her to the door at a bounding run.

Haasterman groaned as his senses returned just in time for him to see the Doctor and the other detainees vanish through the door, which instantly shut behind him. It was as though the wall itself had healed up, becoming just a flat white surface indented with bulls-eye mouldings. A brightly coloured scrap of the Doctor's scarf, snipped off by the closing panel, fluttered to the floor.

Haasterman clambered to his feet and cast around trying to get a handle on the situation. The hooded troops were recovering, picking themselves up from the floor smoothly and with none of the shakiness or shock that Haasterman felt. It was like – it occurred to him only now – they were automata or sci-fi androids: they moved or fell and stood up like humans, but without the barely noticeable little muscular ticks and nuances of humans when they moved or fell and stood. Nothing about them gave off the impression of something actually living inside.

They were all of them, every single one, turning their hooded faces towards Crowley, who stood there, by the console in the centre of the room, with his face in his hands. Haasterman wondered momentarily if Crowley had been blinded by the flash of light – but on closer inspection it seemed as if the man was in the throes of some mental breakdown. His body was shaking violently and the nails of his fingers were digging into the skin of his face hard enough to draw blood.

'Are you OK, Crowley?' Haasterman was concerned. They had never been friends as such, but they had worked together for years and seeing such a familiar human being in this state had an effect that even the deaths of any number of strangers, who are after all just mobile scenery in life, could not approach. 'Are you hurt?'

'No,' said Crowley. It was unclear whether he was responding to the first question or the second. There was suddenly was a quality to his voice that Haasterman found chilling. It was as if something, some entity, had taken control of Crowley's lungs and vocal cords by remote control and was forcing them to speak.

'This cannot happen,' Crowley said, in that remote, dead voice. 'This cannot be. We have waited too long to reclaim what is Ours...'

Light burst from between his fingers. He took his hands away from his face and Haasterman reeled back at the sight of the slack and unnaturally relaxed features. Threads of blood trickled down Crowley's forehead from the deep gouges left by his fingernails, hit the light blazing from his eyes and vaporised with a sound like spit on a hot stove.

'We shall *not* allow it,' Crowley's lungs and vocal cords decided, not loudly but with a rasp of lacerating tissue – and Haasterman realised that what he had thought of as deadness was in fact a kind of physical overload. In the same way that too strong a signal from an amplifier can blow out a speaker, the Voice now speaking through Crowley was simply too *big* for the human biology it was using, and was destroying it while it spoke. 'No, we won't.'

Crowley's feet left the floor. His body hung limply in mid-air, as though an invisible hand had clamped itself around his spinal column and hefted him up. His head, seemingly independent of his body, the neck tethering the one to the other rather than supporting it, tracked about the room turning its lambent gaze upon the assembled troops, whose own hooded faces tracked in unison to follow it.

'*Tracuna macoides,*' croaked the disintegrating voice of Crowley, '*trecorum satus dei!*'

The troopers lurched and contorted, the pop and snap of cracking bone and tearing flesh slightly muffled by their body armour – a mitigation that was utterly counteracted by the fact of their number. Their bodies twisted and transformed, becoming hulking and monstrous as their organs and musculature shifted and reconnected in new, inhuman ways. Several knotted hoods split open under the strain – and Haasterman, seeing the slippery and convoluted forms within, the Marks that branded them, gave an involuntary yelp of fear.

Crowley's head turned to regard him. So did the permutating faces of the transmogrifying troops.

'Ah yes,' said the voice of Crowley. 'We'd forgotten about you, for the moment, Colonel.' A chuckle issued from the ruined throat, conveying that this would have been the best thing Haasterman could have hoped for.

Sweat was springing up on Haasterman's brow; he could feel the sting and the salinity of it. He swallowed with a dry, clicking sensation that felt like somebody had driven a jagged shard of ice into his sternum. He found himself noting, in a detached kind of way, that these were almost the precise physical sensations he had felt during combat, years back in the war, and knew that he had gone insane with fear, frightened out of his mind.

He forced himself to face the transfigured Crowley. 'Stop this now,' he said, while yet another part of his mind wondered how he could have possibly said something so inappropriately banal. 'As your commanding officer, I'm *ordering* you to...'

'Oh, it pleased Us to make use of you,' said the voice of Crowley. 'It amused Us to allow you the semblance of control, but you could never Bind and Command such as Us. And now, We feel – do We? Yes, We do – that your usefulness to Us is at an end. Never fear, though, Colonel, you won't go to waste.' Crowley's hand gestured to take in the monstrous ex-troops who were now furtively edging towards Haasterman and snuffling. 'The procedure of conversion uses quite a large amount of energy,' Crowley's voice said. 'Our minions are hungry.'

While the minions ate Haasterman and fought over the scraps, Crowley's body turned its attention to the wall through which the Doctor had made his escape. The lights from his eyes increased in their intensity. There was a sourceless scream, part organic, part mechanical and part a state of being literally inconceivable to the human mind, and the wall split open, charred and smoking at the edges.

The minions halted in their mastication. The body of Crowley walked to the opening and bent, a little stiffly, to pick up a brightly coloured scrap of knitted cloth. It seemed to twitch a little in his hands, as though imbued with some measure of a fading life of its own. He waved the scrap at the minions, who turned their faces to it and sniffed the air.

'You have the scent?' said the voice of Crowley, now deteriorated into a clotted, only barely intelligible rattle. 'Then *go.*'

Chapter Twenty-Three
Everybody Comes Together

The Whappaho Beach Weekly High School Glee Club Wiener Roast was, by this point, well underway. A number of dorks in trunks and stripy vests were doing some strange variation of the Twist with a collection of girls with bulletproof bouffants and the extensively covering sort of bikinis that would drive any man wild with carnal desire had he the can-opener, or quite possibly the hydraulic jackhammer, necessary to get through them.

On the boardwalk a bespectacled rock-'n'-roll band was playing electric guitars without any amplification leads or, indeed, strings and doing a prancingly choreographed dance that had all the sophisticated sex appeal of Freddie and the Dreamers appearing on an episode of Blue Peter, *without the sophistication or, indeed, the sex appeal.*

Off to one side of this happy group, Dirk Brugman held in a stomach temporarily bereft of corsetry and spoke sternly to his girl, Lana Wilburry, who was wearing the half-inch décolletaged black one-piece and lipstick that denoted a nasty piece of work who didn't appreciate what she'd got.

'Juliette saw you around town,' Dirk gritted, patently trying to be reasonable and control his perfectly justifiable anger. 'Riding around with Ratso Doodie and his gang of roughnecks. You'll be getting yourself a reputation if you're not careful, Lana.'

'And what's it to you?' Ms Wilburry snapped spitefully. 'You're far too busy doing your *science in* your *laboratory. Trying to feed the world's hungry nations with your so-called cheese generator. Hah! You and Juliette...' she made*

*the name sound remarkably similar to 'conniving bitch'...
'are well suited to each other! And now, I think I want to go
for a swim.'*

*She stalked off into the water, barely shuddering as it froze
her lower extremities slightly blue. And beneath the surface,
on a completely different grade of film stock, something
stirred...*

The Doctor had once told Victoria, during a trip to Earth's
twentieth century, that if the contiguous population of five
billion souls, give or take, could have stood together in one mass
they would barely cover an island the size of the Isle of Wight.
Victoria hadn't quite believed him at the time but now, looking
at the bodies as they piled into the Drive-o-Rama – those who'd
had vehicles having by now left them behind – she could see
how such a thing might be possible. She looked at the sea of
bodies and faces, welling ever closer, and knew that she,
together with Jamie and the Doctor, would soon be engulfed.

The people made no sound as they moved – at least, they
made no verbal sound. Their accumulative breathing, the
susurration of it, however, was all but deafening. And still they
moved forward, with unified precision. The mass of bodies
rippled slightly as individual components walked across some
imperfection in the underlying ground, but there was no other
variation to its inexorable pace...

And then the mass, quite suddenly, stopped.

A minuscule piece of it broke away, and walked towards her.
Victoria recognised it as Dr Dibley the Mercy Hill surgeon, all
jocularity gone from him, his face as slack and inanimate as all
the others. He was carrying a big black medical bag.

Dr Dibley halted before the little group of captives and their
guards. His head tracked around slowly, eyes taking in Victoria
to one side, Jamie to the other, finally coming to rest upon the
unconscious Doctor.

'The subjects are not One with Continuity,' his mouth said, in lifeless and unanimated tones. 'They must be Converted so that Continuity shall be properly achieved, in this World and the next.'

As he spoke there had been a change in the motions of the mass behind him, a sense of something passing through it and intermixing with it, like swirls of cream stirred into a cup of coffee. The crowd pressed even closer to itself, if such a thing were possible, gathered itself into itself and began as a whole to *congeal*.

It began to grow in height.

It happened extraordinarily quickly, individual people climbing on their fellows' shoulders and being themselves overrun, in turn, by new people. It was like watching some massive human pyramid take shape in a circus big top… a pyramid so huge that those at the base, men, women and children alike, must surely be crushed by its weight.

As the mass consolidated itself, however, Victoria saw that a glowing was issuing from it, brightening by increments until it rivalled the light from the flickering cinematograph screen on which a young lady was currently being pulled under the water by some hulking form of sea creature. The people themselves, from what Victoria could see of them, seemed more-or-less physically unharmed. Were they being protected in some fashion by the glowing energies that surrounded them? Were they aware now, or would they be aware if they were ever disassembled again, of what was and had been happening to them? It was a horrible thought to consider, either way.

Now the mass heaved and transformed itself, the various human pieces slipping over each other and contorting, reforming the whole into a massive, lumpen and vaguely humanoid shape.

A human shape several hundred feet high.

It turned, slow as the beginnings of a mountain rockslide, and then lumbered off some way into the distance. The ground – the entire world – shook to its footfalls. There was the splintering crunch and crash of crushed and falling trees.

Long before its glowing form could even begin to be lost in the darkness, it stopped, and bent itself down. It picked something up. And then it turned back, once again, and ponderously returned to the open space of the Drive-o-Rama.

Clutched in a massive and rudimentary-looking hand, reminiscent of a child's mitten if the child happened to suffer from giganticism, was the tiny-seeming form of the TARDIS.

'The gateway to worlds other than this,' said the thing that was controlling Dr Dibley. There was, remarkably enough, emotion in its tone. Not so much gloating or triumphant, more a sense of expectation. 'New worlds for Continuity.' It seemed slightly plaintive – as though the thing controlling Dibley was, rather pathetically, anticipating all the new things it would be able to kill and eat.

Dibley's head turned to one of the policeman guards. There was no sense of communication, verbal or otherwise, but the policeman stepped forward and, without preamble, Dibley pulled a scalpel from the big black medical bag and slashed it across the man's throat. Victoria stared, aghast.

The dead policeman fell to the ground, to his knees and then his face, calmly and with no fuss whatsoever. The blood-sprayed Dibley, equally without concern, knelt down and whittled at the nape of the body's neck with his blade. Using a pair of forceps from his bag, he extracted an item from the hole he had made in the back of the policeman's head. It was an egg-sized lump of what Victoria recognised from her travels as electronic circuitry, though she couldn't begin to guess what purpose such an implantational device might possibly serve.

'The link shall be made,' the thing controlling Dibley said, walking to where the unconscious Doctor was held between two guards, and standing behind him. 'The primary subject shall be subsumed within Continuity. It will open the gateway, for Continuity. Continuity will expand.'

Victoria tried to scream to Dibley, to the thing inside him, that it wouldn't work, that the Doctor had already tried and failed to access the TARDIS since they had come here, but it was too late. The scalpel was already plunging for the back of the Doctor's neck.

Chapter Twenty-Four

The Arrangement and Expeditious Disposal of Artefacts

As they turned left at the kitchens and ran through the swimming-pool chamber, leaving the protective influence of the console room behind, the Doctor became aware that certain things were very wrong indeed. This was partly due to his rarefied senses as a Time Lord, and partly due to the basic precognitionary senses available even to humans, which are in actual fact a simple integration, on the deep-subconscious level, of minute nuances of data of which the conscious mind is unaware... but mostly it was due to the fact that the walls were turning themselves inside out at random and the pool was filled with marmosets and purple custard.

'Either the world is going increasingly strange,' he said, 'or I'm going mad.' He thought about it seriously. 'No,' he decided at last, 'I think it's the world.'

He realised that he was talking to thin air – or rather, air that at that moment chose to manifest a shoal of insubstantial lantern fish going by. They popped like soap bubbles when he put his hand through them. The Doctor hoped it hadn't hurt.

Romana was some way ahead, along a corridor that suddenly, despite all probability and visual taste, was walled with variously jarring varieties of tartan. The human woman, Katharine Delbane, was with her, held by an elbow to stop her wandering dazedly off, but there was no – the Doctor looked around – no sign of the Brigadier or the two young men. It was a disquieting sensation, feeling the spaces which had been his home for centuries change around him, without him having anything to do with it – and since the companion who had shared those spaces was at least in sight, he hurried to catch her up.

'You wouldn't have any idea what's happening, Romana, would you?' he said, trying for a tone that would convey he knew perfectly well what was happening and was merely testing her to see if she did, too.

Romana, still moving at a run and by now basically dragging the dead weight of Delbane, turned her head to regard him sardonically.

'I might do,' she said, perfectly calmly, as though her exertions were no more than a gentle stroll. 'Why don't you tell me, so I know I've got it right?'

'No, no, you go first,' said the Doctor, managing to bow with gracious courtesy while in the midst of a full-tilt run. 'Feel free.'

'Well, if you're sure,' said Romana.

'Positively,' said the Doctor.

Martial-sounding music suddenly blared from nowhere and a brigade of ghostly Royal Fusiliers, circa the Napoleonic Wars, trooped in through one corridor wall and out through the other.

'I received another visit from Wblk the High Councilman,' Romana said as they waited for the fusiliers to pass by.

'And did Councilman Wblk have anything interesting to say?' asked the Doctor.

'To some degree, yes. It appears that the anomaly everyone was so worried about, the one created by the Gallifreyan prototype, was actually destabilised by *another* space/time conveyance materialising inside it. A particularly decrepit and ineptly repaired TARDIS, for example, with half its safety protocols disabled or not there at all. Sound familiar?'

'I never did!' said the Doctor indignantly. 'I've never been in a discontinuous singularity in my life. Not one I can't account for, in any case.'

'Well, there's no reason why there should be any overt indication of the singularity's true nature,' said Romana, 'within the singularity itself. Or possibly some future version of yourself is involved. Or you might have just forgotten.'

'There is that, I suppose,' the Time Lord conceded. 'The problem with the occasional forced regeneration is that it leaves you with little time to pick and choose. You sometimes forget to take things along. I've always regretted losing the knack for making soufflés for example; flat as a pancake, they go now...'

'Culinary digressions aside,' said Romana, a little pointedly, 'the fact remains that some version or other of the TARDIS is currently trapped in there and disrupting things catastrophically, with no way into it or out... by conventional means. The only way to access it would be to take another version from some different point on its time line and –'

The Doctor looked at her, aghast. 'You didn't.'

Romana shrugged, and gestured to where one of the corridor walls had spontaneously produced a banjo and was playing 'Swannee River'.

'But that's breaking...'

The Doctor paused and totted on his fingers, '... fifteen thousand, four hundred and seventy-three Laws of Space and Time, not counting codicils.'

'The High Council gave me special dispensation,' said Romana. 'In this case. The idea is that it will create a nexus point, a point of convergence where we can pass from one point on the internal time line to another...'

'But materialising the TARDIS in a space containing itself,' said the Doctor, 'even a discontinuous space, is incredibly dangerous.'

He scowled as the floor turned momentarily into rats' milk cheese. 'If we're not very careful, we could be sucked out of reality like bathwater down a plug hole and end up disappearing up our own interstitial noumena.'

'All the more reason to find the nexus point soon,' said Romana. She looked critically at the barely conscious Delbane. 'I think we'd make better time if we left the girl.'

'Very possibly,' said the Doctor, firmly, 'but we're not going to. We do *not* leave innocent people in danger – especially, so it appears, danger we've contrived to create for ourselves.' He became grave. 'And speaking of innocents in danger – I do hope the Brigadier's doing all right. I hope we haven't finally managed to do for the old chap.'

'This isn't real,' said Danny Slater. 'It's just a dream. It isn't really happening.' It was, if anyone had been counting, the 127th time he'd said it, with minor variations. 'It's not real,' he said for the 128th time as a hydra-like monster appeared, the eyes on its many heads clustered like rings of frog spawn around circular and needle-toothed mouths. 'It's just a dream. It isn't really happening...'

The monster lunged for him but fortunately melted away into plates of manticore sandwiches with little toothpick flags stuck into them before vanishing completely.

Jim McCrae might have thought that his friend had finally and completely lost his mind – had his own mind not been almost entirely focused on his own sense of gut-clenching terror. It seemed to be thinking lucidly, strangely enough; it was just that it couldn't seem to think *about* anything other than the devastating changes in his life.

A leisurely afternoon of surveillance, possibly broken by a two-hour pub lunch on expenses, had turned into one in which he was drugged and abducted by international terrorists and taken to their secret base (his neurasthenically confused mind had thrown up emotional-level interpretations from old spy movies and TV that seemed to fit the observed facts – consoles, hooded troops and hi-tech wall screens) from which he had been plunged into this terrifying hallucinatory hell. It was probably due to some villainous terrorist mind ray or something.

A logical remnant of his mind pointed out that this was probably not a true reading of events. Assassins with three nipples, bowler-hatted henchmen, sexy female double agents with double-barrelled, single-entendre names and such don't exist in real life, so at best this was just the real-life equivalent of such things.

Unfortunately, as that rational piece of his mind insisted on pointing out, one James Angus McCrae was going to have to deal with this using the real-life equivalent of a laser-firing watch and a pocket full of miniature grenades – that is, a market knock-off watch that had the stealth capability of looking a bit like a Rolex, and a pocket containing a crumpled fiver borrowed from petty cash and a handful of loose change.

Dark shapes were coming down the corridor, hard and distinct against the whiteness that seemed to be the default state between transitions. They seemed more substantial, more real and actual, than the other hallucinations. This was not exactly a comfort. McCrae yelped, and tried to push himself back against the corridor wall, which pushed back in lots of complexly shifting little ways.

Later, McCrae was rather proud of the fact that he had unthinkingly grabbed Slater, who was obliviously still saying how this wasn't real and was a dream, and hauled him out of the way of the approaching creatures. It didn't do any good though; the misshapen forms were bearing down on them, unstoppable and snarling, their eyes alight with a hellish glow that McCrae's stern but not particularly lurid Presbyterian childhood upbringing couldn't touch. The way they held themselves and moved, triggered responses that were wired into the human brain when we all lived in the Kalahari, sharing it with carnivores: these were hungry monsters and they were going to pull him down and eat him up…

They passed Slater and McCrae without so much as a sniff. McCrae noticed the rags of combat uniforms still on them.

For a while he leant back against the squirming wall, hardly daring even to breathe – the movie-going portion of his emotions knew precisely what happens to people just as they're heaving that final, as it were, sigh of relief. The shifting, insubstantial visions of the corridor, though, were now something of a relief by comparison. At least, so far, they hadn't actually hurt –

Something else came for him. This time, McCrae screwed his eyes shut and actually screamed.

'Pull yourself together, man!' a voice thundered. 'Carrying on like this, you'll be no use at all!'

McCrae opened his eyes and looked at the man standing in front of him. Vaguely, out of the confusion of recent events, he recognised him as Lethbridge-Stewart, the Brigadier.

'It's not real,' Slater was saying off to one side. 'This isn't happening. It's just a –'

'And you can stop that as well,' the Brigadier snapped. Slater shut his mouth so quickly that the click of his teeth slamming together, and possibly chipping with the force, was plainly audible. It was as if he had been waiting all this time for somebody to simply tell him to stop.

The Brigadier turned his steely gaze back to McCrae. 'You. Name, rank and number.'

It occurred to Jim McCrae that he didn't have an actual *rank* in any recognised sense, his role being defined by duties that were basically those of a general dogsbody, and no serial number save his national insurance number, which in the present trying circumstances he couldn't for the life of him recall.

He attempted to explain this, stammering out something about the function of the Provisional Department, but the Brigadier cut him short.

'It seems that "provisional" is entirely the right description,' he said brusquely. 'Oh well. You'll just have to do.'

The Brigadier gestured down the corridor in the direction the monstrous creatures had gone. 'Thoroughly bad sorts, but I've seen worse. I've no doubt the Doctor can handle them.' He tapped his moustache with a thoughtful finger, obviously considering his line of attack. 'I think our best bet for the moment is to secure the immediate area, see if we can't find a way of calling in reinforcements. Come with me. Well, what are you waiting for? You've been given an order by a superior officer, which by my reckoning, from the shape of you, means any officer at *all*.'

The spaces of the TARDIS formed and reformed as the Doctor and Romana, with an all-but-insensate Katharine Delbane in tow, ran through them. Its internal geography seemed to have undergone some fundamental and basically chaotic shift, so that familiar and entirely prosaic environments like the cloister room, the linking chamber to the eye of harmony, any number of storage compartments, the jungle room, the observatory, the chess hall, bestiary, shoe cupboard and skin museum appeared more or less at random and quite unexpectedly. The other spaces and apparitions were decidedly more strange. They kept up a good pace but were forced to backtrack occasionally and hunt around, following inhuman senses that merely told them they were getting closer to or further away from some region of *wrongness* – wrong in a particular and distinct way – in the TARDIS spaces, as if they were playing an abstract game of 'hot and cold'.

To human eyes, the nexus point of which Romana had spoken would hardly have seemed to be worth the trip. They finally reached a largish, vaulted hall littered with broken fluted-marble columns and items of vaguely Athenian-looking architecture; such ideo- and pictograms as were incised upon them, however, hailed from the non-human minds and hands of ancient Mu.

So far as the visible spectrum of human terms was concerned, it was nothing more remarkable than a hall scattered with oddly chiselled masonry.

'Oh my goodness,' said the Doctor, trying and failing to prevent his body shaking. 'Can't you feel the sheer *power* of the thing?'

'I can feel it,' Romana said. She attempted to inject her voice with a degree of aspersion suitable for answering a patently obvious question – but, rather like the Doctor trying to control his shaking, she failed. The enormity of the thing overwhelmed those senses that could so much as notice it in the first place. This wasn't some mere nexal conduit. This was a Nexus, in the capitalised and archetypical sense – a maelstrom of Universal impact and collision that made the Vortex itself look like the slow seeping of greasy washing-up water from a partially bunged-up sink.

Delbane chose that moment to look up dreamily. 'It's peaceful here,' she said in the disconnected and perfectly calm tones of the lobotomised. 'I like it.'

Then her head lolled again. She stood there, unconscious but upright, held by perfect neuromuscular stillness.

The Doctor and Romana barely paid heed to her, staring as they were into a burning heart of chaos that only they were equipped to see.

'Do we dare?' breathed Romana. 'If we were to step inside, could we possibly survive?'

'Quite possibly not,' said the Doctor cheerfully – although his cheerfulness seemed, at this point, to be not a little forced. 'On the other hand, we'll never know unless we –'

'*Not so fast, Time Lord,*' said a voice behind them. The mouth and vocal cords with which it spoke might have been human, but the sound it made was definitely not. The Doctor and Romana turned to find the monstrous minions spilling through the doorway of the chamber, and behind them, feet floating three inches off the ground, the body of Crowley.

'Do you know,' the Doctor said scornfully, 'if I had a penny for every time some power-maddened villain used those exact same words to me, I'd have... ah, four pounds, seven shillings and fourpence. Do they give you a little booklet with the job or something?' He looked inside the floating figure with his Gallifreyan senses, and didn't like what he saw. The poor chaps Crowley had turned into his minions were the sort of thing he encountered every day of the week, and no problem at that, but the man himself was different. Very different. 'What is it that you want, Mr Crowley?'

'I am not,' the man himself spat, with a disdainful sense of dramatic revelation, 'your "Mr Crowley". I never was your "Mr Crowley"...'

'Oh, I know *that*,' said the Doctor. 'I've known *that* since I said I'd never met the real Edward Alexander Crowley and you agreed with me. I knew the real Crowley for years,' he said in an aside to Romana, who for her part wouldn't know an Edward Alexander Crowley from a Joe Soap. 'Lovely chap, if dreadfully misinterpreted, and a bit too fond of the old laudanum...'

'A puny human fool...' said the body of the man who had hitherto been known as Crowley. He seemed a little put out and deflated that his Final Revelation had been so casually trumped.

'And the fools just keep on coming,' said the Doctor. 'Don't they? I suspected as much from the instant I met you – that patina of suavity was rather too deliberate to be anything other than contrived. I could see from the start that you had no – in every generally accepted sense of the term – bottom. Different biological processes, you see,' he again explained to Romana. 'I think our man here is what is known as a *homunculus* – a rather more advanced form of golem technology, built from organic materials and animated by a demon.'

'That's hardly a scientific description,' said Romana, dubiously.

'Well, call it a quantum-based dynamically self-referential pattern matrix if it makes you happier,' said the Doctor, 'or an Energy Being, or an automemic Entity – what ancient Earth cultures *thought* of as a demon. An Entity who inhabits the homunculus is more-or-less analogous to an AI operating system...'

'Excuse *me*...' the Entitic AI operating system currently operating the body of Crowley appeared to be getting slightly irate at being ignored. One of the minions took an exploratory swipe at the Doctor, who stepped smartly aside so that the minion missed, misjudged the follow-through and ended up injuring its degenerating body quite nastily.

'I beg your pardon,' said the Doctor, brightly. 'So what... - race or species is inappropriate, I gather - so what *variety* of demon are you? The Azrae? The Raagnarokath? The Jarakabeth...?'

'Our name is of no matter,' growled the body of Crowley.

'Ah, so it's the Jarakabeth.' The Doctor turned to Romana once again. 'They don't like their name being spoken, the Jarakabeth.'

Romana nodded intelligently. 'It gives one power over them or some such?'

'No, it just embarrasses them. It's one of those demon names with unfortunate connotations, rather like the English name of Crapper. I beg your pardon again.' This to the demon Crowley, who was by this point looking fit to burst, and who knew what might burst out of him. 'Please, do continue.'

'The man Crowley summoned me,' the demon continued, glowering murderously from his burning eyes. 'Set me to work. I allowed him to think that the feeble bindings he had placed upon me were sufficient. I toiled for him, and when the time came for him to use the shell of my body in the subterfuge of counterfeiting his death, I at last revealed myself in my true Aspect. I subsumed him.'

The demon smiled. 'A flesh and bone container is the same as wood and fungus to me...'

'And you've been passing yourself off as him ever since,' the Doctor finished expeditiously. 'To what end? You haven't exactly achieved Dominion over the Kingdoms of the World and ground them to dust beneath your heels, have you? Skies black with the bodies of the burning dead are slightly noticeable by their absence.'

'That will come,' the demon Crowley said.

'You're a bit inept, in my opinion,' said the Doctor. 'All this time and you haven't even managed to open a proper gateway into the dimensions of Hell. I mean, look what happened to it when even a couple of TARDISes hit it.'

'That too will come.' The demon smiled nastily. 'The Golgotha processes were plunged into disarray by your race's machines, Time Lord, shutting me off from the artefact that was my source of power... but now I shall retrieve it. I will simply step through this *new* portal your Time Lady here has created, and which you seem to be so pointedly ignoring.'

'Oh,' said the Doctor. 'Ah. Do you know, I was rather hoping you couldn't actually *see* that.'

'The eyes, such as they remain, might be functionally human, Doctor,' said the demon. 'I, on the other hand, such as I remain, am not. Soon, now, I shall tear the curtain between the dimensions open wide and engulf your very universe in primal Chaos...'

'And then what?' asked the Doctor.

'What?' said the demon Crowley, a little taken aback by the abruptness of the question.

'Well, if I understand correctly,' said the Doctor. 'you've gone through all these machinations to arrange things so you can open the door to Chaos, utterly obliterating any sense of Order in the universe for all of time. Or not, as it happens, Time being a function of Order. So what, precisely, do you intend to do with the universe then?'

'I shall impose my Will upon it,' said the demon Crowley, firmly. 'I shall take the stuff of Chaos and order it to my liking and desire...'

'No you won't,' said the Doctor, patiently, 'because you won't be there to do it. This is *primal* Chaos we're talking about, yes? No self-referential construct, no sense of identity, even such as yours, can survive in it.'

'I am its master,' the demon said, a note of uncertainty just on the edge of preternatural Time Lord hearing entering its voice. 'It is mine to unleash...'

'That's like saying a gallows won't snap your neck just because you happen to be pulling the lever yourself.' The Doctor snorted. 'Do you know, I really wish that just *once* some megalomaniacal villain bent on destroying the known universe would actually sit down and think it through. It's one thing to be a suicidal paranoiac wanting to switch the whole world off, but if you want to be suicidal you can just kill yourself and let everyone else alone...'

'Silence!' snarled the demon Crowley.

'Twenty-seven pounds, fifteen shillings and tuppence,' said the Doctor to Romana out of the corner of his mouth.

'Oh you'll regret your insolence, Time Lord,' growled the demon, and the glow in his eyes flared bright enough to blind any human eye looking directly at it. Around him, the minions staggered, their twisted flesh withering and flaking as though a process of post-mortem decomposition had been accelerated by time-lapse photography. Both Time Lord and Lady sensed the biologically generated energies as they were sucked from the minions into Crowley's body, building up a charge that made evolutionary back-brain hackles rise in each of them.

The body of Crowley seemed to expand, vulpine, avine, insectoid and reptilian features sliding across his face as though something inside were hunting for a more appropriate form, throwing new forms up at random and then discarding them. The effect was all the more horrifying because of the constancy of the physical expression of pure evil that underlay each abortive transformation.

'I was going to keep you alive,' the mouth of Crowley said, through splintering and shifting teeth. By now, the actual sounds it made were utterly senseless. The thing inside was speaking directly with what passed for its mind. 'I was going to show you the heart of darkness, the screaming and unending night. Now, I think, I just don't want you to be alive.'

Transcendental energies arced from Crowley's body to the Doctor and Romana, blasting them off their feet and making their bodies jerk as though with Saint Vitus's dance. As they lay, stunned, they realised as one that *this* had merely been the sucker-punch, intended to stun them before the major offensive. As one – before they could raise their mental guards – they felt insubstantial tendrils plunging into them. The feeling was not the equivalent of some galvanistical shock, but more akin to the complete opposite.

The interplay of bioneural, kinetic and calorific energies contained within a living individual is, in actual fact, far more complex than a basically meaningless term like 'life force' implies. Be that as it may, it was just that interplay of energies that the Doctor and Romana felt streaming from them, sucked into the body of Crowley for the entity inside it to gorge upon.

'Must... must resist...' the Doctor uttered through gritted teeth, some fading part of his higher intelligence wondering just what it was about situations like these that had absolutely everybody saying things like that. Then that particular part of his higher intelligence shut down. He looked at Romana. She was moaning and her skin was turning dull and thin as energies inside her died...

'*No!*'

The exclamation was so loud and unexpected that everything seemed to pause in momentary, confused silence. For an instant, neither the intangibly attacking nor the attacked could work out quite where it had come from.

The first clue was when the withering minions, every single one, imploded with a smack and a spray of dust, biological energies wrenched from them in one catastrophic discharge, like static electricity earthing through a Marks & Spencer's coat rack.

The second clue was the sense that these energies had not been released by the creature in the body of Crowley who had appeared, after all, to be using the minions as though they were a collection of dry-cell batteries.

The third and final clue was when, from her slumped position off to one side of the chamber, where she had been left and subsequently forgotten about, the body of Katharine Delbane climbed to its feet and then rose higher, floating on a level with that of Crowley, its eyes burning with an entirely similar light.

'*Ramo tath nor gir,*' the mouth of Delbane said. '*Ta lekme Rakthamak di salo man te solo ma!*'

The force of the incorporeal blow knocked the corporeal body of Crowley backwards, tumbling through the air. Both the Doctor and Romana felt the ghostly tendrils linking them to the thing inside Crowley's body whip away from them, leaving deep gouges that had no relation to physicality.

The thing inside Crowley appeared to recover a little; the body righted itself, and the head turned to grin at the advancing body of Delbane through ruined teeth.

'*Little Katharine...*' it said in the voice that issued from its mind. '*Why, I had no idea.*'

'*And that will be your undoing,*' said the voice of Katharine Delbane, or rather the Voice that issued from her. '*It seems that you are as short-sighted as you ever were. You fail to see things even when they are placed before you. Anok ra di samonan ma Kadethed on sami danonat!*'

Again, the body of Crowley rocked backwards in the air, but the creature inside had been anticipating this and rode the blast. Alien energies hummed around the demon, their cycle accelerating as it gathered its forces to retaliate.

'I will try to keep him here,' Delbane said to the Doctor and Romana as they staggered unsteadily to their feet, the thing inside her taking control of her mouth and allowing it to make actual sounds. 'You have a job to do, I think. Go and do it.'

'*Salaki na meh Tononak ti ramen keti lamo dam...*' the thing inside Crowley was saying. Visible energy now crawled around him like a collection of coiling snakes.

'Well, if you're quite certain we can't be of any help...' the Doctor began, caught between the abstract idea of saving the entire universe once again, and the rather more concrete considerations of the battle happening right in front of him.

'Your concerns are elsewhere, now, Doctor,' the thing inside Delbane said, in tones containing an element familiar to absolutely anybody in the as-yet-undestroyed universe, who is about some involved and stressful task and doesn't need well-meaning fools blundering in and trying to help. 'Go and attend to your concerns. I will deal with [uninterpretable name] here.'

'My word,' said the Doctor, unable despite himself to resist commenting upon the sound the 'name' made when filtered through human speech: like an explosive choking drawn out over several seconds. 'It's like the way a cough in a room drowns out every word being said for an instant – the vocal cords producing every sound of which they're capable simultaneously...'

A new sound now came from Delbane, which might be best characterised as the building up of utter blinding rage – and Romana, for one, didn't need anyone to draw her a pictogram to tell her at whom this rage would be directed.

She took the Doctor's arm. 'I think we'd better do what she says. This does seem to be more her sort of thing, and there's nothing we can do to help her in any case.'

'Well, if you really think so...' said the Doctor.

'I do,' said Romana. 'Trust me on this.'

As the battle between arcane forces set to escalate around them, the Doctor and Romana ran to what to a human would be a completely unremarkable and empty patch of thin air, and disappeared into it.

Chapter Twenty-Five
Everything is Happening at Once

In the Lychburg Drive-o-Rama, in the shadow of the massive humanoid creature built from men, women and children, the thing controlling the body of Dr Dibley plunged the scalpel into the back of the Doctor's neck – which suddenly wasn't there any more. Possibly due to the lack of basic human reflexes remaining in Dibley's body, or possibly because the thing controlling it had other things on Its mind to deal with, the body of Dibley lost its balance and fell forward skewering its face, possibly through one of its eyes, on the scalpel still clutched in its hand. From this position there was little to see of a gory or repugnant nature, but the body spasmed and jerked as it expired, the physical shock of its damaged brain shutting down its heart.

The Doctor had come back to life as if he had never been unconscious, shrugged himself easily out of the grip of his captors and avoided the blade that was plunging towards him. Now he looked down at the dead body of Dibley with alarm. 'I, ah, didn't mean for that to happen. Are you all right?'

He bent down to prod ineffectually at the body as though not quite believing that it could go from one state to the other quite so quickly, rather as a man might keep on chatting to some acquaintance for a few moments after the acquaintance had suddenly and unexpectedly died.

'Doctor!' Victoria shouted. Her original reason for the exclamation had been to point out that, while it was all very unfortunate and sad that somebody who had been just about to hack at the little man's neck had dropped down dead, there were several other guards around, two with hands upon herself and Jamie, who might have something less than friendly to say about it... but as she shouted she became aware that the manner of the guards had changed. One of the policemen, who had previously just stood there implacably with her arm in an iron grip, had now let go and was stumbling about clutching its head as if, had there been some sense of human thought inside it, it thought its head might burst. The other guards were behaving in a similar fashion: lurching and stumbling as though in agony, banging their heads on the ground. A thin, keening sound was coming from each of them, as though something inside were trying to scream without quite knowing how to do it.

Victoria ran over to the Doctor, who was still looking down at the body of Dibley with dismay. 'What happened to you?' she said.'I thought you were dead to the world.'

'Oh, I thought it might be an idea to feign unconsciousness,' said the Doctor, vaguely.'I can do that a bit more extensively than most people. The idea was to keep our adversary from picking up my thoughts so that I could catch it unawares when I finally made my move, that sort of thing. Bit of an obvious subterfuge, of course, but I think our chap is getting more and more, well, unintelligent as its world slowly disintegrates around it...'

'Well I don't know about our man getting unintelligent,' said Jamie in a worried voice, drawing their attention back to the massive shape that towered over them,'but I don't think he really needs to be *clever* at the moment.'

The humanoid form was thrashing its limbs, though whether with pain or rage it was impossible to say. It began to *roar*, its human components howling and screaming in unison. In a parody of human demeanour, it turned its massive head to regard the TARDIS that it was holding, and shook the TARDIS angrily. Then it started to pound it against the ground, like an ape trying to break a particularly stubborn coconut.

Victoria tried to ask the Doctor what they could do but however hard she shouted, the multiple roar from the monstrous figure, which seemed to include every possible sound the human voice could make together with any number of entirely inhuman harmonics, drowned out her voice, even to herself.

The Doctor said something, realised that he couldn't be heard, pointed to the monster and then shook his head frantically, waving his hands in a way that seemed to convey that 200-foot-tall giants who happened to be hammering the TARDIS into the ground weren't important. When Victoria stared at him, trying to work out if this was what he really meant, he shrugged, turned to point dramatically at the screen on which the film of the Hell Planet Beyond Time was still playing, and set off for it at a bustling run, not so much as bothering to glance behind him to see if she, Jamie or anybody else was following.

Victoria looked at Jamie, who appeared as puzzled as she was, in the variegated light from the screen on one side and the monster on the other. He shrugged, as had the Doctor, but with the sense of exasperated resignation with which they had both become remarkably familiar at certain times during their travels. Then they both set off after the rapidly diminishing Doctorial form, hurrying to catch him up.

* * *

The Doctor and Romana spilled out of an imponderable hole and landed with a double and not entirely dignified thump on the console room floor.

'I do *not* want to do that again,' Romana said, climbing to her feet and rubbing at her slightly bruised self-regard. 'That bit where the subdimensional soma-monsters lie in wait to suck the lymphatic juices of unwary travellers was particularly tedious – and quite what the *Sontarans* are doing mining the nether regions with soul-catcher bombs I have no idea...'

'Well, the chances are we're going to have to do it again,' said the Doctor cheerfully, as though their unfortunate fifteen-subjective-year diversion in transit, and battle with an entity that for some obscure reason had called itself the Solstice Squid, hadn't happened. 'At least once, at any rate.'

'Please don't remind me,' said Romana. She looked around the TARDIS interior disdainfully. 'This is how you used to have it? I hope so – because I'd hate to think you were intending to do this some time in your future.'

The Doctor looked around slightly more charitably. 'I seem to recognise the old girl. If it's the *me* I'm thinking of, I was far too busy playing my penny whistle to the delight of all around me to bother much with interior decorating.' He watched the external viewing screens until he was sure nothing interesting was going to emerge from the static, then turned to the console and fiddled with it for a while.

'Well, the first problem seems simple enough,' he said. 'The plasmic shell of the old girl is slightly out of phase with the state-vector of her surroundings, occluding her from them and trapping me outside.' He tapped at a keypad and flipped a couple of switches decisively. '*That's* sorted out, at least. All I had to do was reverse the polarity of the...'

The floor of the console room shook and then overturned completely, flinging both himself and Romana off their feet.

* * *

The Mind had never experienced such pain before. In all of Its existence It had never imagined that such agony could be possible. In all of Its killings It had taken both parts, infusing certain qualities of Itself into the murderer, others into the victim, carefully controlling each action and response in what was basically a kind of abstract dance.

None of that dynamic had been present in Its subsumation of the individual mind who referred to itself, when allowed, as Dibley. The Mind had felt the full force of

Dibley's death, and the force of it had driven the Mind all but mad. It might seem strange that the loss of what was, after all, such a minuscule part of Itself would provoke such a strong reaction... but it was the difference between gingerly testing a cup of hot coffee by sipping it, and having that same cup of coffee flung without warning in your face.

In any event, the Mind had been hurt, and hurt badly. In Its shock and pain, all It wanted to do was tear a hole in the World and crawl in and hide. The little blue box in Its Avatar's hand contained the gateway to Worlds within it, and now the Mind, all other plans forgotten, was in an utterly Mindless manner trying to smash it open on the ground.

* * *

As its energies flickered and cracked around it, the thing inside the body of Crowley made the remains of the face grin. *'Oh you're strong, little one, you're strong indeed – but you are younger than me, you have not had experience in the husbanding and direction of your Power. You* never *expend it all at once. You keep some in reserve for use when your enemy's resources are depleted...'*

'Oh yes?' The thing inside the body of Katharine Delbane felt its own power rebuilding, and rebuilding fast – but not quite fast enough. To show any weakness at this point, however, would be a mistake. *'Why don't you try it?'*

The wreck of Crowley's body looked thoughtful for a moment, if scraps of flesh adhering to a living skull can look thoughtful. *'Yes,'* the thing inside him said. *'Yes, I think I will...'*

It was some moments before the thing inside Delbane realised what was happening. It had steeled itself for another destructive blast, prepared with every iota of its being to force it away. It didn't realise it was pouring, actively *forcing*, its life energies into Crowley, who was quietly sucking them in, until it was too late.

'You see, little one?' said the thing inside him, as it sucked the creature inside her dry. *'Always keep something in reserve, and keep it in plain sight, but so that it comes from a direction your opponent has forgotten to expect.'*

* * *

'Avatar?' said Victoria. 'What's an Avatar?' This far from the monster, close to the screen, it was possible to speak and be heard.

'The simple embodiment of some vast and unknowable force,' said the Doctor. 'Not the force itself exactly, but what you might call its *representative* in the world, like the spokesman for some global manufacturing incorporation, or the way a pontiff was once thought to be the living embodiment of God.'

'If that's the *representative* of it,' Jamie said, looking back at the enraged humanoid form, 'then what the hell is the *real* thing like?'

'You're thinking in the wrong terms, Jamie,' said the Doctor. He gestured up at the cinematograph screen which was showing a slimy sea monster, with three eyes and a mouth that appeared to be stuffed with the contents of a tin of raw frankfurters, dragging a struggling girl into a cave containing the silver-painted plywood bulk of a flying saucer.

'Look at this,' he said. 'This is the *representation* of a strip of celluloid, thirty-five millimetres across and running through a shutter at twenty-four frames per second – or the representation of a group of people with hardly any money ineptly play-acting. It depends in which sense you look at it.' He gestured in the direction of the humanoid form, which was now trying a different tack and attempting to unscrew the top of the TARDIS as though it were a pickle jar. 'The size of something isn't the important thing – and that thing there isn't important. The ultimate truth is what matters and its source might be something quite different.'

'And just where,' Victoria said, 'are we supposed to find this ultimate truth?' Uncharacteristically, what with one thing and another, she was feeling distinctly ill-tempered. At some point this... this Avatar was going to realise that the people he had taken captive were missing, would attempt to do something about it, and the Doctor was just standing here and talking in riddles.

'Well, I have my thoughts on that,' the Doctor said. 'I was wrong when I said that the city was the centre of some monstrous killing-bottle, I think. Cause and effect, and the physical law that produces them, work slightly differently here. This is the centre of things and the city lies in every direction from it, while still being in the same place. Do you see what I mean?'

He saw from Victoria and Jamie's blank expressions that they did not. He gestured to the screen again. 'Tell me, do you see anything odd about this? Ah yes, I was forgetting that the cinematic arts are a bit beyond both your times. Let's just say that this thing works by way of light being projected *on to* a screen. Now, does anything strike you as odd?'

Victoria found herself piqued by the Doctor's rather hectoring tone. 'I've seen magic lantern shows,' she told him loftily, 'and they're almost the same. There's nothing here projecting the image from the front, so...'

The Doctor nodded and smiled. 'Precisely.'

* * *

The Brigadier gazed dubiously into the chamber. After a strange and, frankly, not a little harrowing, journey through the TARDIS interior, it looked strangely prosaic and in short, a little disappointing. Fractured marble columns and a floor covered with puddles of greasy ash. The only other things visible were the two figures.

The fact that they were floating, motionless, three feet off the ground seemed almost ordinary. One of them was a ragged horror, its flesh ripped and its viscera exposed in places, items of anatomy hanging by a twisted thread. For all that it was horribly mangled, this body seemed to broadcast a sense of, well… a sense of strength and vitality.

The other was different: the physically intact but horribly withered body of what had once, it seemed, been a woman in a regular army uniform. With a start, the Brigadier recognised it as Katharine Delbane.

Behind him, the Brigadier was aware that the two young men, Slater and McCrae, had taken the opportunity of this apparent lull in events to go limp and dazed again. Well, to hell with them, he thought. He had attempted to instil some backbone into them, to keep them going in the face of adversity, purely out of common decency. Leave 'em to their own devices. This place seemed, remarkably enough, relatively safe for human beings to be in… but the Brigadier had seen enough strangeness in his life to realise that there were other dangers here, other battles being fought, on levels with which human perceptions couldn't cope.

And they were battles, he could plainly see, that Delbane was losing. Delbane might have been in UNIT by secondment, and might – it now seemed – be other than human, or at least caught up in something that was other than human… but she was one of his own all the same. One of what he thought of as his 'men', in an old-school military sense. And so it was in the interests of helping one of his men that the Brigadier stepped forward and grabbed at the floating, mangled man.

What actually happened was this: the thing inside the body of Crowley was fighting the thing in Delbane on any number of power levels, but all of them, so far as human perceptions were concerned, were abstract. In the heat of battle it had entirely forgotten about the concrete, human level. So when the Brigadier so much as touched its barely held-together physical shell, it underwent collapse leaving its true self naked and exposed for an instant. And the thing inside Delbane took that opportunity to strike for all it was worth.

So far as the Brigadier was concerned, the mangled body simply fell rather messily apart, deliquescing and crumbling as it did so. Almost instantly, the body of Delbane was transformed, the flesh filling out and glowing with vitality. Then she fell three feet to the floor and landed in a groaning heap.

* * *

There were no defences, no walls or barriers or steps leading down into a mysterious chamber.

This was simply a place to which, by the basic nature of the world, the people living in that world would never go. It would simply never occur to them, and the circumstances that might have someone wandering in by accident would never happen. It would take a person, or people, not indigenous to that world to so much as intimate that this place could even possibly exist.

Behind the screen was a... monstrosity. That was the only way to describe it. It seemed to shift and melt in a constant state of flux, constantly transforming and reforming, in one sense smaller than a large wardrobe, in another and barely perceived sense inexpressibly massive.

Little details of it were recognisable – in the sense that one saw something and instantly saw what it *was* and what it did. One of those details was the mechanical projector, originally installed when the Lychburg Drive-o-Rama had been built. Its purpose was to back project cinematographic movies on to the drive-in screen every night, which it dutifully did and would dutifully continue to do for all time.

Other elements of the... thing were also recognisable, though not to human eyes or senses.

'It's a TARDIS!' exclaimed the Doctor incredulously. 'The remains of one, at least. At least, I *think* it's a TARDIS. There's something... well, there's something primitive about it, even in this damaged state. Something unfinished, almost as if...'

Abruptly, he stuck a pontificatory finger in the air as recollected inspiration struck him. 'I remember now! I never was much good at history at school, I'm afraid.' He turned to the dumbfounded Jamie and Victoria and, still walking backwards round the... thing while they followed him, began to explain with a rather incongruously earnest enthusiasm. 'When my, ah, people first invented time machines, they had to test them. So they sent out prototypes, you see, so they could see what would happen if –'

'Did they send out beasties in them?' asked Jamie suddenly.

'What?' The Doctor was momentarily nonplussed by the question. 'Why yes, Jamie, I believe that some of the tests were...'

'Like yon beastie over there?' asked Jamie, worriedly.

The Doctor turned.

They had by this time walked around the... thing to a point where they could see another side of it. A collection of cables ran from the twisted and partially melted remains of what looked as if it had originally been a TARDIS console. Squatting restlessly on the console, electrode leads running from it to its head, its claws – of which, as we shall see, it had a multitude – scrabbling at the console controls, was a creature. It was the build of a medium-sized dog, but rat-like in nature save that it had fifteen elongated, partially furred and multiply-jointed legs in an arrangement reminiscent of a spider. Its body was wasted and its fur was thinning and grey. It was obviously extremely elderly, but its eyes glowed with an insane and alien energy, an energy also evident in its mad and dancing scuttle over the console controls.

'As I live and breathe,' said the Doctor, 'that's a Gallifreyan woprat! I thought they were long extinct. This certainly is a...'

He got no further. Victoria, given the tenor of her original times, was not exactly a shrinking violet even in terms of that era. Time and again, on her travels with Jamie and the Doctor, in any number of perilous situations, she had found reserves of courage and fortitude that even *she* had not known she had. There were certain things, however, of which she had an innate and irrational fear. These included rats and spiders. Ordinarily, she would have been quite able to control her fear, but recent events had drained her emotional reserves to the point of debilitation – and besides, if one is innately and irrationally afraid of rats and spiders, how much worse must it be if one is suddenly confronted by some large and madly hideous miscegenative offspring of the two?

And so, not to put too fine a point upon it, she screamed.

The creature turned at the sound and glared at her with an utterly vicious and entirely crazed animal hatred. It rocked back on its multiple haunches then *sprang* at her, uncaring as the wires ripped from its head, its suddenly fang-like, extensible teeth snapping as they sought the throat of this interloper. Its eyes positively *flared* with a brilliant, bluish light that seemed to make something inside Victoria die and lie still, waiting for the creature's teeth and claws to tear into her, tear her to the innards and the bone...

Jamie's dirk thunked solidly into the side of the creature, knocking it out of the air. With a thump the creature hit the ground in front of the... thing it had controlled, kicked its fifteen legs up in the air and expired.

The Doctor looked at the dead creature, aghast. 'Jamie!' he exclaimed. 'Do you realise you've just killed what was quite possibly the last Gallifreyan woprat left in the universe?'

'Good riddance,' said Jamie, shortly. He walked over to the last remaining woprat in the universe, pulled out his dirk and wiped it.

It was at that point that a horrendous sound came from the... thing. A sound like gears clashing in an engine, the sound of sheering, twisting machinery that was bigger than the entire world. Lights stuttered and blazed on the remains of the console to which the creature had so recently been linked, and an oscillating wail began to issue from it.

'Oh dear...' The Doctor ran to the console and stared at the surviving controls and dials with a growing sense of alarm. 'I think we should get out of here,' he said with the quiet control of one who is only being quiet because he fears what he might sound like if that control were relaxed for so much as an instant. 'I have the feeling that our *real* problems have only just begun.'

* * *

The monstrous, composite creature on the other side of the Lychburg Drive-o-Rama screen had collapsed. Fortunately, a little of the binding alien energy that had held it together and protected its individual components from physical harm had remained. The various citizens of Lychburg, however, had lain in unconscious piles, suffering from profound shock and only a very few of them had even begun to stir.

When it began to collapse the Avatar had simply dropped the TARDIS which, in the way that TARDISes tend to do when dropped, had contrived to land safely without squashing anybody flat, and more or less the right way up.

After the death of the Avatar and the obvious malfunctioning of the... thing that it had controlled, every dramatic convention should have had the ground shaking under the Doctor and his companions and, quite possibly, the sky itself falling down around them. There had been nothing of that nature – but the Doctor's sudden sense of utter fear and trepidation had communicated itself to Victoria and Jamie. As they ran for their TARDIS, dodging the citizens who were falling from the monster and leaping over the fallen, the Doctor shepherding them urgently before him, Victoria had been *convinced* that the TARDIS would be in the same effective state as when they had left it: inaccessible, leaving them here with whatever cataclysm the Doctor seemed convinced was going to come.

As it transpired, though, the doors had opened and the only problem about getting inside was a minor log jam, as they all tried to get in at the same time in their haste.

'The breaking of the woprat's control must have opened up the dimensional occlusion that prevented us from getting inside,' mused the Doctor. He stopped and thought about it for a moment, and scowled. 'No. That *can't* be right. That would be complete and utter idiocy, distorted laws of space and time or not.' He scanned the readouts and controls. 'Somebody's been interfering with my console!' he exclaimed indignantly. 'Taking liberties! What a cheek! They've even reversed the polarity of the... oh. Oh my word.'

This last was in response to a display next to which a light was flashing urgently. Text was scrolling down it too fast for either Victoria or Jamie, who had been alerted by his tone and had come to look over his shoulder, to read – and in a language they could not have hoped to understand, even if it had been slower.

'What's wrong, Doctor?' Victoria asked, as the little man glared at the display intently, muttering to himself all the while.

'It seems that the woprat controller was the only thing keeping this little world together,' said the Doctor. 'A crucial element, at least, like the lowest level in a house of cards, or the straw that holds the balls up in a game of *Kerplunk*.'

'Kerplunk?' said Jamie and Victoria together.

'Never mind. The point is that in a matter of minutes – a quarter of an hour at the most – this world is going to collapse in on itself.' He gestured urgently to a wallscreen showing the waking and confused Lychburg citizens outside. 'And all these people are going to go with it.'

Victoria gazed at the screen, the enormity of the situation sinking in. 'There must be a million people out there!'

'Not at all,' said the Doctor. 'There's only two hundred and fifty thousand, four hundred and sixty-one, as it happens. I counted. Come on, you two, we have to do something.' He ran for the TARDIS doors, which opened for him as he drew close to them.

'Do something?' Victoria said, incredulously. 'How can we do something in a quarter of an hour?'

'Thirteen and a half minutes now,' said the Doctor, absently. Suddenly he turned, looked back at her and Jamie and gave them an evilly mischievous grin. 'Oh, you know,' he said airily. 'We'll sort something out. We almost always do.'

After the Doctor and his young companions had bustled out through the TARDIS door, the Doctor and Romana emerged from their hiding place under the console. They had been quietly shuffling around it in a complicated topological manner that allowed them to be on the opposite side to all three of the other people in the room at any time.

'The Avatar!' the Doctor exclaimed, slapping at his forehead with the heel of his hand. 'So *that's* what happened during that business with the Avatar. I knew there was something odd about it, even at the time.' He gave the back of his hand a slap. 'That's for fiddling with my console uninvited.'

Romana looked at him. 'So I take it, since you're still quite obviously alive, you were able to sort out the situation here without any help?'

The Doctor nodded happily. 'As I recall, yes. And incredibly ingeniously, I think, even though I say so myself.'

'So that's *it*, is it?' Romana said rather hotly. 'We get through all this, and our function is simply to open the door to let you in for a grand total of two minutes before you run straight out again?'

The Doctor shrugged. 'It's the little things that mean a lot, they're what count – whether we're talking about *things* in themselves or what people say, think or do. Sometimes, simply being there is enough. And talking of being here, I think we'd better be getting back. Big things are going to be happening, and it might be a good idea to move our own TARDIS out of the way.'

He glanced at the TARDIS doors. 'Besides, I'll be coming back soon and the last thing I want to do is meet myself yet again. I'm a nice enough chap and all that, no question, but you can sometimes have rather too much of a good thing.'

* * *

The Doctor and Romana arrived back in the disrupted spaces of their own TARDIS not quite knowing what they would find. When they had left, a battle between arcane Entities had been raging, and who knew what the outcome had been; which had been the victor and which the vanquished, and what state the TARDIS would be in? Were they looking at a spot of work with a dustpan and brush, Romana wondered, or a yawning rupture into the Dominions of Hell?

As it turned out, the dustpan-and-brush option appeared to be the more appropriate. They fell out of the temporal conduit to find the chamber into which it opened, in an approximately similar state to that in which they had left it. The charred remains of the body of Crowley lay to one side, the living but pale and weakened body of Katharine Delbane to another.

The Brigadier was there, making Delbane comfortable. He was on the point of taking back a proffered hip flask of something which she had obviously refused, and taking a small nip from it himself.

Over in a corner of the chamber stood Slater and McCrae, their manner entirely casual and unconcerned as if it was quite by chance that one of the larger fragments of marble pillar happened to be directly between Delbane and themselves.

'Hello, Doctor,' said the Brigadier as the Time Lord walked over to him and Delbane. Long exposure to the man who had once been his scientific adviser had left him able to deal with people appearing out of apparently thin air with almost complete equanimity.

'I don't think you've been entirely straight with us, Miss Delbane,' the Doctor said, with mock sternness after assuring himself that she was basically all right, in the physical sense at least. 'Who exactly are you? Or should I say, *what* are you?'

'*I am of the Conclave of That Which Shall Not be Named,*' her mouth said, the thing inside speaking through her. It made her mouth smile slightly. '*The Jarakabeth. You think of us as demons, as Evil, but that is not so. We merely wish to live. The one you knew as Crowley was an Aberration. I am one of those who were set to watch Him, to keep him from doing Harm. And now that task is fulfilled. The usefulness of the Delbane-construct has ended...*'

'Construct?' the Doctor said. 'You're saying that Delbane is – that you're inhabiting a homunculus, like Crowley?'

'*The Delbane-construct is more sophisticated in its origin and nature,*' said Katharine Delbane's mouth. '*It has memories and its own thoughts which, although generic and incomplete, are remarkably detailed. Katharine Delbane thinks she's real. Now that her usefulness to the Conclave is ended, I shall bury myself deep, and she shall live out her natural life and never think of Me again.*'

'You could simply let the construct die,' mused the Doctor absently, 'and move on – not that I'm suggesting you do anything of the kind,' he added as his ears suddenly caught up with his mouth.

'*The Jarakabeth are effectively immortal,*' said Delbane's mouth, pointedly, '*and as effective immortals we can afford to be kind. That was what the one you knew as Crowley failed to understand. Katharine Delbane shall live out what she thinks of as her life, however real that life might ultimately be.'*

Delbane's eyes closed.

Delbane opened her eyes.

'What the hell's happening?' she said. 'The last I remember, Crowley was pointing a gun at us. What's happening?'

'It might take some time to explain...' said the Doctor.

A massive shock, from somewhere unseen and nearby, shook the room.

'Time we don't have at the moment,' the Doctor said, gently but insistently helping Delbane to her feet. 'We have to be going. Prepare yourself for something not a little strange. It's time we got back to the console room, Romana...'

* * *

In the Golgotha Project command post on the edge of the Lychburg crater, Dr Sohn watched as the readouts and alarms went crazy. She was alone. Colonel Haasterman had told her to evacuate the post and she had sent the other Section 8 technicians on their way, but she could no more have abandoned her position than she could have abandoned her right arm – no, not her arm, her head and her heart. Haasterman might have wanted her out of harm's way, and his concern was touching, but this was... well, it was her *post*.

The gauges had long since gone off the scale. It didn't matter. Sohn had actually felt and *seen* reality changing around her. Through the lead-crystal viewing ports, before the blast shutters had racked themselves up, she had seen the Lychburg Discontinuity transform itself into what had appeared to be a small blue box. And then the box had transformed into a pyramid. And then the pyramid had changed to an hourglass, and then a big three-dimensional model of a ridiculously grinning purple dinosaur...

The lights went out; first the fluorescent strips that lit the room and then, one by one, the tell-tale lights of the displays. As Dr Sohn sat in the darkness waiting for the end, the unearthly screaming from the Discontinuity, even through the blast shutters and soundproofing, rose to an ear-piercing, unendurable pitch...

And then, quite simply, stopped dead.

Epilogue
But There's One Thing

When the forces of Section Eight arrived at the site of the Lychburg crater, stopping to release one Dr Sohn from the locked-down observation bunker in the process, they found, instead of the crater they had been quite reasonably expecting, the ruins of a small city.

This was doubly surprising, since before the accident that had created the crater in the first place, Lychburg had been a small town of the sort that would be described as 'rural' by the kind and have the unkind making jokes about worried agricultural livestock.

The ruins contained more than two hundred thousand people – fifty thousand more than in the original experiment, as though some process had been operating to spontaneously generate them whole. All of them were unharmed save for the occasional minor injury no worse than a broken arm or leg, and all of them were in a state of extreme confusion. It was almost impossible to get coherent statements, and the details of their last hectic moments before the Lychburg Discontinuity turned itself inside out were merely another datum to add to an already chaotic list.

The sheer number of these 'survivors', made the more dramatic and draconian methods of keeping the events of which they were a part under wraps, unworkable. In effect, they were simply allowed to collect what possessions they had – or at least, those possessions of an unclassified nature – and let go. They disappeared into the great mass of Middle America, there to find – or fail to find – jobs, homes and new lives. Lychburg was left utterly deserted, at least in terms that human beings can ordinarily perceive.

A Ghost Town.

Where are they now?

Dr Sohn is now teaching traditional weaving techniques at a small arts and crafts college in Minnesota. She has absolutely nothing to do with the hard physical sciences and – strangely enough for one with such an 'arty' avocation – nothing whatsoever to do with mysticism of any kind, even New Age mysticism.

The molecules of Colonel Haasterman, intermixed with the molecules of the decomposed subhuman minions who had eaten him, were swept up from the TARDIS floor and saved, with ecology-conscious rectitude, for recycling.

You just wouldn't want to know what they were recycled into.

Katharine Delbane is now a captain in a revitalised and EC-supplemented UNIT which, at time of writing, is still commanded by Brigadier General Lethbridge-Stewart.

The entity that lived within her seems to be lying dormant, possibly busy digesting what remains of the entity that lived in the homunculic reproduction of Crowley. The real Aleister Crowley is, of course, long dead, and any resemblance to him and the homunculus is purely coincidental.

As for the Doctor, the Doctor and his companions of various age, sex and species...

* * *

Victoria lay back in the marble-sided bath that was the size of a small swimming pool and let the tensions of her recent adventures ease away. The unguent she had added to the warm, soapy water came from the twenty-second century, she knew, and she imagined all the tiny things in the apparently clear, pinkish liquid working themselves inside her skin and crawling over her muscles and tendons, chemically stripping them and replacing them with microscopic shreds of new material.

All of a sudden, she didn't feel like a bath any longer. She climbed out and towelled herself briskly, not feeling as if she were trying to get little things out of her skin at all. She wrapped herself in a bathrobe and padded out into the corridor that led to her room.

Jamie was sitting on a chair in the corridor, writing.

'The Doctor told me to do it,' he said with a shrug. 'I thought I'd better go along with it. He seemed in a bit of an odd mood.'

Victoria glanced at the words painstakingly printed on the sheet of paper:

I MUST NOT STICK BIG KNIFS IN EXTINCT ANIMALS JUST BECAUSE I DONT LIK THE LOOK OF THEM.

I MuST NOT STIK BIG KNIVES IN ESTINCT ANIMALS JUST BECAS I DON'T LIKE THE LOOK OF EM.

I MUS NOT STICK BIG KNIFES IN EXTINCT ANIMALS JUsT BECAUSE I DON'T LIKE A LOOK OF THEM…

… and so on, with the minor variations in spelling and punctuation of one only exposed to the joys of literacy in later life.

Victoria sighed and moved on; sometimes the Doctor was too like a supercilious old school teacher for words.

As she passed what was usually, in the strange spaces within the TARDIS, a cloakroom closet she heard within it the sound of a rather mournful penny whistle. She paused for a moment, considering, then opened the door.

The Doctor was hanging by his knees from a coat rail. On the floor of the closet were stacks of writing paper, each stack coming up to Victoria's hips. The visible pages were covered with tiny, neat copperplate writing reading:

I must not, through my own carelessness and conceit, allow the deaths of innocents that can in any way be prevented.

I must not, through my own carelessness and conceit, allow the deaths of innocents that can in any way be prevented...

The Doctor regarded her owlishly, and dropped the penny whistle. It fell directly into his breast pocket even though he was upside down.

'I failed,' he told Victoria, simply. 'That man, Dibley, wasn't evil, wasn't in control of himself, wasn't even *there*, and I was responsible for his death.'

He looked so forlorn that Victoria was moved to charity.

'Things could have been worse,' she said. 'It was an accident, and nobody - even you - can guard completely against accidents. And think of all the people you saved. The way you managed to get all those two million people into the TARDIS in five minutes flat, to ride out the transformation of their world. It was - well, the way you did it would never have occurred to me in a million years, if at all.'

'Well, there is that, I suppose.' The Doctor brightened a little, flattered despite himself.

'It was a work of the purest genius,' said Victoria, 'believe me.'

'Oh, I wouldn't go as far as that,' the Doctor said. 'It was just a little something that occurred to me on the spot.'

He became cheerful with a suddenness that was shocking, as if an electrical switch had been thrown on a nature that was quite simply unable to live in the past, no matter how hard it might on occasion try.

'Well, we're not doing any good just moping around,' he said, swinging himself down from the coat rail.

He clapped his hands and rubbed them together, the little twinkle back in his eyes. 'You know, I've been thinking about what I did wrong in repairing the TARDIS the last time, and *this* time I really, truly, absolutely, positively think I know what it was...'

* * *

'And where shall we go now?' asked the Doctor, who was sitting in a stripy deck chair by the pool, a frosted glass of iced tea in his hand, a new hat – which he was trying on for size before he would allow it out in public, and which he would be testing in this manner for several years before he might feel it was ready – pulled down some way over his eyes so that only his nose and mouth were visible. 'Somewhere fun and relaxing, I hope.'

'Do you know,' said Romana, languidly sculling around on the pool itself – the heavy water with which it was filled was of such a molecular weight that she didn't so much as break the surface, 'I don't feel like relaxing at all, somehow. I'm feeling that I'd really *like* to get involved in some sudden and perilous adventure. Maybe we should start doing something to find the Key to Time again or something. Something,' she continued sourly, 'that doesn't involve us ending up as nothing more than glorified doormen.'

'Well, as I said before', said the Doctor, 'we can't always expect to take what you might call a proactive role. Sometimes, in this life, we're lucky if we can so much as work out what's going *on*, much less whether what we do has an effect. As a man with a big beard, whose name I unaccountably forget, once said: great events are the result of the interactions of people who are largely indifferent to each other.' The Doctor smiled to himself. 'I wouldn't worry about it. I'm sure that something will turn...'

'*Up* has no meaning, Doctor!' said a squeaky little voice, suddenly.

'And neither for that matter has *down* or *sideways!*'

Standing on the edge of the pool was what looked to be a little man, less than three feet high. At least, he was presumably a little man: he was covered from head to toe in a voluminous and rather grubby raincoat and a Sam Spade fedora hat.

'You have been taken…' The little man paused dramatically. '…Out of three-dimensional space by the Committee for Paradimensional Affairs, and so you shall remain here until you agree to do our bidding…'

'You see?' said the Doctor. 'What did I tell you?'

Appendix

Astonishing Stories of Unmitigated Science!
The Giant-sized Monthly for the Fan of the Future who Knows what He Likes

Compiler's Note: Following the involution of the Lychburg Discontinuity, a number of items were left in a transitionary state - that is, caught and fixed between two different levels of reality. Many of these items are of interest only to molecular physicists - a tyre iron or a slice of processed cheese, for example, being basically the same in any real sense, no matter how 'real' it ontologically is. Randomly hybridified organisms like the so-called 'pigrat' did not survive for long, and certain other items containing the possible seeds of new technologies were instantly classified by the powers that be.

Surviving artefacts where the primary function was and is to display some form of information, however, are slightly more interesting. There are BetaMax videotapes of Hollywood action movies, for instance, where the characters seem to stop in the middle of the pyrotechnics, say 'I've had enough of this' and walk off the screen. There are murder mystery books where, halfway through, the narrator tells us that we must be incredibly stupid if we haven't solved the mystery yet, names the murderer and stops dead, leaving the remainder of the pages blank.

We present here, in the interests of completeness, excerpts from one such surviving artefact, an issue of the popular science-fiction magazine, Astonishing Stories of Unmitigated Science!

* * *

From the Editor's *Astonishing!* Desk

Greetings and welcome to the latest thrilling issue of *Astonishing Stories of Unmitigated Science!* We here at *Astonishing!* have worked real hard to put this month's issue together; the linotype is set and ready for the presses and all systems are 'green for go', despite the sad news that our most gracious publisher of many years, Goblinslather Press, has declared bankruptcy following the disappearance of its honoured founder, Arlo Goblinslather, in a tragic ornithopter accident over the Malagasy South Seas. Our new proprietors, Wamco Holding Properties Inc. (Korea), share our God-given dream of bringing quality SF to those who are not only fans but also discerners, but have told us that we have to cut our costs by way of a drastic trimming of our page count, word rates and permanent editorial staff. There was some consternation about that in the *Astonishing!* bullpen, I can tell you! But our little family rallied together and we are proud to present a collection of tiptop yarns by all-new writers which continue in the finest *Astonishing!* tradition of E. Dan Belsen, Charles 'Bubba' Delancey and Podmore Sloathe! None of whom, unfortunately, appear in this issue for contractual reasons.

So let the so-called critics in their decadent ivory towers gnash their reefer-stained teeth at the so-called 'pulps' for all they like! For all their lit'ry talk of the transcendence of content over form, the telling particular and litotes, they are nothing but denouncers who will never understand how a monthly like *Astonishing!* can do its tales in the Scientific Method that only the cleverest and most technically educated geniuses can truly do. They sit there with their fountain pens and little gilded pocketbooks, drinking their prissy little cups of tea and absinthe, getting their so-called 'ideas' from the funny papers and this World Wide Internet of theirs, and I'll bet they couldn't work a basic piece of engineering equipment like a slide rule if their worthless lives depended on it.

Fear not though, readers, *Astonishing Stories of Unmitigated Science!* will be around, now and for ever, to show them the error of their ways! The Manifest Destiny of Mankind (and Womankind, too!) awaits! On with the chronicles of our glorious and indomitable Future!!

'Jolly' John F. McMacraken, Editor-in-Chief

* * *

Snail Women from Uranus
by Norbert Edgar Trant

(Hideous galactic aliens are come to defile our fairer human sex, and nothing within the power of mortal Man to stop them! How this horrifying and seemingly insoluble problem is solved can only come from a plot twist so devilishly original and ingenious that only a mind such as that of Norbert Edgar Trant *could have ever possibly thought it up. The prolific Mr Trant has sent us, without fail, a new and meticulously handwritten manuscript from his home in Westlake Falls, Virginia, for every month since our first ever publication, which we have always looked forward to and read with lively interest. This is his first appearance in the pages of* Astonishing! *itself.)*

The stars were bright that night, whole constellations and the galaxies in them shining in the pitch-black sky and laying there like scattered jewels on velvet, shining down on the sleepy little town of Kitchen Falls, set deep in the majestic forests of Kitchen Falls. Still and quiet, the stars were fixed for all eternity – but something else moved through the sky, slashing across it and leaving a fiery screaming trail in its very vacuum. *This* was no brightly boiling furnace of the nebulas…

it was a spaceship! An alien spaceship... and who knew what crawling, slithering terror and horror those alien monsters who were in it would bring...?

Norman Manley wasn't thinking about aliens, for all he had just been to see a movie about them at the Kitchen Falls drive-in. The movie had been *Snail Women from Uranus*, starring Candy Crawford and Lara Dane, and the thrusting womanly globes thus on so blatant display had made him feel real frisky. You could see through their tops and everything. This had given Norman some Ideas, so he had tried to touch the pliant orbs of the girl he was with, but she had slapped him hard and raked his face with her nails until it started to bleed. She really *had* wanted Norman to touch her, the girl, whose name was Myra Monroe, had then explained, but she was an old-fashioned girl with lots of primitive sex hang-ups, and she could not be doing with anything like that until she was respectably married.

Well, Norman had plenty of other girls whose minds had not been canalised with illogical and outmoded sex-ideas that had no place in the New World Order of the Atomic Age, so now he was driving his bright red 'hot rod' automobile into nearby Stovetown to meet one of them. Her name was Dorothee McShane, and she was a stripper in a bar called the Beer Cellar, which she did because, apart from the money, she really *liked* to do it and it made her feel real hot. She was a real 'swinging' lady, and once they had even done sex right there on the stage, after the bar had closed and the lights had gone out.

That was why the existence of aliens – though as a 'switched on' kid who listened to the radio news, he knew it was impossible that they should *not* exist – was the last thing on Norman Manley's mind... until he turned a corner in the narrow country road, and something landed in the woods off to one side in an explosion of fire and with a devastating *crash!* Instantly, Norman made his 'hot rod' squeal to a stop, dived through the door and started running through the woods as fast as his well-muscled athlete's legs and firm young buttocks could carry him.

'It must be a crashed jet plane out of Table City Air Base!' he thought to himself grimly, and vowed to retrieve the unfortunate pilot, if the pilot had survived, even at the cost of his own life! The giving of his own, he thought, to save one of those brave boys who even now stood as the final bastion between all that was decent and good and the Godless foreign hoards, would be a life well spent indeed.

What he found, however, was something different. Instead of the crashed and mangled remains of an air plane, a shining ovoid squatted in the burning scrub and maples, resting on tripodular support struts. Norman was no fool. He recognised this thing for what it was instantly. 'Aliens!' he snarled. 'What hideous deeds can they be up to here?'

And it was then that a hatch opened in the side of the ovoid with a hiss of noxious alien gases. And something came out of it… something so monstrous and horrible that to even begin to describe its monstrous and horrific form would drive you mad with the suppurating horror of it! And Norman Manley clawed at his eyes and screamed as if his lungs would burst…

The next day, Myra Monroe was behind the soda-pop stand in the drugstore that she worked in, when Norman walked into it wearing his best suit of clothes, carrying a marriage licence and a gold ring with a diamond as big as a tree-snipe egg that must have cost every cent of a year's pay from his fancy job, and asked her if she would do him the honour of becoming his wife.

No girl could have resisted! 'Yes!' Myra cried. 'Oh, Norman, let us get married right away!'

They were married an hour later by the Justice of the Peace, and set off for their honeymoon in the swanky Kitchen Falls

Hotel, which stood on the top of a mountain outside of town and which had more than fifty different rooms and bellhops who all wore little hats. Black storm clouds were gathering, however, and it was a dark and stormy night when they at last reached their room and got ready for bed.

'Oh, Norman,' Myra said, coming from her foamy bubble bath and sitting on the big wide bed in a little lacy negligee, 'you have made me the happiest girl in all the...'

There was an explosion of lightning and thunder outside. The girlish delight in Myra's voice trailed away, and her eyes went wide at what the lightning had so horrifically revealed.

'I am not your "Norman",' said the thing as it lurched towards her, a snarling grin upon its face and a hellish light inside its eyes as they ran all over her delectable female form. 'I have merely taken control of the puny *hu-man* who you know as Norman's body. I am a space alien, from a galaxy so many miles away that your mind cannot imagine them! I am Queegvogel Duck Duck Duck Duck Duck Duck Seven, come to kill all Earth men and to *breed* with all Earth women...'

Myra Monroe looked a little strangely at the thing who had once been Norman Manley, through narrowed eyelids. 'Oh, do you really bloody think so?'

'What...?' The thing inhabiting Norman's corporeal form seemed a little nonplussed by this sudden change in tone, and made to take an involuntary step back, grazing a calf quite nastily on the corner of the minibar. 'What are you – ?'

'I don't think so,' Myra said, reaching for the zipper in the back of her neck, and pulling off her Human Being suit. The thing that had been Norman Manley stared, aghast, at the form that lay within, a creature now bulking itself outwards on a telescopically articulated, polysilical skeletal structure, internal organs unfolding in some dimensionally complex manner as though from nothing, a retractable carapace extending over them, encasing them, effectively, in a sheath of living armour...

'Fifteen thousand years,' the monstrous creature snarled, looming over the now quite frankly terrified thing that had once been Norman Manley, jagged-talon'd claws clenching and unclenching as though only the merest thread of self-control prevented it from tearing him apart. 'Give or take. That's how long we've been working with our guys – and it's a thankless bleeding task, I can tell you. I mean, we've only just got the buggers to the point where they put the bleeding *seat* up, let alone down afterwards! So if you think we're gonna let a bunch of little sods like *you* come in and have us start again from scratch, you've got another think coming…'

The creature put its face close to that of what had once been Norman Manley. 'So come and have a go if you think you're hard enough, slime boy, or, tell you what, why don't you just piss off back where you came from?'

If active and sufficiently advanced satellite-based tracking systems had been trained on that particular area of the North American continent, they might have have tracked the vector of a sad and rather diminutive glowing ovoid as it rose and set a dispirited and vaguely elliptical course for the far side of the moon, where a larger vessel waited. Once line-of-sight transmission could be established, and had they been capable of registering the correct frequencies, the radio-telescopic dishes of humanity might have noted and decoded the exchange detailed below.

But they weren't and they didn't and they weren't, and so they didn't:

'Report, Queegvogel Duck Duck Duck Duck Duck Duck Seven,' said a brusque and somewhat atonic voice from the mother ship. 'Is the world of puny humans ripe for foul unending domination?'

'Yeah,' said another and slightly more enthusiastic voice, 'and are there any *girls* down there, Queeg?'

'It's no go, guys,' said the voice of Queegvogel Duck Duck Duck Duck Duck Duck Seven. 'It's just no good. They have weapons down there.'

There was a brief, contemplative pause.

'What sort of weapons?' said the first voice from the mother ship.

'Horrible obliterating weapons of devastating and utter death, OK?' said the voice of Queegvogel Duck Duck Duck Duck Duck Duck Seven. 'Can we go home now?'

In the Honeymoon Suite of the swanky Kitchen Falls Hotel, Norman Manley woke up and rubbed at the back of his head, which hurt real bad, like he had been drinking beer. 'My God,' he said to himself. 'What happened? What did I *do* last night..?'

He realised that he was not alone, and that this other was not looking at him in a particularly friendly manner.

'You married me,' said Myra Monroe, coldly.

'Oh,' said Norman, and with a remarkable sense of self-preservation, began to think of ways he could back-pedal right from the start.

* * *

Termination on Golgotha
by Dexley Blandings

The assault craft ploughed into the swamp with an explosion of sludge and superheated steam. Concussion-bolts detonated and a Teflon-coated butterfly hatch racked itself back and up into its housing in the polyceramicised, fractured-prismatic shell.

John Daker worked the action on his pulse-pump, slamming a subatomic charging cell into the inject-breech and priming it. He dropped from the hatch, the shock-pads of his boots taking the impact on the soft, still steaming ground.

The Golgothian wildlife shrittered and whooped in the swamp around him. Daker flipped a switch in his helmet and a sensor-readout unfolded on the virtual screen chipped into his brain, behind his eyes: a troupe of inquisitive fomprats were circling cautiously off to one side, but, given their carrion-eating nature, there would have to be one Sheol of a lot more of them. Daker himself would have to be dead before they'd feel brave enough to move in. Daker shouldered the pulse-pump, quickly double-checked the other systems of his power armour's anti-personnel package, and set off in the direction of the transponder-blip he'd tracked in orbit.

At last, he thought, after a quarter of a galactic-standard century of searching, after twenty-five Earth years of following a hopscotch interplanetary trail, of hunting down rumours, of dead ends, wild goose chases, red herrings, dead ends, dead red herrings and of beating people viciously in 473 separate planetary and/or orbitally based space bars... At last he neared the end of his search; the termination of that long, long arc through space and time that had begun with the destruction of all that the young John Daker had held dear.

Even now, wading through the fetid swamps of Golgotha, the memories came back to plant hooks in his cythernesically implanted mind, and score it.

Memories of the blasted ash and rubble that had been his homeworld: the bones protruding from the ash; finding the remains of his mother, father, grandmother on his father's side, brother, half-sister and beloved tame pararat, Cyril, and the abominable things that had been done to them before they died. Memories of the brutish minions who had broken his legs and hands and left him for dead. Memories of his discovery by the emergency-service forces of Earth: of his recovery and enlistment; his desertion and his wanderings thereafter, making his way through the violent chaos of the Galactic Hub and out into the even more violent, lawless tract-gulfs of the Outworlds... all the while searching, never giving up, searching for the creature that had done this to him.

Searching for Volok.

And finding him. 'It ends here,' Daker snarled, baring his teeth behind his impact-visor, though there was nobody to see or hear him. 'It all ends here and now.'

The hut was strangely small and unprepossessing, little more than the size of a sublight SAD pursuit ship, its irregularly octagonal form lifted from the swamp on pilings cut from some local equivalent of wood. A shallow flight of mismatched steps led to a blank, stout-looking doorway.

Daker mounted the steps and hammered on the door with the stock of his pulse-pump. 'Open up! Open up you bastard!'

After a few moments, the door opened with a squeal of rudimentary hinge-springs, to reveal a hulking and Gorgonic form, its claws and the individually cantilevered incisors of its jaws clotted with festering gobs of fleshy matter and with old, dried blood, its eyes burning with an ancient and unknowable hunger that seemed a form of madness in its own right.

'Can I help you at all?' it said. It was wearing tartan carpet slippers, and was in the process of removing a triocular set of eyeglasses, which it now began to polish with a little cloth. A pipe depended from one corner of its slavering jaw, a particularly pungent variety of alien shag burning in the bowl.

'I want Volok!' Daker snarled, levelling the ejection vent of his pulse-pump at the monstrous form. 'Volok the Riever! World destroyer! Volok whose hands run wet with the blood of a million women and children! Give him to me now...'

The creature frowned as though in momentary puzzlement. 'Excuse me one moment.' It turned its horrid head to shout back into the reeking dark beyond the door. 'Del*bert!*'

There was the sound of movement inside the hut; a muffled crash and muttering.

'Delbert!' the creature shouted again. Its voice devolved into a coldly murderous growl. 'Come out here. I want to *talk* to you…'

A second creature appeared. Though equally horrible in form, it was smaller and seemed to be younger than the first one. 'Yes, Dad?' It looked past the other, caught sight of John Daker and visibly blanched. 'Oh…'

'I'll "oh" you, you little bugger!' the larger monster cried, belabouring the smaller one about the head and shoulders. 'You've been sweeping across the worlds of Man like a corrupt and all-consuming fire again, haven't you! Grinding the bones of mothers and their sons beneath your iron heels!'

'Aaow, Dad!' cried the younger, clutching at its head protectively with its jagged claws.

'What did I tell you about turning the skies black with the bodies of the burning dead?' the older creature thundered menacingly.

The younger looked down at its monstrous feet and muttered something sullenly.

'I can't *hear* you…' growled the older creature.

'All *right!*' the smaller creature snapped. 'No-turning-the-skies-black-with-the-burning-bodies-of-the-dead-if-I-want-to-live-under-your-roof. *OK?*'

'Kids, eh?' said the older creature, turning its attention back to the now completely astonished Daker. 'Can't live with 'em, can't put a blaster-bolt to the back of their heads and put them down.' It took the younger by the ear and dragged it back inside the hut. 'Please accept my most profound apologies. Won't happen again.' It slammed the door behind it.

Daker looked at the flat expanse of wooden door.

'Um…' he said.

* * *

Books from the *Astonishing!* Bookshelf
Reviewed by Stanford Groke

It's been something of a thin month for books, what with one thing and another. The big-shot houses seem to have misplaced our name on their review list, with the result that we have yet to receive copies of their latest output. Never fear, though, reader; judging from their efforts of the recent past, such output will consist of such perversion and squalor in the guise of 'psychology'; such subversive, Godless propaganda and such so-called 'speculation' that flies in the face of all we know to be good and decent in the mind and heart of Man; such filth that would make the mind sick just from the reading of it, that the loss of them can only be a blessing.

To make up for that, we have two real treasures for you. *The Best of Astonishing!* (Goblinslather Press, 445pp), in which you can read and savour again all the highlights you have read and savoured in these very pages. From Wiblik's justly famous and Nebula Award-winning 'Robot is Intransigent', to Grand Master Henshaw's 'The Precise Ballistic Ellipsoid from the Asteroids to an Orbital Circumlocution of Io', to the far-out brain feverings of Blandings' 'Wardrobe Eating Nanny's Arm', this surely is an indispensable compendium for historians of the SF form. [*Unfortunately, due to an error in the production stage, all bound copies of this book have been pulped and are no longer available - Ed.*]

Our second book is of another stripe entirely. While not being science fiction in the proper sense, *Future Impact: The Apocalyptic Backlash* (PractiBrantis Enterprises SA, 414pp) by Dr John Smith, is of vital importance to all those interested in the future of mankind and what futuristic things it will bring.

Dr Smith, as readers of these pages will know, has long led the life of a recluse, disappearing for years at a time in the company of his young 'assistants', appearing in public only sporadically to originate such neophysical concepts as the cheese drive – first championed in *Astonishing!* – the discovery of Pellucidor and the PractiBrantic processes that have informed one-tenth of the American-speaking world. For years now, it seems, Dr Smith has been secretly refining and expounding his theories as to just what, precisely, has gone wrong with the world – and now, at last, in *Future Impact*, he presents his conclusions.

As we grow older, says Dr Smith, the world makes cumulatively less sense. Things you used to buy for a penny become ridiculously expensive on the level of a factor of ten, Empires set to last a thousand years collapse seemingly overnight, the young people with their pompadours and electrical beat-combos begin to talk in what, increasingly, becomes gibberish to any sane mind, peppered with a blasphemy and outright filth that seems to come about as a matter of course. For too long, says Dr Smith, such phenomena had been dismissed as market-forces-driven monetary inflation, the social dynamic or being a senile old bugger who should do the world a favour and just die.

The truth, as detailed in *Future Impact*, is somewhat more alarming.

The world as we know it, Dr Smith asserts, is being actively invaded by Futurity. Far from merely, as we once thought, travelling through time at a second per second, we are in fact *accelerating* through time at a second per second per second, the physical matter of the universe falling through the fourth dimension towards some unknowable end like a collection of ornamental balls dropping to a concrete floor. And at some point – Dr Smith estimates it as within a decade – we're going to hit it.

The effects of this catastrophe are being felt in our own time, the shock and shards of it rebounding to intersect with and impact upon our time line – discrete packets of what can only be called *para*reality which, in the same way that humour operates by the collapsing of some textual structure under reality, turns the very world around us into dumb and incredibly rotten old jokes. As proof, Dr Smith presents excerpts from any number of popular publications, the products of and mirrors of our world, the texts of which show such inconsistencies and glaring shifts in tone for it, cumulatively, to be virtually inconceivable as the mere result of the intransigence of writers, the incompetence of editors, or production errors.

The future, without question, seems bleak – or possibly not. Loath to end on such depressing terms, Dr Smith provides one possible solution, involving the cooperation of all nations and the sinking of all private resources into a project to tunnel into the earth, extract its molten core and mould it into a massive grappling hook, which will then be fired back through time in the hope that it catches on to something and brings the temporally headlong plunge of Planet Earth to a stop. Indeed, he speculates that with the collapse of the more monolithic world powers and the animosity between them, the increasing disappearance of the high-profile rich under mysterious circumstances and the fact that there seems to be less and less actual *money* around these days, such plans might already be secretly in effect.

Of course, Dr Smith concludes, the ultimate result would be a planet hanging on a line and swinging back and forth through Time. So, whoever you are, wherever you are, it might be an idea to make sure you're doing something nice – reading this fine issue of *Astonishing Stories of Unmitigated Science!*, say – because at any moment you might suddenly find yourself doing it over and over again, for ever.

About the Author

Dave Stone is truly a prince amongst men, and women for that matter, and they all agree that he is quite possibly the highest pinnacle to which humanity can ever hope to aspire in form, thought and deed. Swordsman, bon vivant, polymath - these are just some of the words he knews how to spell. All of which makes the current unavailability of half of the eleven-odd books he's written more upsetting. He also writes comics.

Rumours that he personally ended World War II, the British Slave Trade and that he single-handedly pulled down the Berlin Wall with a pickaxe are entirely true, but he doesn't like to talk about them. Mr Stone is currently living in a cardboard box under the Plaistow New Road underpass. When asked to comment on this new work, *Heart of TARDIS*, he said, 'What? Who? Buy me a drink you b——.'

We wish him well.

PRESENTING

DOCTOR WHO

ALL-NEW AUDIO DRAMAS

Big Finish Productions is proud to present all-new *Doctor Who* adventures on audio!

Featuring original music and sound-effects, these full-cast plays are available on double cassette in high street stores, and on limited-edition double CD from all good specialist stores, or via mail order.

Available from April 2000
RED DAWN

A four-part story by Justin Richards.
Starring **Peter Davison** as the Doctor
and **Nicola Bryant** as Peri.

Ares One: NASA's first manned mission to the dead planet Mars. But is Mars as dead as it seems?

While the NASA team investigate an "anomaly" on the planet's surface, the Doctor and Peri find themselves inside a strange alien building. What is its purpose? And what is frozen inside the blocks of ice that guard the doorways? If the Doctor has a sense of deja-vu, it's because he's about to meet some old adversaries, as well as some new ones...

If you wish to order the CD version, please photocopy this form or provide all the details on paper. Delivery within 28 days of release. Send to: PO Box 1127, Maidenhead, Berkshire. SL6 3LN.
Big Finish Hotline 01628 828283.

Still available:
THE SIRENS OF TIME (Doctors 5,6,7)   THE LAND OF THE DEAD (Doctor 5, Nyssa)
PHANTASMAGORIA (Doctor 5, Turlough)   THE FEARMONGER (Doctor 7, Ace)
WHISPERS OF TERROR (Doctor 6, Peri)   THE MARIAN CONSPIRACY (Doctor 6, Evelyn)

Please send me	[ ] copies of *Red Dawn*	
	[ ] copies of *The Marian Conspiracy*	[ ] copies of *Whispers of Terror*
	[ ] copies of *The Fearmonger*	[ ] copies of *Phantasmagoria*
	[ ] copies of *The Land of the Dead*	[ ] copies of *The Sirens of Time*

each @ £13.99 (£15.50 non-UK orders) - prices inclusive of postage and packing. Payment can be accepted by credit card or by personal cheques, payable to Big Finish Productions Ltd.

Name...

Address...

Postcode..

VISA/Mastercard number..

Expiry date...Signature...

For more details visit our website at **http://www.doctorwho.co.uk**